SURVIVAL

GENOSKWA
BOOK THREE

HEATH STALLCUP

Copyright © 2024 by Heath Stallcup

All rights reserved.

No part of this book may be reproduced in any form or by any electronic or mechanical means, including information storage and retrieval systems, without written permission from the author, except for the use of brief quotations in a book review.

1

Albany, NY

Patricia Murphy double-checked her notes before reaching for the car door. She opened it cautiously and stepped out, looking for oncoming traffic. Just as she shut the door, her cell phone rang.

She wasn't surprised to hear Hector on the other end. "Well?"

"Not yet. I just got here."

"Are you sure you have the right address?" His voice sounded even more nervous than she felt.

"My sources are rarely ever wrong." She swallowed hard as she looked across the street at the unassuming house. "Wish me luck."

"Call me back as soon as you're done."

"Yep." She pressed the end call button and slipped the phone into her raincoat pocket. The light mist of drizzle wetted her shoulders as she crossed the street and pushed open the small picket fence gate.

The sudden creak of old hinges made her stiffen, afraid that announcing her arrival would somehow jinx her ability to do what needed to be done.

She trotted up a recently swept walkway to the porch, her heels clacking on the cement. She took the few steps two at a time, stood under the portico, and did her best to screw up her nerve.

She stepped forward, pressed the doorbell, and stepped back. She waited nervously for somebody to answer then pressed the button again. Straining to listen, she didn't hear a chime from within so she resorted to knocking.

Her gloved hand muffled the sound somewhat but a moment later she noticed shadows moving inside the house.

She took another step back from the door and squared her shoulders, clearing her throat as the locks inside turned. She planted her best smile as the door cracked and then opened.

A weary eyed gentleman stood inside, wiping at his mouth with a paper towel. "Can I help you with something?"

She cleared her throat again and held her hand out. "My name is Patricia Murphy." The man stared at her hand and then looked up at her, his brow raised.

"So?"

She slowly lowered her hand and licked her lips nervously. "Are you, by chance, FBI Special Agent Dale Archer?"

Dale sat in his worn out recliner, a napkin covering the now cold TV dinner as Patricia quickly went over the highlights of each of the files. More than once he opened his mouth to say something but it only seemed to spur her to speak faster, forcing more information out before he could object. Dale finally held his hands up in surrender as he scooted to the edge of his seat. "WHAT, exactly, do you want from me?"

She stared at him blankly, her mind racing. "Your name is mentioned more than—"

"I can neither confirm nor deny—"

She stood up quickly, scattering the files across the coffee table and floor. "My brother *died* out there."

Dale locked eyes with her and did his best to show no emotion. "And I'm sorry for your loss." He motioned for her to sit back down and she slowly lowered herself to the cushion. "I had friends out there as well." His voice took on a softer yet more somber tone. "And I tried to warn them. They refused to listen to anything I had to say."

She tugged at one of the files on the coffee table. "You told them, 'We've been warned,' correct?" She returned his gaze and held it. "Did these things actually talk to you?"

Dale shook his head and sat back, trying to think of a way to make her understand. "You ever watch the old Westerns? You know, the black and white movies where the white guys first meet the Indians and neither one can understand the other?" She gave him a confused look but nodded. "They used a rudimentary sign language to get their messages across, and somehow it worked. Same thing."

"You're telling me these Genoskwa communicated to you in sign language?"

He sighed heavily and wiped a heavy hand over his brow. "Come on, Patricia. Stop being so literal here." He sat forward and scoffed. "Stop being a damned reporter for a minute and try to hear what I'm trying to tell you."

She suddenly felt patronized and her anger started to flare, but she opted to be professional and stomp that fire out. "You have to work with me here, Agent Archer. Until I got these files, I thought, like every other sane person, that these things were nothing more than legend and drunken hallucinations."

Dale sighed again as he sat back. "And I'll never understand how you got your hands on this information."

She lowered her eyes and shrugged. "Honestly, I thought it was Johnny sending it to me...until I read his name on the casualty list."

"Had to be Ford then." Dale reached for the cold coffee and took a pull.

"You knew David?"

He nodded as he set the cup down. "He and I went way back." He caught her gaze and offered a soft smile. "I'm sorry I didn't really know your brother, but if Ford chose him as his second then he must have been a real stand-up guy."

She offered a sad smile. "A real Boy Scout that one."

Dale suddenly sobered and came to his feet, gripping the coffee cup. "I'm certain you realize that if I comment on any of the information in these files, I could lose my job." He stepped past her and into the sparse kitchen, pouring another cup.

"I'm not asking to verify anything, Agent Archer." She stood in the doorway of the kitchen, her eyes searching his face as she screwed up her courage. "I want you to take me out there."

ARCHER COULD FEEL his blood pressure threatening to blow through the roof. "*Are you fucking nuts?*"

"I'm not intending to go to war with them, I simply—"

"They don't *care* about your intentions. The minute you step into those woods, you are fair game!" He threw his hands into the air. "Literally!"

"I have to verify—"

"If the report says that your brother is dead, then he's dead, lady. That's something the Bureau ain't gonna get wrong."

Her face solidified into a mask of anger. "How DARE you bring my—"

"YOU'RE the one who came knocking on my door and—"

"If I'm going to report on this then I have to know it's REAL!" she screamed, stomping her foot. Dale sobered and stared at her for a moment.

"Wait…you want to report on…*this?*"

She huffed then took a deep cleansing breath. "Somebody sent this information to me for a reason. Regardless of their intentions, I intend to see it through." She spun and pleaded with her eyes. "For all we know, that was what they wanted when they sent me—"

"Woah, woah, woah…back up the truck a minute." He held his hands up and moved closer. "Let's just take this one bite at a time."

She held a finger up. "Somebody sent this information to me, a reporter, for a reason." She popped another finger up. "There's enough information here to write an actual book, but I need to condense it down into an article…possibly a three part series, but regardless—"

"And you don't need to go traipsing around in those woods to do that."

She narrowed her eyes at him. "And three, I need verifiable, tangible, undeniable proof that this story is the truth."

He raised his brows at her. "And your brother dying out there isn't enough?"

Anger flashed in her eyes for a brief moment before she scoffed and turned away from him. "Low blow, Agent Archer." She took another deep breath and let it out slowly before turning back to face him. "I need to see for myself. If that many people were out there, they'd have left a trace. A…a bullet casing, or a…a… candy wrapper or—"

"Any hunter could have left those things."

"Exactly! That's why I need to comb those woods and look for something I can tie directly to the Bureau." Her eyes suddenly turned sad and her shoulders slumped. "And I need to do it before the government can get out there and sanitize the area."

Dale groaned as he dumped the coffee in the sink and planted his hand on either side of the counter. He hung his head and squeezed his eyes shut. "No."

"What?"

He nodded slightly. "You heard me. The answer is no."

"But I have to…" She stepped back and squared her shoulders. "You can't stop me from going out there. Those are public lands and—"

He spun so quickly that she was startled. "You're right. I can't stop you." He crossed his arms and looked down at her stoically. "But I also do not have to escort you out there and risk both of our lives just so you can…" He trailed off, not wanting to belittle her justification.

She stepped back and stared at him, her mouth opening and closing, but no words squeaking out. She finally nodded slightly and offered a weak smile before turning and scooping up the fallen files. "I should have known better than to come here." Emotions that she had fought to keep in check suddenly began to surface and she found herself sniffling to keep from crying. "Not all FBI agents are cut from the same cloth as Johnny." She slid the files into a pile and squeezed them together before forcing them into her leather satchel. "I'm sorry I wasted your time, Agent Archer." He watched her glance around the living room then turn for the door. "I'll see myself out."

Dale watched as she tugged the door open and stepped through the small vestibule then out onto the porch. He could see the rain had given up the slow drizzle for a torrential downpour, but she didn't slow as she marched to the gate and let herself out.

He stood in the doorway and peered through the foggy single pane window as she fought to enter her car and then eventually pulled away. He stepped back and closed his eyes for a moment. If he helped her find what she was looking for and something happened to her, it would be entirely his fault.

Then again, if he *didn't* help her and something happened to her…

Dale rolled his eyes and groaned.

FBI Field Office, Albany, NY

Interim Director David Stanton rifled through the files scattered across the desk and growled low in his throat. "No wonder nothing ever got—" He was interrupted by a knock on the doorframe. He looked up to see Dale Archer standing in the open doorway. "Archer, come on in."

"Troubles, sir?"

"I just…" He sighed heavily and sat down quickly. "The filing system here is abysmal, but we'll get it polished up."

"How are you fitting in here, sir?" Dale asked politely.

Stanton shrugged animatedly. "I know I'm just acting director here, but between the two of us, I hope and pray they don't offer the job to me. I prefer the climate of New Mexico."

"You could always decline the position, sir."

Stanton gave him a droll stare. "Son, when the Bureau makes you an 'offer,' it's not really something you can refuse. Unless you're as high up as you ever want to go, in which case, feel free to say no."

"Ah. I didn't realize…"

"It's an unwritten rule." Stanton sat up straighter and checked his tie. "I'm certain that's not why you came by."

"Uh, no." Dale looked away, unsure how to start the conversation. "I had a…" he cleared his throat nervously. "A visitor drop by my house."

Stanton raised a brow. "And this is something you feel is reportable…why?"

He looked up and locked eyes with the man. "It was Special Agent John Murphy's sister."

Stanton's features slacked for a fraction of a moment before going stoic again. "Okay. And?"

"She knows her brother is dead."

Stanton's brows knit. "How? We haven't made any of the familial contacts yet."

"Somehow she intercepted a data burst that was intended to go to HQ, sir." Archer did his best to show no emotion. "She knew he was reported as KIA. She also had copies of *all* the current case reports."

Stanton couldn't hide the reaction this time as his stomach fell. "How?" he practically whispered.

"That, she didn't know." He took a deep breath and prepared to drop the other shoe. "She's a reporter. At the Daily Informer."

Stanton leaned forward and rubbed at his eyes with his palms. "Oh, dear lord…." He suddenly sat up and looked at Archer. "What did she want?"

Archer sighed and offered a gentle shrug. "She wants me to take her out there."

"What on earth for?" Stanton stood and pushed his chair away. "If she has the reports then she knows how deadly those things are." He paused and turned to stare at Archer again. "She wanted you to verify the information, didn't she?"

Archer shook his head. "No sir. She seemed convinced that the files were accurate and authentic. She wants to get out there and find the physical evidence she would need to go to print."

"Go to..." he trailed off, the words sticking in his throat.

Archer nodded. "Although she is certain the files are authentic, she needs tangible proof that the events that occurred out there, in fact, occurred."

"Proof?" He reached for his chair and slowly sat down. "You do realize that we are weeks...possibly a month away from getting a qualified cleanup crew out there?"

"Sir?"

Stanton found it hard to swallow. "As it stands, the remains of every agent, their weapons, their satellite uplinks...hell, their change of socks...it's all still out there."

Archer sat forward in his chair. "Sir? Why the hell hasn't there been a recovery effort?"

Stanton's face fell. "Do you realize just how many highly trained agents, not to mention the mercenaries that Davidson brought in, were LOST out there?" His jaw quivered as his anger grew. "To a bunch of...rock tossing, spear chucking...cavemen!"

Archer came to his feet and sighed. "Sir, I'm requesting permission to take a few days off."

Stanton came to his feet and locked eyes with Archer. "You can't take her out there, Dale."

Archer gave him a knowing look and cracked a smile. "I have no intention of it, sir." His smile spread.

SURVIVAL

"I intend to take her as far away from the altercation as I possibly can."

Stanton nodded slightly. "You'll need props. Believable ones."

"I'll go by the range and get a variety of spent brass, sir."

"And trash." He snapped his fingers. "Those energy bars the SWAT teams are always chewing on. The ones that make 'em fart like draft horses."

Archer chuckled under his breath.

Stanton pointed at him. "And clothing."

Archer nodded again. "I'll hit the lockers on the way out, sir. I'll get whatever looks good."

Stanton slowly sat down and sighed. "If you can get those files from her…" He let the sentence hang.

Archer gave him a knowing nod. "I'm not sure that will be possible, sir, but if I can, consider it done."

"Then go. Take as much time as you need, Agent Archer."

2

NEW YORK CITY

PATRICIA NEARLY JUMPED when someone pounded on her front door. She nervously looked around the cluttered room, picked up a tennis racket, and practiced swinging before she moved to the door. She stood to the side and peered through the peep hole before relaxing and dropping the racket, kicking it away from the door.

"You startled me," she said, smiling.

"Your bell doesn't work." Dale nodded to the device hanging out of the wall with wires disconnected.

Patricia winced. "Yeah, I was going to try to fix that, but…" she trailed off, shrugging. She suddenly stiffened and tried to give him a determined look. "I haven't changed my mind about going out there."

"I have." He pulled his sunglasses down and tucked them into his shirt pocket. "If you went out there and something happened—"

"Say no more!" She nearly hopped up and down. "I

don't care about your reason, I'm just happy to have you." She pulled the door open more and stepped aside, allowing him entrance.

Dale hesitated and cast a look around as he slowly entered. "Were you robbed?"

She shut the door and locked it quickly then spun and gave him a surprised look. "I don't think so."

Dale stepped deeper into the mess and avoided a stack of magazines tied with twine. "Hoard much?"

Patricia stifled a laugh. "Sorry. No, I just…" She took a deep breath and let it out slowly. "I decide to do something and before I can finish, something else pops its head up. It's like life is a hydra or something." She kicked the magazines to the side. "Recycling," she chuckled.

Dale squared his shoulders and nodded. "Okay. So when are you wanting to do this?"

She held a finger up and brushed past him, moving into the living room. She motioned toward her backpack. "I'm almost packed."

"So soon?"

She unzipped the pack and started pulling out items. "I've got bug spray, bandaids, batteries, toothpaste…" She continued to dig in the pack, pulling out items as she went. "Socks, undies, bra…" She paused and blushed slightly, shoving the bra back into the bag. "Not…that you…needed to know that."

Dale nodded knowingly. "Any chance you've been diagnosed with ADD?"

She scoffed as she glanced around the room. "Actually, it was ADHD with an emphasis on the H. Where did I put that machete?"

"Machete?" Dale stepped back and cleared his throat. "Okay, how about this? Do you have a tent?"

She stared at him blankly. "Um."

"Sleeping bag?"

Her face fell. "No."

He took a deep breath and glanced at the items she had pulled out of the bag. "What are the batteries for?"

"Flashlight!" She beamed and sat up straight.

"Okay good. What kind of flashlight?"

Her face fell again. "I…don't actually…have one." She cleared her throat nervously. "I don't have one *yet*."

Dale's face dropped and he groaned inwardly. "Okay, how about your toothbrush? You have the toothpaste."

Her smile wavered as she slowly turned and leaned to the side, staring at the bathroom. "I think it's still in there."

Dale felt a laugh try to form in his chest and he quickly quelled it. "Okay, how about we make a list of items you might need, rather than just grabbing things at random?"

Her smile returned and she gripped the backpack, shaking it out into the rest of the mess on the floor. Dale felt all humor leave the situation when a Beretta 9MM fell to the floor with a loud clunk. His eyes darted between it and her before he slowly stood. "I don't think you'll be needing—"

"Those things killed my brother." She grabbed the pistol and held it to her chest. "I'm not going out there unarmed."

Dale chewed at his lower lip. "It was in the bottom of your backpack." He gave her a knowing look. He could almost see the lightbulb go off when the realization struck. "Is that thing legal?"

She gave him a droll look. "Of course it's legal. Johnny bought it for me when I first became a reporter—"

"I mean is it legal with the state?"

She sighed and rolled her eyes. "I have a permit. Somewhere."

"Fine." He held his hands up and made a tentative step toward her. "May I?"

She handed him the pistol and he ejected the magazine. "There's no bullets in here."

"Oh, they're in the top of my closet." She smiled sheepishly. "I don't keep it loaded. I wouldn't want to actually shoot someone."

Dale felt the need to sit down and slowly lowered himself onto her couch. "Okay. We have a lot of work to do here."

"Hector, Tommy, Al, and myself." She took a deep breath and let it out slowly, her medication taking effect.

Dale nodded as he jotted notes in his notepad. "And who are they?"

"Hector works the police beat at the paper. Tommy is a friend of his that knows how to track stuff. And Al used to be with the SAS. He was a pilot or something."

Dale raised a brow. "SAS? As in British Special Forces?"

She nodded as she sipped the coffee. "Yeah, he was here in the States years ago doing some kind of training with SEAL team support guys. That's when Johnny and him hit it off."

Dale rolled the pen between his fingers. "An SAS pilot? He was probably special forces flight. They go by SFF."

"That sounds right." She sipped again and glanced at the clutter, wincing. "Sorry about the mess. I wasn't expecting company."

"No worries. I've seen worse, trust me." Dale went back to the list. "And this Tommy?"

"Tommy Youngblood. He's Native American. Supposed to be an expert hunter and tracker."

Dale jotted a note in his pad then flipped it closed. "And that's it. Five of us?" He gave her a knowing look. "Don't you think it would be easier if it was just the two of us? We could slip in and out, and with a little luck the 'squatches would be none the wiser."

She gave a gentle shake of her head. "Hector was the one that provided the ability to decrypt the message, so he's invested in the project. Tommy and Al are two people Johnny trusted, so…"

"I understand that, but…" He trailed off, trying to think of a valid reason to leave the others behind. "If there's any backlash to your story, they could be implicated." She opened her mouth to argue but he held a finger up, stopping her. "Not to mention, if anything happens to these guys, it's on us. Both of us. The only reason I agreed to escort you out here was because I honestly assumed it would be just the two of us. Nobody else would be risking their heads." He shrugged. "Literally."

"I don't plan to take root out there, Agent Archer. Just in and out. Hopefully less than a day. A few extra people are also extra eyes to help me locate whatever I need to verify my story."

"Understood. And, you can call me Dale." He stood and flipped shut the notebook in his fingers then slipped it into his shirt pocket. "The problem with the best laid plans is things never go according to them. We can go in there expecting to be in and out and something will inevitably happen that extends the trip. Hence the tent and sleeping bags. We need to plan on staying a few days at least. That means food, water, a change of clothes, everything we might need."

She stared at him wide-eyed. "I really don't want to be out in the woods at night with them."

"Neither do I." He raised a brow at her. "But it's better to be prepared."

She nodded absently. "Like a condom, right?"

He chuckled lightly. "Exactly. Better to have one and not need it."

"Than need it and not have it," she finished the expression as she stood and set her coffee down. "I'll call the guys and let them know you changed your mind. I'll also tell them to pack for a multi-day stay, even though that is not the plan."

"Right." Dale sighed then turned for the door. "Oh yeah." He turned back to her. "Transportation?"

"Tommy has a four-wheel-drive SUV. It should carry all of us and our gear."

"Great. What time?"

"I'll text you when I know for certain. Early, I'm sure."

Dale gave her a slight nod and then headed for the door. "Oh yeah, one more thing." He glanced over her shoulder to the pistol lying on the table. "Do you know how to use that thing?"

She nodded. "Johnny used to take me out regularly to the range. I'm actually not a terrible shot."

Dale raised a brow and swallowed hard. "If you insist on bringing it, please keep it secure."

"Understood."

Dale methodically packed his gear, moving from one side of his room to the other, collecting the few items he felt he might need. As he prepared his pack, he slipped the Bluetooth device into his ear and tapped the number for the regional office.

"Director Stanton, please. It's Special Agent Archer."

A moment later Stanton answered. "When do you depart?"

"In the morning." Archer paused and closed his eyes, still unsure how to bring up the issues that had arisen. "There's a problem though."

"Spill."

Archer sighed and sat on the edge of his bed. "She's got another reporter coming with—"

"No problem. Reporters are stupid. You should be able to—"

"Negative, sir," Dale cut him off. "In my experience, good reporters are anything but stupid. Plus, she's bringing an Indian tracker and an ex special forces guy."

Stanton was quiet for a moment. "What are their names?"

Dale flipped open his notepad. "The tracker is Tommy Youngblood." He could hear tapping on a keyboard in the background.

"Nothing on him. Is he local?"

"No idea, Director."

"Interim director," Stanton corrected. "What about the other guy?"

"Ex SAS or SFF. Al Briese." He flipped the notepad closed and settled in while Stanton searched.

"Oh, man. This guy has a history."

"Talk to me, boss."

Stanton took a deep breath. "Okay, Albert Briese. Born in London, grew up in the United States. Father was German, mother was from South America. Moved back to Britain just before high school. Exceptionally high marks. Joined Her Majesty's Royal Marines, spent eight years with the SAS, expert in tactics and demolitions. Finished university early with a degree in aeronautical engineering. Rejoined the service and was assigned to Special Forces Flight." Stanton paused as he read through a list of ratings Briese had attached to his license. "This guy has been busy. He now runs a consulting firm, mostly working with government agencies and…"

"What?"

"Military. He teaches techniques and tactics to our special forces pilots and boat crews."

"Boat crews?"

Stanton scoffed. "I see where our original plan is out the window. There's no way you're going to redirect her group without raising a ton of suspicion."

"Or plant believable evidence with this tracker fellow." Archer sighed heavily. "Okay, so considering this

Briese is the real deal, odds are that Tommy Youngblood is as well."

"Roger that." Stanton sat back in his chair and ground his teeth. "I'm open to suggestions."

"So am I, sir." Dale wiped at his eyes and glanced around the room. "So I take them where they want to go."

Stanton sat forward audibly. "*Do what?!*"

"Director, we can't get a cleanup crew out there for weeks. Odds are the mountain apes are still in the area." He paused a moment to let the pieces fall into place.

Stanton's voice became soft and quiet. "Are you implying what I think you're implying?"

Dale hung his head and sighed. "Sir, the problem could very well take care of itself."

"What about you?"

Dale swallowed hard. "I'll do what I have to, sir."

Stanton groaned low in his throat. "I don't like this."

"Neither do I, sir. But considering the circumstances…"

"And if the creatures aren't still in the area?"

"Then we deal with the fallout of her story." Dale stood and began to slowly pace his room. "We could send a high altitude drone to search for their heat signatures."

Stanton nodded to himself. "I'll get on that. I can't guarantee we can get one, but I'll pull whatever strings I can. As soon as I have an answer, I'll let you know."

Archer took a deep breath. "It would be good to know what I'm leading them into."

"And maybe you can use that intel to create a workable exfil plan."

Dale blew his breath out hard and reached for his phone. "Text me when you have something."

"Good luck out there, Archer."

"Thank you, sir. I have a feeling I'm going to need all the luck I can find."

3

ALBANY, New York

DALE SAT in the rear booth of a greasy spoon diner, sipping coffee and staring at his phone. He glanced out the window and noted the sky was slowly growing lighter. The sun would be up shortly but it would mostly be hidden behind clouds. The fog had turned to mist and set a chill in the air. Winter was nearly upon them. He'd only been up for a couple of hours and his day was already crap.

The front door dinged and Patricia stuck her head in, giving him a curt nod before she stepped back out and waited. Dale dropped a five on the table to cover the coffee and grabbed his duffle bags.

Stepping outside he saw Patricia standing next to two other men, chatting quietly. Dale measured the men as he approached and set his things next to a lifted, early 90's Suburban. "I take it this is our ride?"

Patricia turned with a smile and quickly introduced

the two men. "This is Tommy Youngblood and Albert Briese."

Dale extended a hand, locking eyes with both men as they shook. "And Hector?"

"He should be here any moment." Patricia glanced around and then offered a crooked smile. "Where's your car?"

Dale shrugged slightly. "You said we had a ride so I Ubered here." He glanced at Tommy. "Is that a problem?"

Tommy shook his head, "Not by me."

Patricia chuckled to herself. "No, I only meant we'll have to follow Hector back and—" She was interrupted by the extremely loud exhaust note of a quickly approaching vehicle. She actually cringed when a lifted, yellow, balloon tired, short wheel based pickup covered in chrome swerved into the parking lot and Hector waved excitedly. "I borrowed her from my cousin!" he yelled through the open window. "She's made for going offroad!"

Dale raised a brow and scoffed. "The whole plan was to sneak in and sneak out." He turned to Patricia and grimaced. "They'll hear us coming a mile away."

"I'll talk to him." She stepped away from the group and had to crane her neck to look up at Hector in the driver's seat.

Tommy opened the back of the Suburban. "You can load your gear here."

Dale scooped up his bags and noted the rear of the Suburban was empty. "Uh…didn't Patricia tell you guys to pack for a couple of days? Just in case?"

Tommy hooked a thumb to the roof rack. "All taken care of."

Al stepped closer to Dale and quietly cleared his throat. "Tricia says you're FBI." Dale was actually surprised he didn't hear much of an accent.

He nodded as he pulled the door shut. "Yeah. And you were SFF?"

Al replied with a curt nod. "She said that these things were able to take down a helicopter gunship?" His eyes narrowed as he spoke and he studied Archer's body language as the man quickly decided how much information to release.

"That's what the reports say." He stepped away from the rear of the Suburban and lowered his voice. "I had friends out there. People I would trust with my life." He took a deep breath and let it out slowly. "If they say that these cavemen took down a helicopter with a giant spear, who am I to question?"

Al considered the possibility and nodded slightly. "That must have been one hell of a spear. The Lexan screens for helicopters are thick. Strong enough to withstand bird strikes at three hundred miles an hour."

Dale felt a smile tug at the corners of his mouth but fought the desire. "I don't know any birds that can fly that fast."

Al nodded. "That's why they're over-engineered. To prevent that from ever being a possibility."

Dale offered a weak shrug. "I'm no expert on any of that. But I would guess that a sharpened spear refuses to flatten when it meets glass. Birds? Not so much."

Al raised a brow at him but said nothing. He made a slow turn and stepped to the front passenger side of the vehicle, claiming "shotgun" without muttering a word.

Dale turned back to find Hector quietly arguing with

Patricia. He groaned inwardly and injected himself into the situation. "What's the problem?"

"He's insisting on taking this thing, and I told him that—" Dale held a hand up, cutting her off.

He turned to Hector and shook his head. "We need to make a quiet approach."

"And we still can. But there's no way we should go into those woods with only one way out." His eyes bulged as he spoke. "I read those reports. Those things smashed and flipped over cars like they were nothing. I want a lifeboat in case the *Titanic* over there sinks."

Dale's head dropped and he stared at the parking lot asphalt for a moment. "How about once we reach the trail into the woods, you park that thing and ride in with the rest of us?"

Hector smiled broadly as his shoulders lifted. "Hey, man, that sounds like a plan to me." He nudged Patricia with the back of his hand. "I'll follow you."

She glanced at Dale and then sighed as she turned for the truck. "We're ready. He's going to follow us out there."

Tommy's eyes widened. "In that?"

"He's leaving it at the trailhead and will ride in with the rest of us." She reached for the door handle and had to hop to enter the lifted Suburban.

Dale gave Hector a quick glance. "Tell me you came prepared."

"Oh yeah, yeah, man. She told me to pack for a couple of days, just in case." He smiled broadly as he jumped back into the bright yellow beast. "I'm all good."

Dale reached for his phone the moment it chimed. He read the quick text then hit speed dial. "Archer for Stanton."

A moment later Stanton picked up the phone. "That was quick."

"We're already on the road. Did you find out anything?" He noted Tommy studying him in the rear view mirror.

"I called in every marker I had. Even had to create a few new chits with the right people."

"But?"

Stanton sounded relieved over the line. "A high altitude drone with IR capabilities did a survey of the area. Massive numbers of heat signatures were leaving the zone with the majority of them headed west."

Dale felt a smile forming. "That's good news then."

"I would say so. However, there's still a good number of the creatures still in the area."

"Define 'good number.'" Dale's brows knit.

"Apparently it was hard to get an exact count due to the canopy density, but our best guess is somewhere between eight and nineteen."

Dale nearly choked. "That's a pretty big spread there, boss."

"I'm sorry, Archer. That's the best I could get from them." He sighed heavily into the phone. "Trust me, I pressed for better intel, but they just couldn't make that call. They kept saying the canopy was too thick. Some of the readings could be a very large creature, or it could be more than one in close proximity to each other."

Dale growled low in his throat. "Okay. We'll work with what we have. Thanks, Director."

"Interim—" he started to correct him. "I will say this. Judging by the number of creatures leaving the zone, there must have been a pretty big population of those things there." He cleared his throat nervously. "I'd guess they stripped the area of resources early into this battle."

Dale squeezed his eyes shut and ground his teeth. "Except for the hundred or so people they killed."

Stanton was silent for a moment. "I had forgotten that they were supposed to be cannibals."

"Carnivores. *Cannibal* suggests eating your own kind. They may be smart, but I'm not ready to give them human status yet."

Stanton took a deep breath and blew it out hard. "Be careful out there. Try to bring those people back alive."

Dale raised a brow at the comment. "What about the story?"

Stanton scoffed. "I think enough blood has been sacrificed to keeping these things trapped in lore. Let the chips fall where they may."

Dale nodded slightly. "Understood, sir. Try to get some sleep."

Stanton scoffed. "It's a whole new work day. I'll coffee up and be in standby mode. If you can get a signal, check in once in a while."

"Copy that, sir." Dale heard the line go dead and clicked off his phone.

"The office?"

He turned to see Patricia studying him. He gave her a slight nod. "Boss had a drone do a flyover. They said that the grand majority of them are leaving the area."

Al twisted in the front seat and gave him a shrewd look. "Were they reinforcements for the indigenous, or forced to leave the area due to a lack of resources?"

"No idea." Dale slipped his phone back into his pocket and met the man's gaze. "But they're reported to be meat eaters. All the people they killed could have fed them for some time."

Al glanced away and considered his words. "Makes sense." He turned back and faced the front again stoically.

"Did they have any idea how many were still out there?" Tommy asked, glancing in the rear view mirror.

Dale offered a tight lipped smile. "Anywhere from a dozen to a dozen and a half." Tommy nodded slightly before turning his full attention back to the drive.

"That's not very precise," Patricia quietly stated.

"They blamed the canopy. Blocked too much of the heat signatures. They just couldn't get a clear enough read to say for certain."

Patricia sat silent for a moment before turning back to him. "Is that a lot?"

Dale felt there was a hidden meaning to the question but he wasn't sure what she was asking. "In my opinion, one is too many."

She gave him a surprised look. "You'd rather they all be dead?"

Dale raised a brow at her. "Not…exactly. I'd simply rather we didn't have to risk facing any of them." He cleared his throat and turned away. "I'd rather they all left the area and hid deeper in the woods."

She felt the need to pat his hand and started to reach out, but thought better of it. "I'm sure we can be in and out before they even realize we're there."

Dale sighed as he watched the world zip by his window. "I certainly hope so."

Deep in the Catskills

"It sorta stands out like a sore thumb." Hector kicked absently at the tire of the custom yellow 4X4. "Maybe I should drive it a little further off the road?"

"It will be fine." Dale held the door of the truck open and waited for Hector to shut off the engine. "Come on, man. We're burning daylight here."

Hector groaned and shut off the engine then glanced around the cab for a place to hide the keys. "The sun visor? Or is that too much like the movies?"

Dale rolled his eyes. "Drop 'em in the floor for all I care. Just move." He stepped away from the truck and shot Hector an annoyed look.

"Man…" Hector whined as he pulled open the ash tray and hid the keys inside. "You have no idea how much fun driving that thing is."

"Well, if we hurry, you can drive it back to town in just a few hours." Dale tugged open the rear door of the Suburban and raised a brow at the reporter. "The sooner we get there, the sooner Patricia can document the scene, the sooner we can leave."

Tommy appeared beside Dale and shot him a

concerned look. "There's been a lot of traffic along this trail recently." He glanced back to the well-worn trail. "Lots of heavy vehicles."

Dale nodded as he glanced over his shoulder. "They should still be there. My boss said it could be weeks before they can get a team up here to sanitize the area."

"Sanitize?" Tommy gave him a dubious look.

"It just means retrieve all the junk that was left. Try to make it look like nobody had come out here."

"Why's that?" Patricia asked accusingly. "What are they trying to hide, other than bigfoots?"

Dale groaned and gripped the door tighter. "Wrong choice of words on my part." He took a deep breath and locked eyes with her. "A lot of equipment was left out here. Weapons, tech, and the like. They'll need to retrieve as much as they can. To keep hikers and campers safe if nothing else."

She scoffed as she turned away from him. "How many hikers and campers do you really think will come out here once they find out there's a tribe of killer cavemen?"

Dale felt his jaw tighten and had to bite his tongue to keep from snapping at her. "Well, I can guarantee you one thing. The minute you report that there *is* a tribe of bigfoots out here, every wacko in the city is going to throw on their hiking boots and backpack and come out here hoping to catch a glimpse of one. Your article is going to be one huge invitation to the stupid to come out here and get eaten."

Al offered a quiet chuckle. "Survival of the fittest, am I right?"

"What's that?" Dale asked, his temper still trying to rise.

Al simply shook his head. "Social Darwinism." He offered a grin. "The stupids will come out here and your Sasquatches will thin their ranks. Remove the dumbest from the gene pool." He shrugged. "Survival of the fittest."

"Hey, man." Hector pointed to some of the smaller nearby trees. "Do you think we should like, cut some limbs or something to try to hide the truckBig Bird?"

Dale turned and shot him an angry glare. "Get in the goddam truck already." He held the door open more and stepped aside. "Or you'll be walking into the camps."

"Alright already!" Hector slammed the door of the pickup and then gave it one last longing stare. "My cousin did a helluva job fixing her up, didn't he?"

Dale turned to Tommy. "Let's go. He can walk in." He slid into the rear seat and slammed the door, locking it behind him.

Tommy smiled as he walked around to the driver's door and slid in. "That's cold man."

"If he wants to stay back and make out with that overdressed piece of crap, he's not getting a cheer squad." Dale crossed his arms and exhaled forcefully. He refused to turn and look at Hector as he slid in on Patricia's side.

"I just don't want anything to happen to her, ya know. She's not mine." He turned to stare at the truck one more time.

"Then you should have left it back in the city," Dale muttered through gritted teeth.

"It's going to be okay, Hector." Patricia shot him a soft smile. "Trust me. It's far enough off the road that nobody will mess with it."

"I sure hope so." He sat back in the seat and tried to relax. "I just wanted us to have another set of wheels should the creatures...you know. Bash this one or something."

Tommy glanced in the rear view mirror at him. "They better not or they'll get a size twelve in the ass."

Al turned and gave him a sardonic smile. "Can you really kick that high?"

"Black belt, baby," Tommy grinned at him. "I can do a flying heel kick like you wouldn't believe."

Dale rolled his eyes again and stared at the ceiling of the truck. Somehow he felt like the lone chaperone on a school field trip and all of the kids forgot to take their medication.

4

Deep in the Catskills

As the Suburban slowly advanced over the rocky terrain, the pair of black government Tahoes began to come into view. "We got company," Tommy muttered.

"No, we don't. Don't stop." Dale locked eyes with Tommy's reflection in the mirror and he gave him a knowing nod. "In and out, remember?"

"Yeah, you got it, bro." Tommy slowed the truck and stared at the destroyed vehicles. "Was that a *trailer*?"

Dale groaned inwardly. "Yes. They brought four-wheeled ATVs with them to go deeper into the woods."

"Oh, man. We shoulda done that." Hector sucked at his teeth as they passed the destroyed vehicles. "I bet my cousin could fix those."

"Those would have been from the initial team, correct?" Patricia stared at Dale for confirmation.

Dale nodded slightly. "That was Gamboa's team."

"And they were the first to make contact with these…" She checked her notes quickly. "Genoskwa?"

Dale hemmed a moment then shook his head. "Actually, no. The initial contact would have been made by the group that Allen and his team came out to investigate."

"Ah, yes. The suspected 'terrorist training camp' mentioned in the reports." She jotted something in her notes and then reread it, nodding. "But Gamboa and his people were the first Bureau folks to make contact."

Dale nodded. "To the best of my knowledge, yes."

Al pressed the button to roll the window down and stared into the deep shadows of the woods. "Surprisingly dark, considering the time of day."

"It's the clouds, man," Hector stated matter of factly. "And this mist. Makes everything gloomy as hell."

Dale sighed to himself. "Actually, the woods are so thick that it's hard to see very far into them even in broad daylight. When my team inserted, it was a clear, sunny day, but under that canopy? It can feel like it's the dead of night."

"Noted," Al quietly replied, his eyes scanning the interior of the woods as they pushed on.

"How much further?" Hector asked, pressing his knees closer together.

Tommy shrugged, glancing in the rear view toward Archer. "How far is it?"

"Not far. It seems like the Tahoes were about halfway between the main road and Gamboa's camp."

"What about the camp that my brother set up?" Patricia asked.

Dale shook his head. "I really don't know how deep

they went. All I know is they had some heavy trucks in and out, so their trail should be easy to find."

"Hey man, pull over. I gotta pee." Hector reached up and unlocked the door. "Too much coffee on the drive in."

Tommy groaned quietly as he slowed the Suburban to a stop. "Be quick."

Hector scrambled out of the truck and slammed the door behind him. The occupants all cringed slightly at the unnecessarily loud noise. Tommy checked the surroundings as Hector made his way to the rear of the truck.

"I'm sure the engine is every bit as loud out here." He glanced at Dale in the rear view mirror. "Don't you think?"

Dale sighed and sat back in his seat. "I think we'll be lucky not to be seen."

"They're nocturnal, yeah?" Al asked, staring out the window.

"Yeah, but I'm pretty sure they set up a guard to keep an eye on things while the others sleep. I mean, when we were out here it was like we were constantly under surveillance." He shot Patricia a furtive glance. "My team was attacked during daylight hours, so I have no doubt that at least some of them are already aware of us."

Hector appeared by Tommy's window and startled him. "I can't go. It feels like I'm being watched."

Tommy rolled down the window and raised a brow at him. "You probably are being watched." He nodded towards the woods. "Birds, squirrels, woodchucks, and probably a Sasquatch or two are all wondering why we stopped so you could wag your flag at them."

"I'm serious. I can't go if something's watching me. My roommate had this dog once—."

Dale leaned forward and gripped the back of Tommy's seat, pulling him closer to the window. "Squeeze it out or get back in the truck. Every second we waste out here is just more time for them to become aware of our presence."

"Oy, take yer piss or load yer arse in the truck." Al shot him a serious stare. "This is no time to be fuckin' about."

Hector seemed to dance in place a moment then cursed under his breath as he trotted to the back of the truck again.

Patricia leaned forward, craning her neck to look at Al. "Was that finally an accent I heard?"

Al chuckled quietly. "Too many years in service. When I get stressed, it tends to slip."

Tommy studied the mirrors and then sighed heavily. "Should I leave him?"

"No!" Patricia replied a bit too quickly. "I'd have too much explaining to do back at the office."

Dale huffed and reached for the door handle. "Enough of this bullshit."

The door opened before he could grip the handle, and Hector scrambled back in. "Oh man, do I feel better."

"Everything come out okay?" Tommy asked sardonically as he put the truck back into gear.

"Just a heads up, I'll probably have to go again pretty soon. That happens when I hold it too long."

"Tough shit, mate," Al replied loudly. "This time you'll just have to piss yer pants."

Hector's face fell. He suddenly leaned toward Dale. "You said we weren't far, though, right?"

Dale pulled away from Hector's hot breath and winced. "Dude…"

"Relax. We're almost there," Patricia pushed him back slightly. She continued to stare out the windows, her mind seeing movement in the shadows that wasn't there.

"Starting to become real to you?" Dale asked quietly.

Without facing him, she nodded slightly, her hands instinctively gripping her satchel tighter. "I guess what I imagined isn't quite the same as reality."

"It rarely is," Dale softly replied.

"What the actual fuck?" Tommy slowed the truck and came up behind a line of vehicles trapped behind a fallen tree.

Al reached beside him and unzipped a bag. He removed an MP5 and charged it as he opened the door to step out. Dale's focus jumped between the line of trucks and the fact that an ex-SFF pilot was carrying a full-auto machine gun in the presence of a federal officer. It was bad enough that an untrained reporter had brought a weapon into the woods, but this?

"Yeah, what the actual fuck?" Dale hissed and hurriedly extricated himself and approached Al. "Tell me that's a semi-auto civilian version."

Al glanced at the selector switch on the side. "Christ, I hope not." He shot Dale a crooked grin. "Relax, mate. I'm licensed for—"

"Not in the state of New York, you aren't." He could feel his temper start to rise and a dozen arguments were running through his mind when Patricia cautiously stepped between them.

"Actually, he is. I researched him before contacting him. His LLC also has a Federal Firearm Special Occupational Tax that—"

Dale spun on her. "There are still *rules* you have to follow with an SOT, and you can't just be carting around a fuckin' machine gun wherever the hell you want to!"

"Uh, guys." Tommy stepped closer and held his hands up. "Rather than argue about this, shouldn't we be figuring out a way around that?" He pointed to the blocked trail. "And, um…agent Archer? There are a shit ton of guns just lying in the dirt over there."

Dale turned shocked eyes to him. "Say again?"

"Yeah, man. There's a bunch of guns scattered everywhere. A lot of dry blood, too."

Hector groaned something in Spanish and made the sign of the cross as he cautiously stepped forward. "Unless you brought chainsaws and a tractor to pull these out of the way, I don't think we're driving any closer."

Dale turned to Patricia. "Tell me this is enough proof for you." His eyes pleaded with her, but his stomach fell when she turned and raised a brow at him.

"I need to see where the camp was." She saw his expression change and stepped closer, lowering her voice. "I need to know that everything in those documents was real."

Dale groaned and rolled his eyes. "Fine." He glanced at the sky and shuddered. "We better get moving. Everyone grab their gear." He stepped toward

SURVIVAL

Al and pointed a finger at the weapon. "You and I aren't done with this."

Al gave him a crooked smile. "Actually, we are." Dale spun back ready to give him a ration of shit when Al leaned in and lowered his voice. "She's right. I am licensed and this is completely legal. I also have a team of lawyers who love chewing up and spitting out entire federal agencies. One lone FBI agent wouldn't even be an appetizer for them." He stepped past Dale and towards the truck. "Consider your career, Agent Archer."

Dale watched the man start pulling gear from the roof of the Suburban and had to close his eyes and count silently to bring his blood pressure down. "Pick your battles, Dale. Pick your battles."

"WOULD YOU LOOK AT THIS?" Tommy quietly asked. He held a carbine up that had been bent into a neat half circle, its plastic furniture broken or missing. "These things must be strong."

"You have no idea," Dale responded, his eyes bouncing from the surrounding woods to the damaged vehicles.

Patricia gasped and turned away from one of the bigger trucks. "Oh my god."

Al stepped closer and noted the thick tree trunk jutting from the shattered windshield. He stepped closer and craned his neck to peer inside the cab. "Driver's missing."

"Yeah, missing a lot of blood," Hector added a bit

too loudly. "There's gotta be a gallon of it ran out the door."

Patricia had to keep her emotions in check as her imagination attempted to run away with her. Visions of her brother being physically tortured kept popping into her mind, and the toll for fighting it all was higher than she had allotted.

"You okay?"

She turned to see Dale studying her and gave him a feeble nod. "I keep thinking of Johnny. What he must have gone through."

Dale patted her shoulder. "I'm sure he gave as good as he got."

She stopped walking and turned to peer past him at the tree trunk stabbed through the front of the two-ton truck. "Somehow, I don't think he could have." She felt her jaw quiver and she clenched her teeth to stop it. "I think they were all outmatched."

"They're strong," Dale quietly responded, "and smart as hell. But that isn't what gave them the advantage."

"Oh?"

Dale continued to scan the tree line. "They were defending their home. We were the intruders."

"I got something." Tommy waved them over. "This was a trap." He pointed to another fallen tree, blocking the truck's retreat. "Also, that…" he pointed to equipment and personal belongings scattered into the trees.

"Why would mountain gorillas go through their belongings?" Al asked as he stopped to pick up a torn duffle.

"Maybe they were looking for food?" Hector toed a

smashed MRE package. "I mean, even the bigfoots have to eat, right?"

Dale stiffened and kept his opinions to himself. He didn't need to share the Iroquois belief that the Genoskwa were cannibals; he'd already warned them sufficiently. "We should go." He gave Al a knowing look before turning to march past the kill box.

"Madre de Dios…" Hector whispered. "Tahoes, two tons…a fucking Winnebago? Talk about government surplus. My cousin would go nuts."

"Any idea how far it is?" Patricia asked.

Dale sighed heavily. "I'd say an hour's hike to the first camp, but I have no idea where exactly the agency set up theirs."

She rifled through her satchel and withdrew a copy of a topographical map. "I printed this from the download."

Dale studied the map for a moment and turned a slow circle. "I'd say we're not far at all." He nodded to Al who was bringing up the rear. "You SAS types are good at reading maps, aren't you?"

"I've been known to, from time to time."

Dale handed him the printout. "What do you think?"

Al ran a finger along the edge of the map and then reached into his bag. He withdrew a small device and punched in the latitude and longitude printed on the map. He waited a moment then shook the device. "My GPS is acting up."

Patricia snapped her fingers. "I remember reading something…um…" She dug into her satchel again and withdrew a small notebook. "One of the reports said that there were magnetic fields that interfered with their communications and other electronics." She looked up at him expectantly. "Could that be it?"

Al's features knitted as he studied the screen. "This is supposed to work directly with the satellites."

Dale held his hand out. "May I?"

Al handed him the bright yellow plastic device and Dale flipped it over, removing the battery cover. "Usually on the inside, they'll print...yeah." He held it out for Al to see. "There, where it says 4G and 5G bandwidths? They'll use cell signals to contact a local router rather than direct read from satellites." He put the battery cover back on and handed it to him. "It makes them more affordable. The manufacturer doesn't have to have to provide the power and processor capability for actual satellite connection. It's faster and cheaper to use a cell signal."

"Great," Al groaned as he dropped the device back into his bag. "So much for high tech, eh?" He turned his attention back to the map and tried to study the terrain. "This would be a lot easier to do from the air, but..." He turned another slow circle and then landed his finger on the map. "My best guess."

Dale studied the position and then handed it back to Patricia. "If the Bureau's coordinates are correct, and I have no reason to think they're not, then we're about an hour-and-a-half's hike from where they set up camp."

She took a deep breath and then squared her shoulders. "Let's push on then. The sooner we get there, the sooner we can leave."

"Great," Hector stated. "I gotta pee again. Nobody watch!"

5

Deep in the Catskills

AL MANEUVERED CLOSER to Dale and lowered his voice. "Do you feel like we've got eyes on us?"

Dale nodded slightly then glanced back at the reporters. They were huffing to keep up, struggling with their packed gear. He looked ahead at Tommy, taking long strides, obviously used to trekking over rough terrain.

"I have no doubt they're watching us."

Tommy suddenly stopped and held a hand up, stopping them. He studied the woods ahead and squinted, catching remnants of shadows as they shifted deeper into the forest. "We have company."

A loud wood knock echoed through the forest and Dale felt the hair on his neck stand on end. "They're announcing our presence."

"So much for in and out, eh, mate?" Al stepped around him and approached Tommy. "How many?"

Tommy slowly shook his head. "I can't tell, but they're out there." He continued to stare into the woods and felt a cold chill run up his spine. "I get the distinct feeling we aren't welcome here"

"What is that sound?" Hector asked as he approached the other men. "Tell me you hear that."

Al and Dale both shook their heads, but Tommy craned his neck and turned his best ear towards the woods. "It's almost like a *growl*."

Patricia groaned slightly and pressed a hand to her temple. "Oh my…what the hell?"

Dale spun and reached for her arm. "What is it?"

"It's like the worst migraine and…" she trailed off, wincing as she lowered herself to one knee. "I think I'm going to be sick."

Hector suddenly turned and bent over, his pack threatening to send him ass over tea kettle. He planted his hands on his knees and hurled, spewing the remains of his breakfast into the sparse grass.

"Oh man…I've heard of this." Tommy pressed his fingers into his ears and began to spit as his mouth salivated.

Dale eyed Al and gave him a tight-lipped smile. "Infrasound. It's a defensive thing."

Al raised a brow at him. "Too many years of flying multi-engine craft and shooting high caliber weapons. My hearing is shot."

Dale took a deep breath and let it out slowly. "Yeah, mine is shot too, but you'll start feeling it." One hand pressed to his gut while the other pressed at his temple. "Trust me."

Al slowly shook his head. "Sorry, mate. I don't feel a —" His features suddenly sobered and the color drained from his face. "Bloody hell." He spun to the side and threw up in the grass, his body bent over, his skin breaking into a cold sweat.

"How do we make it stop?" Patricia asked as she continued to spit into the grass.

Dale groaned inwardly and reached for the shotgun slung over his shoulder. He aimed it haphazardly toward the forest ahead of them and began firing randomly into the darkness. He knew the odds of hitting anything were slim to zero, but he also knew that the creatures had previously abandoned their infrasound attacks, once they were fired upon.

Once the shotgun was empty, he switched to the short-barreled M4 and sprayed the surrounding woods again. A moment later the group was struggling to catch their breath, the pain and pressure in their heads subsiding and their queasiness easing. Dale stood and stretched his back, breathing heavily from the mouth. "That may not stop them for long."

"This ain't good," Hector said as he continued spitting the bile from his mouth. "They definitely know we're here." He turned to Patricia and pleaded with his eyes. "We should go. Like, now. We can..." he stammered as he tried to think clearly, "we can come back with a drone and fly it over the campsite."

Patricia spat again and wiped her mouth on the sleeve of her flannel overshirt. She sniffed hard and blinked away tears as she shook her head. "Drones won't work out here." She took a deep breath and let it out slowly as she looked at Dale. "Did you ever recover the drone you brought?"

"Actually, no." He took another deep breath and

continued to stare into the woods. "There was too much interference with the remote."

Hector stiffened. "Hey, I read those same reports. The feds used drones all the time. Th-they used them for thermal readings and, and..." He struggled to think as the panic continued to rise inside. "They had that contractor guy from the city come in, and his drones worked."

Dale turned and raised a brow at him. "What contractor?"

Hector shrugged. "I dunno. I mean, I don't remember. I just remember reading about it in the write-up."

"Davis," Patricia answered. "Larry Davis. I remember his name but I don't recall the company he was with."

Tommy turned and held his hands up, catching their attention. "Look, we can stand here and discuss all of this really interesting stuff, or we can get our asses to the camp, verify what you need to verify, and get the hell out of here." He hooked a thumb over his shoulder. "Something tells me that those guys are going to lose patience with us really quick if we don't get out of their territory."

Dale adjusted his pack and sighed. "They're already losing patience with us." He stared into the darkness and prayed that the monster that had allowed him to leave before didn't recognize him this time around. He knew in his gut that there was no way the beast would grant him a second reprieve.

Patricia stood on shaky legs and took another deep breath. "Then let's carry on, shall we?" She stepped past Hector and approached Al. "Gentlemen, care to lead the way?"

SURVIVAL

Tommy gave her a look that Dale couldn't quite read before he turned and took point again. The group trekked forward with Hector giving the occasional surprised gasp or groan. More than once he whined that he didn't want to be there.

Patricia could take only so much before she stomped her foot and spun on him. "You brought that god-awful truck out here. If you don't want to be here, feel free to turn around and go back." She glared at him as she spoke. "Believe me, we won't hold it against you."

Hector stammered a bit before glancing back over his shoulder then turned to face her. "No. I, uh…I don't want to go back by myself."

"Then for the love of Pete, keep your whining to yourself. Please?" Hector opened his mouth to say something then quickly closed it. He pursed his lips and gave her a slight nod. "Thank you." She spun back around and began marching again.

Al chuckled to himself as he sidled next to Dale again. "She's got a set on her, eh?"

Dale gave her a furtive glance then shrugged. "She's determined. I'll give her that much."

Tommy slowed as he rounded a bend and whistled low. "More trash."

Dale slowly approached with his carbine at the ready. "Report," he whispered as he came up behind Tommy.

"Just trash bags, man." Tommy stepped aside and sighed. "Like, lots of them. Looks like some animal tore into them."

Dale froze and slowly lowered his rifle. "Those were body bags."

Al stepped around him and the sight made him

catch his breath. "How many people did they lose on this op?"

Dale felt his chest tighten. "All of them."

Tommy stepped aside as Dale and Al moved forward, taking in the black plastic shards scattered over the trail, in the grass, and some were even hanging from trees.

"If these are body bags…" Al trailed off, hoping Dale would pick up on the question.

Dale sighed heavily and felt a sudden weight press down on his shoulders. "According to Iroquois legend, the Genoskwa are cannibals." He took a deep breath and blew it out slowly. "Red Moon said his tribe had stories of them eating people."

Al's brows knit. "Wait. If they're cannibals, then they also eat their own?"

Dale shook his head. "No, they…" he trailed off, as frustration rose. He closed his eyes and counted silently. "The natives called them cannibals because they considered them to be a type of people. Barbaric, violent, cunning people, but…people nonetheless." He poked at a shred of plastic with the barrel of his carbine. "Stone giants."

"Ah, yeah," Al replied quietly. "She told me that part. They apply a plaster to their middle that looks like rock, right?"

Dale nodded. "Impervious to arrows and deflects most small arms."

Tommy stiffened. "Stone giant men?" He seemed to pale and his shoulders slumped. "My people have stories of them as well."

"Your people?" Dale raised a brow.

"The Tuscarora. They're…we're part of the Iroquois

tribe. They called the stone giant men Ot-nea-yar-heh." He scoffed silently. "If I'd known they were real and that was what we were facing out here, I wouldn't have come."

Al gave him a stoic look. "Well, you *are* here. Better make the best of a bad situation."

Tommy's face fell. "What the hell is that supposed to mean?"

Dale stepped between the two men. "Let's not do this, okay? Let's get her to the campsite, document whatever she needs to, and get the hell out of here." He gripped both men by the shoulders. "Okay? In and out, remember?"

"Too late for that," Hector quietly added. "They already know we're here."

"There was no avoiding that," Dale snapped. He caught himself and took a deep breath. "Look, emotions are running a bit high right now—"

"I'm cool as a cucumber, mate." Al shot him a sardonic grin. "But I catch your meaning. Let's shove on."

Tommy stared at the back of the man's head as he turned and began pressing on through the sea of shredded body bags. He glanced at Dale with a worried look. "Do you think they collected the dead to…" He swallowed hard. "To eat?"

Dale shrugged. "One can only assume."

Tommy nodded quickly. "So, maybe they won't be too hungry for a while." He offered a sheepish grin. "Maybe they won't need to add us to the menu."

"Hope for that if it makes you feel better."

"Can we take a quick break?" Patricia asked, limping. "Somehow I got a rock in my boot."

"Yeah, let's take five." Dale shrugged off his pack and gripped his carbine as she sat and began to unlace her boot.

"We should be close," Al stated as he studied the map again. "I'd say maybe a click and a half."

"The sooner we can get this over with, the sooner my heartrate can go back to normal," Dale replied. He glanced over Al's shoulder as Tommy crept closer to the middle of the rocky trail. "What's he doing?"

Tommy suddenly turned and gave them a worried look. "They're back." He made a slight motion with his head, pointing to their right.

"Of course they are," Hector groaned as he moved closer to Patricia. "You know, drones may not work, but I'd foot half the bill to just rent a helicopter ride out here."

She shot him a dirty look as she dumped her boot then quickly tugged it back on. "It's not the same and you know it." She grunted as she tugged the laces tighter and tied them. "I want to place my hands on the stuff, not just see it from a distance."

Hector shot her a bug eyed glare. "Helicopters CAN land, ya know!"

"Hold it down," Dale shushed them as he slowly advanced to Tommy's position. "What are you seeing?"

A snap in the darkness had all eyes turned in that direction and Tommy winced. "There they are."

A high-pitched "whoop" echoed through the trees

and Dale suddenly felt the hair on his neck stand on end again. "My adrenaline system is never going to be the same," he quietly groaned.

An answering "whoop" came from the other side of the trail and the group realized they were surrounded. Al stiffened and brought the barrel of the MP5 up as he scanned the shadows. "They're flanking us."

"I think they've had us flanked the whole time," Dale replied. "Let's get going." He reached down and gripped Patricia's arm, lifting her to her feet. "We need to move it. Double time."

"I like that idea," Tommy shot back as he turned and practically jogged along the trail. "I think there's a clearing ahead. I see sunlight."

"Motherfucker!" Hector yelled as he crumpled to the ground.

"Up and at 'em, amigo," Al stated as he reached for the man's arm. "No time for twisted ankles today."

"No, man. Somebody threw a rock at me," Hector whined as he came to his feet. "Fuck me, that hurts." He rubbed at his thigh as he tried to fall into step behind the taller pilot.

Dale moaned inwardly. "Oh yeah, they like to throw rocks." He turned and raised a brow at Al. "Sometimes they throw really big ones."

"How big?" Al asked as he push-pulled Hector along with him.

A loud *thump* sounded nearby and Al spun to see a small boulder roll onto the trail. He froze and stared in the direction it had come, unable to see the culprit.

"That's on the smaller size of 'em," Dale responded. "The faster we move, the harder it will be for them to hit us."

"I can't run with all this shit on my back, man!" Hector yelled from the rear.

Tommy shouted and slid to a stop at the head of the pack. A tall tree trunk cracked in the darkness, raining leaves and pine needles down on the path. He stepped back just as the trunk crashed across the trail ahead of him. "I think they're trying to box us in!"

"Or they're trying to tell us to go back," Patricia offered as she went around him. The group of men watched as she trotted towards an area of the trunk that was limbless and quickly hurdled over it. "We're burning daylight, gentlemen!"

Tommy shot Dale a surprised look and stared in awkward amazement as he ran to catch up to her. He leaped over the trunk and quickly closed the gap. "She's nuts," he muttered.

"We all are for being out here with her," Hector complained as Al practically pushed him over the trunk.

"Hustle up, friend," Al shot him a grin. "Wouldn't want to be left behind, now would ya?"

Tommy felt a knot form in his stomach and fought the urge to run in the other direction. "You're all fucking nuts, you know that?"

He planted his hands on the trunk and hurled his legs over. He could smell the fresh pine sap and happened a glance toward the fallen tree's base. It had to be a solid foot thick, but it was twisted and snapped six feet from the ground. He stared in awe at the damage, but for the life of him, he couldn't spot the creature that had felled it.

"Why the hell am I out here again?"

6

Deep in the Catskills

The group slowed as they approached a clearing. Tommy smiled as the sun's warming rays saturated his skin, warming him in the glow.

"Man, you don't realize how chilly it is in the shadows until you get into the light."

Dale scoffed to himself. "You don't realize how chilly anything is when you're running for your life." He glanced at Patricia tugging her pack off. "That was pretty decisive to just hurdle the tree and carry on."

She walked a slow circle, her hands planted to the small of her back, trying to take slow and even breaths after the run. She barely glanced at Dale before she nodded. "With or without you boys, I plan to carry on with the plan." She took another deep breath and forced it out slowly, doing her best to lower her heart rate. "Maybe it would be better if it were just me."

Both Dale and Al raised a brow at her but it was

Hector that spoke first. "Are you seriously that nuts?" He chuckled cynically as he approached her. "One person? On their own? Out here? Against...those things?"

She felt her anger begin to rise. "You ask that because I'm a woman? Maybe they wouldn't see a female as a threat."

Hector scoffed and shook his head. "Male, female, it wouldn't matter. You're just meat to these things. Do you think a hunter cares if the rabbit is a female?"

"This is my mission and hunter or prey, it makes no difference to me."

He threw his hands up. "Christ on a cracker, Patty, you got a fuckin' screw loose."

"Okay, that's enough." Dale stepped between the two and gave Hector a slight shake of the head. "We all knew what we were signing up for when we agreed to come out here."

Hector scoffed again. "Fucking boogeymen is what I was told. Nobody believes in that shit."

"And yet, here we are." Dale shot him a stern look. "Doesn't matter *what* you believe, they're out there, and they're not happy that we're in their territory."

Al appeared at Dale's side. "Did you see the size of that boulder they threw?"

Tommy suddenly stiffened. "Did you check the trunk of that tree? It was at least a foot thick and it wasn't just pushed over. I saw the break point and I'm telling you, it was twisted and...*ripped* apart."

"That's not possible," Hector finally interrupted. "Nothing has that kind of grip strength."

Dale held a hand up, trying to keep the discussion from escalating. "We don't know what happened. That tree could have been diseased or dying or—"

"Fuck you, man. I SAW it." Tommy sneered at him with contempt. "I smelled the fresh sap and I saw the break point. If you don't believe me, hike your happy ass back there and check it yourself."

"I think this break is over." Patricia gave them all a stern look. "We should get moving." She hefted her pack and slug it over her back again.

Dale sighed audibly then gave her a curt nod. "On the road again." He glanced at Al. "How far did you say it was?"

Al pulled the map from his vest pocket and unfolded it. He glanced around at the terrain then turned and pointed. "About a click as the crow flies." He raised a brow at Dale. "I'm not so certain I'd want to risk marching through dense woods though."

"Agreed." Dale hefted his pack and slung it over his back. "We stick to the trail."

"Some trail," Tommy scoffed. He kicked a small stone from his path. "Let's get this shit over with."

Hector nearly jumped when a tree knock echoed behind them. The crack of wood on wood sounded like a baseball bat had been used, but was almost as loud as a gunshot. He clutched at his chest as he stared back into the trees. "That sounded close."

Al slid his arm back into the strap of his pack and glanced at Dale. "They're announcing us again, aren't they?"

Dale nodded. "My bet would be that there are more of them ahead of us." He sniffed the air and winced. "Catch that?"

Al's features twisted and he held the back of his sleeve to his nose. "Whoo! That is ripe."

"They're closer than we thought," Dale whispered.

"If you can smell them that strongly, they're right behind us."

Al tugged his shooting glove tighter and licked his exposed trigger finger, holding it in the air. "Wind is from the east."

"Good thing we're headed west." Dale tugged at Al's arm. "Let's get moving. Maybe we'll get lucky and they'll drop back."

Tommy stood still in the path, staring straight. "There's movement ahead."

Dale grunted as he marched past him. "I'd expect nothing less." He glanced back at the kid. "Coming?"

Tommy's head slowly shook "no" but his mouth replied, "Yeah. Right behind you."

Patricia froze and fought the urge to stare in the direction of the "whoop" she heard in the woods. She nearly jumped when Dale marched past her. "We know they're out there. No reason to freeze up."

She shook her head fearfully as she took off again, catching up with him. "It just caught me off guard." She offered a nervous smile. "Believe it or not, when it goes quiet for any length of time, I can almost forget that they're out there."

Dale tugged the straps of his pack tighter. "Yeah, I know what you mean." He glanced behind them and then turned his attention back to the trail. "You can almost convince yourself that you left them behind."

She chuckled low and nodded. "'Almost' being the key word there."

"Hold up," Tommy quietly said, holding a fist in the air.

"Movement?" Al asked.

Tommy shook his head quickly and then glanced around at the darkening trees. "More debris, but…"

"But?" Dale repeated.

Tommy glanced back at him. "What time do you have?"

Dale peered at his watch. "A little past five, why?"

Tommy looked up at the sky beyond the canopy. "Is it getting dark already?"

"It can't be that late," Patricia tugged her phone out and stared at the time on the lock screen. "How did it…" She turned and searched Dale's face for answers he couldn't give.

Dale stepped around her and approached Tommy. "What kind of debris?"

"Just stuff. Like the streets after 9-11." He nodded ahead and Dale maneuvered around the tall, lanky, young man. He stared at hundreds of sheets of paper, rustling in the gentle fall breeze.

Al stepped around the two men and bent to retrieve a sheet of paper, still damp from the morning dew. "It's wet." He lifted it and spread it out over his open palm. "Log entries." He handed the sheet to Dale.

"This is part of their transmission logs." Dale lowered the paper and peered further along the path. "Are we at the edge of the camp?"

Al shrugged slowly and bent low, peering just above the tallest grass. "There's been a lot of movement through here." He stood and sighed. "Can't tell if it was from humans or not."

Tommy moved slowly forward and pushed the taller

grass aside, studying the ground below as he advanced. "Both." He bent low and spread the taller grass to the side. "Here's a huge barefoot print sunk in over part of a boot print." He turned back and raised a brow at Dale. "At least we're on the right path."

Dale handed the log page to Patricia. "You'll want to see this, I'm sure."

She took the page and studied it a moment. "Is there something in particular here that I should notice?"

Dale almost appeared to be looking down at her. "It's part of the proof that you needed to see and touch." He nodded to the page. "You might document that." He turned from her and continued moving along the stony trail. "Eyes open, people."

Tommy fell into step behind him, his hand instinctively hovering near the grip of the pistol strapped to his leg. "It's awfully quiet."

"A little too quiet," Al responded softly. "You would expect birds…insects. Something."

Dale spun around and faced the group. "Welcome to Dog Town, people."

FOB Dog Town

Patricia broke into a trot and passed Tommy and Al. She slowed as she approached Dale and stared past him. "Oh my…"

"Yeah. The bigfeets made a real mess of things." Hector was huffing as he broke past the edge of the trees and stared at the wide clearing. He could tell that at one time, the camp had been set up with some kind of purpose. The larger tents were in different stages of still standing. The portable buildings looked like they had been pushed off of their concrete block foundations and personal items were scattered across the area. "Place looks like it was bombed."

"Not too far off the mark, Mr. Ramirez." Dale moved around the man and tiptoed to reach a dark piece of cloth moving in the breeze, stuck to the corner of one of the converted shipping crates. He stepped back and opened up the dark material. "This was somebody's undershirt." He checked the inside, near the label to see if a name was stenciled inside. "Part of their tactical uniforms." He let the shirt fall to the ground as he made a slow circle, taking in the damage.

"Holy shit," Tommy gripped a pole and tugged it free from one of the metal doors. "Somebody shoved a tree right through…" he paused as his eyes focused on the tip. "This was a spear." He turned, ashen faced, and met Dale's gaze. "Did you know they had spears?"

Dale looked away and nodded. "Yeah."

Tommy hefted the piece of wood. "This thing has to be, what…ten feet long?" He held it out to Dale. "Check it out. It's thicker than the barrel of a baseball bat." He couldn't hide the anger and frustration in his voice. "You knew about this and you didn't think to inform the rest of us?"

Al moved past the angry young man. "Wouldn't matter if he had told us."

Tommy spun on him, the point of the spear aimed toward Al. "What do you mean, 'it wouldn't matter'? Of course it matters." He threw the spear to the ground. "These things can use weapons."

He spun and took an angry step towards Dale. "What else can they use? Bows and arrows?"

Al gripped Tommy's upper arm and spun him around. "It DOESN'T matter. It doesn't matter if they had muskets or machine guns. We're here to do a job."

"Speaking of," Hector began, turning to face Patricia. "How about you do what you need to do so we can get the hell out of here, okay?"

Patricia nodded nervously, her eyes locked on Tommy and Al. She broke her gaze from the two men and began to rifle through her satchel. "Document." She swallowed hard. "Document everything." She pulled out small cameras and handed one to Dale. "Here." She turned to Hector and handed him one. "Take this. Document everything." She stepped closer to Tommy and Al, both still locked in a staring contest. She thrust the small camera into Al's face. "Here. Take it. We need to document everything."

She gently pushed the two men apart and handed Tommy a camera. "Everything. Even if it looks like trash, snap a picture of it." She stepped back and raised her voice. "These are just digital cameras. They're cheap and somewhat disposable. Not a lot of features, but with the upgraded memory cards, they can probably hold between three and four hundred photos."

Dale turned the device over in his hands and raised a brow at her. "You want us to…" he trailed off.

"It will go a lot quicker if we all do it." She gave him a weak smile. "And it will keep us busy for an hour or so." She glanced at Al and Tommy. "Less chance of butting heads, right boys?"

Tommy rolled his eyes and huffed as he walked away. Al watched him go then turned his attention to the camera. "Just point and click?"

"Yes. They're not fancy, but they take decent pictures." She nodded toward the old logistics building. "I'll start here. The rest of you, just pick an area and start snapping pictures. Even if it looks unimportant."

Dale sighed heavily and then turned for what was left of the mess tent. He began to snap pictures of the outside then tugged at the broken wooden door that someone, or some*thing*, had pulled from its hinges. "They're probably going to fire me for giving aid to the enemy for this."

"How many fucking people did they have out here, anyway?" Tommy stretched his neck and rolled his shoulders. "That collapsed tent over there…there must have been at least a dozen beds in there. And there are a lot more tents just like it."

Dale sighed heavily and rubbed a rough hand over his weary face. "They had over sixty operational personnel. Plus support staff." He caught the look of confusion on Tommy's face. "They had sixty SWAT guys. Five teams of twelve."

Al stepped out of another tent. "And a metric shit ton of weaponry." He gave Dale a perceptive look. "There are empty armament racks in there. And that's not all. They had munitions."

Dale nodded knowingly. "They came loaded for bear, that's for certain."

"Wait a second," Hector interjected as he approached the trio. "They had guns…like, a LOT of guns. And explosives? And somehow these bigfoots just ran them off?"

"Killed them," Dale corrected, "all of them."

Hector's face went pale, and he spun around looking for Patricia. "This ain't cool. This ain't cool at all." When she emerged from an overturned shipping container, Hector pounced. "Did you hear what they said? The FBI had SWAT teams, a shit ton of guns, and even explosives, and these things killed them *all*." His face turned stern. "We need to get the hell out of here."

Dale glanced at Al then turned and stared at the setting sun. "Not tonight, we don't."

Hector's eyes bugged and he turned a panicked expression to Dale. "Whatchu mean, 'not tonight' *vato*? These things will—"

"He means," Al interrupted, clamping a firm grip on Hector's shoulder. "That it wouldn't be prudent to try to sneak out of the forest at night while those things are out there."

"The fuck you say?" Hector pulled away from him. "You really think they'll try to stop us if we're *leaving*?"

Tommy stepped closer and caught Hector's panicked gaze. "You saw that line of trucks and SUVs that were blocked off? The trees fallen in front and in back? All that blood? The guns lying in the dirt?"

"Yeah? So?"

Tommy's face went stoic. "They were trying to leave."

Hector felt his chest tighten and his guts cramp. "We're so screwed…that's it, man. We're dead."

7

FOB Dog Town

As the sun slowly sank below the western horizon, Dale and Al cleared most of the trash from the logistics center. The modified double shipping container was the most solid thing left standing at the camp. As the men dragged the last of the cots from the team tents into the building, Al went to work trying to fix the door so that it could be shut.

Patricia appeared near the entrance with a broad smile. "There were a lot of MREs left in the back of the cafeteria. I grabbed a box."

Dale reached in and plucked one of the heavy plastic envelopes. "Vegetarian lasagna?" He dropped the packet and reached for another. "Chili Mac?" He gave her a knowing look. "There's a reason these were left behind."

"I don't care." Hector reached into the box and

plucked one out. "I'm sick of candy bars and protein snacks."

Dale watched him for a moment and tried to stifle his smile. "He'll find out." He took the box from her and set it on the folding table. "I don't suppose there's a beef ravioli in here?"

Patricia shrugged. "I saw a meatball, but I'm not sure if there's more than one."

Dale smiled as he plucked one out. "Cheese tortellini. Not terrible." He nodded at her. "Thank you."

"How would you grade the meatball in marinara?"

Dale ripped open the packet with his teeth. "Seven and a half out of ten." He glanced at Hector trying to read the heating instructions in the low light. "That lasagna is about a four. It will keep you from starving, but unless you have cast iron guts, you'll be making mad dashes to the latrine."

Tommy stepped into the building and sighed. "The latrine is trashed. We'll just have to find a bush to go behind."

"I think that has it." Al stood back and swung the door shut, latching it. "Not perfect, but it should keep a majority of the bugs at bay."

Patricia patted his shoulder. "Not a lot of insects this late into Fall, but I appreciate the effort."

Hector sat cross-legged in the corner of the building and tried to make his trembling hands work. "We're not going to survive the night, are we?"

Al turned and leaned in the doorway, his eyes searching Dale. "Normally, I would say that if we leave them alone, they'll leave us alone, but..." he trailed off, searching Dale for input.

"But he's right. Normally, I don't think they'd be a

problem. But considering that every human that has come out here in the last month or so has waged war with them, we might be in for an eventful night."

A noise echoed from outside and all heads turned for the open door. "Was that a water drop?" Patricia asked.

"Too loud," Tommy whispered as he edged toward the opening.

"Too creepy," Dale added, glancing at Al.

Al shrugged. "I've no idea what that was," he whispered.

Another loud water drop sounded, as if in answer to the first one. Tommy stiffened and slowly reached for the door. "I think they're communicating our location."

Dale stepped up beside him and blocked him from closing the door. "Sealing that won't stop them." He stepped out into the brisk night air and glanced in either direction, his eyes adjusting to the darkness. "They know we're here. There's nothing stopping them from surrounding us and…" he trailed off, his mind refusing to revisit the horrors he knew the creatures were capable of.

"And what, mate?" Al asked.

"Doing whatever they want." Dale stepped out further into the darkness and squinted in the low light. "I see movement in the trees."

Al removed his infrared camera and brought the monocle to his eye. "I see a lot of heat out there, but it's fading fast."

"Fading?" Dale reached for the camera and peered through it. "Where the hell are they going? They know we're here."

Tommy appeared beside the two men and cleared his throat. "Since they have the upper hand regardless, I say we follow them. See where they go and what they do."

"Why the hell would we do that?" Hector hissed. "Those things killed an entire army and you want to tail them? What are you, nuts?"

Al smiled. "Well, if Hector's against it, I say we do it." He patted Tommy's shoulder as he stepped past him. "I'll lead the way."

"Wait!" Patricia whispered loudly. "I want to go."

Dale gripped Tommy by the shoulder and pulled him close. "I'll stick with them. Why don't you hold back and keep an eye on Hector. Make sure he doesn't do anything stupid."

Tommy's face fell. "Why me? It was my idea to follow them."

Dale shrugged. "You really want to leave all of our gear in one room with somebody on the edge of panic?"

Tommy's shoulders slumped and he slowly turned around. "Fine."

"That a boy." Dale winked at him. "We'll be back before you know it. I'll have Al record whatever we find."

Tommy waved them off as he stepped back into the shipping container. "Where's the food?"

PATRICIA CROUCHED between the two men and peered over a tall rock outcrop. The trees were thick around them, but ahead was a taller rock outcrop in a clearing. The Genoskwa shuffled around the clearing, their heads down and their shoulders slumped.

SURVIVAL

"What are they doing?" she whispered in Al's ear. The man barely shook his head as he slowly brought the thermal camera back up to his eye and pressed the record button.

Dale placed a gentle hand on her shoulder and pulled her back slightly. "Stay low," he whispered.

A series of guttural clicks had the creatures stop moving and a huge, reddish-brown male limped to the middle of the group. Even from forty yards away, the trio could hear the creature's heavy breathing as its chest expanded and collapsed.

He looked up into the canopy and Patricia's eyes followed his. It took her a moment to notice, but smaller creatures were either sitting or standing in the thicker branches of the bigger trees. She stifled a gasp as the huge male began to mumble something.

The sound was familiar, yet like nothing she had ever heard before. It seemed to have the structure of language—but in the most basic and guttural sense of the word. The more she listened, the more she realized that the giant male was creating sounds as he inhaled, rather than on the exhale. The whole idea made the back of her throat itch.

She winced as the sounds increased in volume, growing as if reaching for a great crescendo. When he stopped speaking, the others began to rock forward and back, humming something just below her hearing.

She turned wide eyes to Dale who stared open-mouthed. He glanced at her and offered a weak shrug.

A sharp wail snapped her head back to the ceremony, and she watched as a shorter and thinner Genoskwa threw her head back and shrieked. A moment later Patricia knew why, as two males carried in the dead body of one of their own.

Patricia stared in horrid fascination as they gently lay the body to rest in a shallow hole. The wailing Sasquatch knelt beside the body and gripped its lifeless hand in her own.

As the two males carried in another body, a second female began to openly cry out. The great sobs racked her form until she collapsed next to the other grieving female. The second one reached upward and cupped the head of the lifeless body as the two males reverently laid the corpse next to the first one.

Patricia suddenly felt like she was intruding on something very private. A ceremony that she had no business even knowing about, much less observing. She slowly pulled away from the outcrop and tugged at Dale's sleeve. "We need to go," she whispered in his ear.

Dale held a hand up, stopping her. His eyes were glued to the ceremony. When the two males gripped one of the boulders at the end of the outcrop and began to pull it over to cover the dead, he tapped Al's shoulder and motioned him away.

The three of them quietly slipped out of the forest and made their way back to the clearing that separated the camp from the trees. They practically ran across the grassy knoll until they were back at the edge of camp. It was only then that Patricia felt safe enough to speak. "Did you just SEE that?"

"See it?" Al responded. "I recorded it."

Patricia paced quickly in a wide circle. "These aren't just dumb animals out here." She spun and glared at Dale. "Tell me you didn't know."

He gave her a surprised look. "Didn't know what?"

"That they were *spiritual*!" She had no idea how to deal with the myriad of emotions that continued to surface as she paced. "Tell me you didn't know they could speak!"

Dale gave her an exaggerated shrug. "I read one of Gamboa's team members' oral report that said they heard what sounded like speech, but..." he trailed off, unsure what to say next.

"Oh my god," Patricia exclaimed as she stopped pacing and bent over, her hands planted on her knees. "Oh my god."

"You just said that," Al stepped out of swinging range in case she was actually listening.

"Oh...my god!" She looked up and her face was pale. "This...this changes everything!"

Dale's feature's twisted. "How so?"

"I mean, it has to, right?" She began talking so rapidly that neither man was certain he could listen fast enough. "I mean, they obviously aren't dumb animals; they have ceremony and pomp and circumstance and bury their dead and they mourn and they can SPEAK!" She took a deep breath and began to pace again. "Oh my god...they speak! I have no idea what they were saying, but they not only spoke, they were singing something and...and it sounded like it was just a tune...but there could have been words to it, right? Like words we don't understand but they understand and—"

"Stop it!" Dale gripped her arms and locked eyes with her. "Have you taken your medication?"

She continued to stare at him, confusion written across her features. When realization set in, her features turned to scorn. "How dare you ask me—"

"Have you taken your medication?" Dale asked

again, his voice steady and even. "You tend to go off the rails when you've forgotten your meds."

Her lower jaw quivered as her brows knit and Dale felt like she was about to blow her top when she suddenly sobered. "Yeah, I need to take it. Thanks." She pulled away from him and stepped into the logistics building.

Al raised his brows as he passed by. "Brave move."

Dale sighed heavily and wiped a calloused hand over his face. "She was about to spin out."

"Obviously." Al stepped closer and lowered his voice. "But she's not wrong. It is pretty incredible what we just witnessed."

"Yeah, I don't think we were supposed to see any of that."

Al scoffed. "Ya think, mate?" He hooked a thumb towards the tree line. "Those things had to know we were there. They've known our every move since we arrived. What are the odds they wanted us to see that?"

Dale's brows rose. "What makes you think that?"

Al crossed his arms and clenched his jaw. "You really think that they made those funny noises outside our camp just moments before they all broke away to have a funeral? And none of them thought to set a sentry to make the sure the hairless apes didn't crash the party?"

Dale opened his mouth to argue but couldn't. He closed his mouth and let the words marinate a moment. "You really think they wanted us to be there?"

Al shrugged. "I wouldn't hazard to guess what goes through the mind of one of them, but it makes sense."

"To what end?" Dale turned to face him. "I mean, what purpose would it serve?"

Al toed at a stone near his foot. "To show their humanity?"

"Humanity?" Dale scoffed, fighting the urge to break into full-on laughter. "What humanity? They *eat* people."

"So do other humans." Al sighed heavily. "Look, I'm just saying, it's their woods. They've known our every move before we did." He hooked his thumb back toward the logistics building. "You heard those weird water droplet sounds. They had to mean something."

"And you think they meant, 'hey, hairless assholes, you're invited to a funeral'?"

Al shrugged. "Okay, okay, maybe it was their way of calling their sentries off the watch to come and pay their last respects. Who knows?"

"Exactly. Who knows."

"Look, mate. I'm just saying that maybe what we just witnessed was meant for us to see."

"Okay." Dale tossed his hands in the air. "And now we've seen it. So?"

"So?" Al gave him a curious look. "What do you mean, *so?*"

"So. Exactly what I said." He took a deep breath and let it out slowly. "What purpose did it serve?"

"Maybe they want us to know that.... You know, that maybe we're not so different from them."

Dale chuckled as he patted Al's shoulder. "Except we don't swing from trees and pull people's heads off their shoulders."

Al gave him a serious look that faded into a deadpan stare. "Not anymore. Now we drive around in SUVs and shoot each other, and our rocks tend to be nuclear."

Dale turned and stared back towards the woods and

rapidly darkening sky. "Come on. We need to settle in and pray they let us leave in the morning."

Al watched him step into the shipping container building and disappear into the darkness. He turned slowly back to face the woods and offered the creatures a curt nod. "I see you."

8

FOB Dog Town

Patricia was bent over the computer replaying the recording, doing her level best to take in every nuance. "What is that they're singing?"

"I just hear grunts," Hector reached into the box for another MRE. "Sounds like the monkey cage at the Bronx Zoo."

She shushed him and waved her hand in his direction. "I've almost got it."

Tommy stood behind her and studied the images on the screen for the tenth or twelfth time. "It almost sounds like a song, doesn't it?"

"Like, I should know this, right?" She turned and looked at him expectantly. "Like, it's just out of reach."

Tommy crossed his arms and nodded to the screen, "Run it back again."

"Oh, for piss' sake." Al stood and exhaled forcefully.

"It's not a bloody hymn. They're just mourning their dead."

Patricia paused the video and raised a brow at him. "You're telling me that you can't hear a melody in that?"

"That's exactly what I'm telling ya. Good luck trying to make something out of nothing." Al stepped to the exit and pushed the door open. "I need some air."

"Hold up. I'll come with." Dale stood and reached for a bottle of water. "It's kind of stuffy in here."

Hector leaned to the side and loudly passed gas. He stared at Patricia and Tommy with wide eyes. "That was supposed to be silent."

Tommy rolled his eyes and then pointed to the door. "Maybe you should do that out there. They weren't wrong about this room being stuffy."

Patricia waved him on. "Please, go. I really want to hear this."

Hector groaned as he came to his feet and grabbed another MRE, tucking it under his arm as he walked out. He stepped into the chilly night air and took a deep breath. "Smells a lot better out here than in there." He turned and gave the two men a cheesy grin. "Who knew MREs made you fart like that. Talk about friendly fire."

Dale groaned inwardly and turned away from the smaller man. "I think I'll sleep out here tonight."

Al nodded as he scanned the trees for movement. "That might not be a bad idea." He glanced at Dale then hooked his chin towards the edge of the clearing. "They're back."

Dale squinted in the low light and couldn't be sure if the moving shadows were his mind playing tricks on him or if something was out there, hovering just beyond the tree line, hiding in the dark.

"Are you sure?"

Al nodded and glanced at the nearly full moon. "I can feel their eyes on us. They're out there."

"So, has Patty lost her marbles or what?" Hector asked, sliding in between the two men.

Dale raised a brow and stepped aside, creating a bigger gap for the reporter. "If she says she hears music, then she hears it. One man's tune is another man's noise."

"I saw part of that video. You guys sure got close. It was like I was there, ya know?"

Al cleared his throat slightly. "It's called zooming in." He turned and gave Hector an annoyed look. "Most cameras can do that these days."

"Yeah, I know. I mean, of course." Hector stammered for a moment. "I just can't believe you were close enough to record them making noises and shit."

Dale stepped to the edge of the bull pen and studied the base of the overturned antenna tower. "With the damage they did here in the past, I'll really be surprised if they don't pay us a visit tonight."

"You know, I read your original report," Al quietly stated, eyeing him carefully. "It was part of the file dump that Tricia received."

Dale glanced at him, his curiosity up. "And?"

"And I read about how they released you…after they showed you their dead."

Dale came to his feet and gave him a curious look. "Okay. And?"

Al shrugged. "And, I'm thinking, what if that's why they allowed us to observe what happened earlier."

Dale's brows knit. "I'm not following you."

Al chuckled to himself as he closed the distance

between them. "Consider the possibility. They showed you their dead the first time. They... 'explained' to you why they did what they did, yeah?"

Dale shrugged. "That's what it seemed like."

"And this time, they allowed us to watch them lay their dead to rest." He crossed his arms and looked at him expectantly. "Perhaps they needed for us to know why they did what they did."

Dale scoffed. "I am more than capable of putting myself in their shoes. From their perspective, strangers came in and killed one of their own. They got revenge. Then more strangers came, threatening their way of life. Then more and more and..." he trailed off, looking away. "From their point of view, they were protecting what little they had."

"And maybe, by allowing us to participate in their ritual—"

"Ah! We didn't *participate*, we *observed*. From a distance."

"Whatever, mate. There's no way they didn't know we were there. They allowed it to happen."

Dale rolled his eyes. "Your point?"

"I'm just...I know it's a reach, but, what if they were letting us know that enough was enough? No more killing."

Dale stifled a laugh and had to turn away. "Please tell me you aren't serious."

Al shrugged. "Anything is possible."

"Not this time." Dale turned back slowly and locked eyes with the man. "They're animals. Yes, they bury their dead and yes, they appear to mourn them. But that's as far as it goes. These things eat people."

"Eww," Hector interjected quietly.

"Yeah, eww. *They eat people*. Rip their friggin' heads right off. Pop 'em like a grape." He stepped closer and lowered his voice. "Don't forget for a single moment that they're anything but animals. Because I promise you, the moment you start giving them the benefit of the doubt, it will turn around and bite you in the ass." He turned and walked away, leaving the two men to themselves.

Al stood at the edge of the bull pen and stared out across the clearing. "Then why haven't they killed us yet?"

Patricia leaned closer to the speakers and hummed along with the creatures. "I think that's it." She glanced at Tommy. "What does that sound like?"

Tommy shrugged. "It almost sounds like Irish or Scottish music." He gave her a sheepish smile. "I used to like this little red-haired chick and…" He cleared his throat nervously. "Anyway, yeah. She used to listen to that stuff."

Patricia nodded as she turned back to the computer. "You're not far off. I hadn't made the connection until you said that, but you're not wrong. It does sort of sound Celtic."

"Or Gaelic?" Tommy offered, listening again as she replayed the video clip. "Is there a difference?"

"Probably." She barely glanced at him. "I have no idea what the difference would be, but…" she held a finger up then replayed the last few moments of the video. "It's hard to tell where they take the melody once the wailing starts."

"What if we ran it through a sound filter? Maybe we could isolate the music part."

"I like the sound of that, but I'd have no idea what software to use."

Tommy grinned as he whipped out his cell phone. "I know just who to ask." He ran through his list of contacts and tried to call. "Oh, yeah." He closed the call app. "No signal."

"I suppose we can try when we get back to civilization."

"You're assuming we make it back," Tommy's voice grew somber. He nodded to the computer. "You see how upset they are. If they blame all humans for what they've lost…" he trailed off.

Patricia reached up and closed the laptop before turning to him. "I don't think we're at risk." She came to her feet and searched his face. "I mean, I could be wrong, but…" she glanced over his shoulder toward the door then lowered her voice. "I felt like we were supposed to be there. To see what they were doing."

Tommy hiked a brow at her. "After they threw rocks at us? And made us barf on ourselves on the way in?" His features turned from questioning to disbelief. "They're animals, Patricia. They're primates. Mountain gorillas." He shrugged. "Nothing more."

"You don't believe that for a moment." She stepped back and shook her finger at him. "I looked up Native American lore on Sasquatches and they believe that they're wild creatures, but still men."

Tommy scoffed. "Maybe that's what Wikipedia says, but I can tell you that the relatives I have who still believe these things exist? They don't consider them human. They're little more than two legged wolves. A smart, strong, HUGE two-legged wolf, maybe, but not human."

She pointed to her computer. "You saw what they were doing."

"Yeah, and I've seen momma cows cry out and moo for their calves when they're pulled off the teat to be weaned. It's instinct to care for your young. But that doesn't make them people."

"I have no doubt that other animals can feel some form of empathy, but to blindly associate them with wolves?"

Tommy scoffed as he leaned back on the table top. "Wolves are smart as hell. They're cunning and communicate with other pack members so easily that it's almost like they have telepathy, and they definitely look out for their pack. I'm telling you, Patty, if wolves had thumbs, they'd be the dominate life form."

She rolled her eyes and waved him off. "You can't see the forest for the trees."

"I can see both quite clearly." He pushed off the table and sighed. "You're anthro…" He paused to think for a moment. "Anthromorph…"

"Anthropomorphizing," she finished for him. "And no, I'm not." She sighed heavily and hung her head as her gears nearly spun out of control. When she looked up, she was smiling. "Okay, what makes a human a human?"

Tommy stared at her with a blank expression. "I don't guess I really know."

Her smile softened slightly and she sat back down gently. "Humans are primates, but so are monkeys and apes. In fact, I've read that genetically, we're only a fraction of a percent different in our DNA."

Tommy nodded. "I think I read something like that, too, only I'm pretty sure they said that we're more closely related to dolphins than we are to gorillas." His smile turned into a smirk.

Patricia nodded. "It may well have said that, but consider that chimpanzees are our closest relative in the genetic tree."

"Fine, but that doesn't make them human."

"Maybe not. But they still have social relations, they have hierarchies, they have familial connections that—"

"But they're not *human*." He crossed his arms and stood rigid.

"Fine. But they're clearly closely related to us. We're related to *all* of the great apes, but we're distinguished from them because we have a more highly developed brain and the capacity for articulate speech and abstract reasoning."

"Okay, but that doesn't make chimps human either."

She pointed to her computer. "But these...they're different. Closer to us." She held her hand up to keep him from interrupting. "We heard them speak...sort of. And they were singing—"

"Humming," he quickly corrected.

She shrugged. "Possibly, but chimps don't hum. Maybe we couldn't understand the words, but I'm telling you, there's a melody. Either way, they have the ability to understand and conceptualize *music*. That's a trait showing abstract reasoning."

Tommy shook his head and smirked. "I still think it's a stretch to call them human."

"I'm not, though. I'm saying that they're human-LIKE. They share a lot of the same distinctions. A lot of the same attributes that set us apart from wolves."

SURVIVAL

Tommy raised his brows and sighed heavily. "I guess I can see where they might be closer related to us than a chimp—"

"Exactly!" she cut him off excitedly. "Closer. Not the same, just closer." She stepped toward him and locked eyes with him. "Jane Goodall was convinced that chimpanzees have a soul. Their behavior is so human-like that she felt they must have one." She raised a brow at him. "And if the Genoskwa are more human-like than a chimp…" she let the sentence dangle.

Tommy's eyes narrowed. "You think these things have a soul?"

She smiled broadly. "It's not out of the question."

Tommy scoffed as he turned to leave. "If they have a soul, then they're all going to Hell for what they've done."

"Maybe," Patricia answered, "but we'll be right behind them."

9

FOB Dog Town

"Want me to take the first watch?" Dale asked quietly.

Al shook his head slightly and raised the thermal camera to his eye again. "Not necessary." He lowered the camera and sighed heavily. "They're definitely out there, but they're standing still."

"Watching us."

Al nodded slightly. "They haven't made a single move towards us." He raised the camera again and shook his head. "Perhaps because they see us milling about outside?"

Dale shrugged. "Perhaps, but…"

"But?"

"Even though the biggest part of their clan has left the area, just one of the larger males could make short work of us if they wanted."

"Agreed." Al lowered the camera and wiped at his eyes. "What are you thinking?" He turned and raised a brow at him. "You are the closest thing to an expert that we have out here."

Dale couldn't hide the surprise from his face. "Me? I'm no expert on—"

"Mate, you faced these things and lived to tell the tale."

"Yeah, because they let me go."

Al scoffed. "Doesn't matter, now does it? You lived." He turned back to the tree line and scanned it again.

"That doesn't make me an expert." He crossed his arms and squeezed them tightly, fighting off the chill of the night air. "There's no way I could second guess these things."

"It's difficult to get an exact headcount. I know how big they can be, but the heat signatures are broken up by the brambles."

"Best guess?"

"Five. Maybe." He lowered the camera again and turned to face the other side of the camp. "I wonder…"

"What?" Dale fell into step with him as they crossed the bullpen and cleared the nearly destroyed structures.

Once they reached the beginning of the clearing on the opposite side of the camp, Al began to scan the trees again. "Nothing on the east side." He turned and squinted in the darkness to another side of the camp. "I need to get to higher ground."

Dale glanced around at what was left of the camp. "Probably the shipping containers."

"The logistics building or the other one?"

Dale craned his neck to look and compare the two. "Either, I think. They're about the same level."

Al walked to the closest container and tested the bent and twisted door. "I think it will hold me." He stuffed the thermal camera into his satchel and gripped the top of the door. With a slight hop, he scrambled up and onto the roof.

"Better view?"

Al peered through the camera and nodded. "Oh, yeah. I've got almost a three hundred and sixty..." he trailed off as he studied the view. He stepped toward the end of the container and paused. "North side. We have another heat signature." He lowered the camera and glanced over the edge of the container to Dale, standing on the ground. "There's only one, but it's massive."

"The one with the limp that we saw at the funeral?"

Al shrugged and brought the camera back up. "Could be. Too hard to tell. He's not moving."

Dale scratched at his chin. "One to the north, a handful to the east, but nothing west or south. What do you think that means?"

Al shrugged as he turned off the camera and slid it back into the satchel. He bent over and gripped the roof of the container before sliding his lower body off the edge. He dropped effortlessly to the ground and dusted off his clothing. "My guess would be that wherever these things call home, it must be in one of those general directions."

Dale closed his eyes and tried to remember what little information he'd come across from Ford's excursion out here. "I think there are mines to the east." He shook his head. "Or they could have been to the west." He huffed in frustration. "I don't remember."

"Not important." Al clapped his shoulder as he walked by. "It's all supposition at this point anyway." He paused by the door of the container then slowly turned to face him. "Except...I do recall one of the reports saying that they chose to gas the females and little ones in the mines." He turned to face Dale. "Do you think they're guarding the entrances to prevent something like that from happening again?"

Dale shrugged animatedly. "Brother, I have no idea."

Al considered the possibility a moment longer then shook it off. "Again, it doesn't matter."

Dale gave him a surprised look. "How's that?"

"Neither option serves us in our primary goal."

"Oh? What's that?"

"Surviving the night out here." He smiled at him as he walked away.

Dale entered the logistics building and paused long enough to grimace. "Dear god, what is that stench?"

Tommy hooked a thumb over his shoulder to a cot in the corner. "Hector. Ate himself silly on MREs and now he's tooting like the little engine that could."

Dale's features twisted and he stepped closer to the door opening. "Briese is taking this watch. He's tracking a handful of the creatures along the tree line." He waved his hand in front of his face and wiped at his eyes. "Good grief! My eyes are burning. What the hell did that guy eat?"

Tommy shrugged. "I hardly notice him anymore. Either you get used to it or it burns out the nerve endings in your sinuses."

Patricia walked by, humming to herself, still

watching the video on her computer. "Now I've got this song stuck in my head."

Dale stretched his neck and followed her to a cot. "So, do you have everything you need to verify your story?"

She sat down and closed the computer, setting it aside. "Yes...and no." She gave him a sheepish grin.

Dale felt his shoulders slump and he wiped a calloused hand over his face. "Okay, what else do you need? We'd really like to march out at first light."

She pulled her feet up onto the cot and sat cross legged. "After seeing what we saw?" She gave him a tight lipped smile. "I'm thinking of taking the story in a different direction."

"Do tell," he deadpanned.

"The Genoskwa have souls now," Tommy loudly interjected.

Dale turned and gave him a confused look. "Excuse me?"

"Ask her." Tommy turned his attention back to a rifle he'd found outside the building, hoping to get it back to working condition and praying he wouldn't need it.

Dale turned raised brows to her and gave her an expectant look. "What is he saying?"

She chuckled to herself then leaned forward, lowering her voice. "That was just us bouncing ideas back and forth."

"And these ideas have made you want to change your story...to what?"

She cleared her throat and leaned forward. "Rather than how the Bureau screwed the pooch and got over a hundred people killed out here…" she trailed off, almost unsure how to proceed.

"Please, go on."

She lowered her head and sighed. When she looked back up, she had an expression he couldn't quite read. "An expose. A story on how the Genoskwa are real, living, breathing, nurturing creatures that—"

"Wait, what?" Dale came to his feet. "How do you go from 'war between humans and monsters' to touchy-feely bullshit about the big cuddly motherfuckers that ate my friends?"

She gave him a dirty look. "If I wrote something like that, people would flood the area wanting to find their own proof, or hope to 'meet' one." She shook her head. "No, I want to document how the government knew they were real, prove to my readers that they are real, but at the same time, conceal *where* they are so they're left alone."

Dale hung his head. "That is the stupidest damned thing I think I've heard in a long time."

"Told you," Tommy called out, pretending not to listen.

She sat up straighter and raised a brow at him. "And you think a story about how inept the Federal Bureau of Investigation is would be better? Do you think your bosses would agree?"

Dale groaned as he slowly sat down on the cot beside her. "So, you want to leave out the 'inept' part and focus on the monsters?"

She shrugged slightly. "I might mention the inept stuff." She turned from him slightly and stared off toward the door. "But I think the focus should be on how closely related these things are to people."

He stared at her incredulously. "Close…to people?"

She rolled her eyes and huffed. "I've already had this out with Tommy. He thinks I'm an idiot."

Dale nodded slightly. "I think I could co-sign that one."

"Oh, for…up yours G. Gordon." She huffed as she hopped up from the cot and grabbed her computer. "You wouldn't know a good story if it bit you in the ass."

Dale squeezed his eyes shut and silently counted to himself before he stood and followed her back to the table where she was now staring at her screen. "Okay, I apologize." He sat down slowly, trying to read her reaction. "It's just that these things are a sensitive subject to me. A lot of very good people lost their lives out here—"

"They invaded someone else's borders and were beaten back." She turned and gave him a serious look. "It doesn't matter that they're less civilized. This was *their* territory and the American Government invaded."

Dale realized his mouth was hanging open and had to shut it. He glanced at Tommy who shrugged slightly before turning his attention back to the weapon.

"So, they're like…Afghanistan?"

"No, they are indigenous *people* who protected their land and their way of life from an armed aggressor." She turned back to him and smirked. "And did so against superior weaponry, as well."

Dale blew his breath out hard and slowly pushed up from the chair. "Okay…regardless of what your story is, what else do you need so we can leave?"

She paused for a moment and tapped a fingernail against her front tooth as she thought. "I'm not sure." She immediately turned her attention back to her computer. "But I'll know it when I see it."

"Y-you…" Dale stammered, wide eyed. "You do realize that the longer we're out here, the higher the odds are of us being killed, right?"

She took a deep breath and turned to face him standing over her. "If these things wanted us dead, we'd be dead."

"No doubt. No sense in pushing our luck out here."

"Feel free to leave whenever you wish, Agent Archer." She turned her attention back to her computer. "I'm staying."

DALE PACED OUTSIDE in slow circles, mumbling under his breath as his mind tried to piece together Patricia's thinking.

"You're going to plow a rut into the ground, mate."

Dale looked up and saw Al sitting atop the second container, the thermal imager hanging from his neck. "I tried to pin her down on when we could get out of here and…" he trailed off, unable to finish.

"Let me guess. She doesn't know?"

"Not just that, she's changing her story. She wants to make the Genoskwa seem like misunderstood natives. Civilized teddy bears."

Al raised a brow. "Okay, that's a bit of a stretch. I'm only going by the reports she had, but these things seem like they're anything but warm and fuzzy."

Dale forced himself to stand still and allowed the chill night air to permeate his coat. "I don't understand her thinking." He sniffed hard to avoid a runny nose and looked up at Al. "I mean, I should be grateful that she's not planning to rake the Bureau across the coals and make us look stupid."

"But?"

Dale looked away. When he looked back, his face was a mask of anger. "To portray these things as anything other than the violent, malicious—"

"Heads up!" Al brought the thermals to his face and peered across the clearing. He scrambled to his feet and searched to the north, hoping the bulky heat signature was still present.

It wasn't.

"What's up?"

Al lowered the thermals but continued to stare at the tree line. "I caught movement in the dark. When I scanned with these, the group had moved off."

"Why do I sense there's a 'but' coming?"

"But…the big one that was at the north is now registering where the group was." He glanced at Dale and shook his head. "I don't know why, but it felt unnerving."

Dale dug into his satchel and pulled out the infrared monocular. Peering through it, he could see the huge male standing just inside the trees. It wasn't trying to conceal itself; it gently swayed side to side. "What the hell is it doing?"

"Slow dancing to a song we can't hear?" Al shrugged. "Maybe it's drunk?"

Both men watched the creature again and nearly jumped when it clearly raised an arm and pointed back towards the main road. Dale felt a lump form in his throat that he couldn't quite swallow down. "Tell me you're seeing this."

"Aye, mate. I'm seeing it." Al lowered his thermal and glanced at Dale. "I think he's inviting us to leave."

"Yeah, I think you're right." Dale glanced up at Al and sighed. "We might have to drag her out kicking and screaming."

Al nodded. "Better we drag her out squalling than carry her off in a bag."

10

FOB Dog Town

"I don't care what you saw." Patricia planted her hands on her hips and set her jaw. "I still need to verify the chopper crash, I need to—"

"You're not listening to me!" Dale could feel his blood pressure rise along with the volume of his voice. "That thing just gave us a 'get out of the woods alive free' card and you want to ignore it?"

"You can't possibly know what that gesture meant." Her face reddened as her anger grew. "And how dare you yell at me like that. I invited you along, but you didn't have to come."

Dale's mouth fell open and he glanced at Al who simply shrugged and stepped back. "I've got nothing, mate."

Dale took a deep breath and counted internally. When he opened his mouth, his voice was soft and gentle. "Tomorrow morning, as soon as the sun is up, we're packing out of here." He held a hand up to cut her off. "If you want to stay on your own, feel free, but I'm leaving and I'm taking whoever wants to stay alive with me."

Tommy's hand shot up as his eyes darted between the two. He slowly lowered it and shook his head. "I... didn't have a question. I just prefer to remain breathing."

"That's two of us," Dale stated quietly. He glanced around the room.

Hector sat on the edge of his cot and rubbed at his hair. "Sorry, Patty. I wanted out of here ever since we arrived." He looked up at her with reddened eyes. "Count me in as well."

Al nodded as he stepped forward and placed a gentle hand on her shoulder. "I think it best we take the opportunity as it's presented."

She turned and glared at him. "You, too?" She scoffed as she pulled out from under his hand. "I thought you were Special Forces. You're not supposed to be afraid of anything."

He offered a wan smile. "One thing about special forces is, we're trained differently from your average foot soldier; makes us canny. Those smarts have kept me alive a lot longer than I should have been. And this time, my gut is telling me we need to leave."

"I don't understand," Dale interjected. "You got enough proof to write any story you want. What is your real objective here?"

She stared at him blankly for a moment then seemed to snap out of it. "I have no other agenda than proving the information sent to me was factual."

"And you've got more than enough to do that." Dale

crossed his arms and raised a brow at her. "Your actions aren't matching your words."

"I don't answer to you—" She took a half step back and shook her head. "Fine. You want to leave? Leave. I don't care." She turned and threw open her leather satchel. She began to collect her belongings, tossing them haphazardly into the bag. "I'm staying until I'm satisfied I've got everything I need."

Dale shot Al a knowing glance then turned back to her. "What are you not telling us?"

She huffed as she latched the cover on the satchel. "Right now, I'm not even speaking to you." She slung the satchel over her shoulder and stepped toward the door. "You can infer whatever you like from my lack of conversation."

The four men stood back as she stormed out of the logistics building. Al moved toward the door and watched as she stomped her way to the one tent that was still standing and jerked the door open. "Yeah, mate, she's roiled."

"Tell me it isn't just me that senses she's holding back."

Hector laughed as he rolled forward to a standing position. "She's not holding back. She's mad-mad."

"I meant that she's withholding information." Dale stepped toward the door and peered across the bullpen. "She's got an agenda and I, for one, would like to know what it is."

Tommy sat down at the table to finish putting the rifle together. "Well, her brother was killed out here."

"So were a lot of other good men." Dale slowly shook his head. "No, there's something else going on with her."

Hector moved to the main table and pulled another MRE from the box. "I don't know about you guys, but these things aren't half bad."

Tommy groaned. "Dude, come on. You're about to kill us in here."

Hector stared at him with confusion. "There's plenty left." He turned to Dale with raised brows. "We're leaving tomorrow, si?"

"That's the plan."

Hector grinned as he sat on his cot and ripped open the heavy plastic container. "Then there's still plenty for everyone."

Tommy worked the action on the rifle and then came to his feet. "I'll take the watch." He shot a nasty look toward Hector. "At least I can breathe out there."

DALE JERKED awake and rolled off the cot, his hand instinctively reaching for his rifle. "What was that?"

Al scrambled for the door and pushed it open slightly. "Something struck the outside wall." He glanced toward Dale. "Hard."

Dale was on his feet and checking his watch. "It's after three."

Al glanced over Dale's shoulder and saw Hector sprawled out over his cot, snoring softly. "How did he sleep through that?"

"Who cares?" Dale pushed past him and stepped out into the brisk night air, pulling his coat on as he stepped away from the building. "Tommy, what was that?"

He waited a moment then craned his neck to see better. "Tommy?"

Another loud noise had Al nearly jumping out the open doorway, his MP5 scanning the area. "Tell me that was Mr. Youngblood."

"I wish I could." Dale reached for the big steel door and pulled himself up far enough to peer across the roof of the structure. "He's not up there."

"He was." Al stepped away and began maneuvering to the side of the steel container.

"What's with all the noise?" Patricia stood in the doorway of her tent, squinting in the darkness.

"Tommy's missing," Dale replied as he stepped toward her. "Something hit the side of the logistics building and woke us." He nodded toward the tent. "You'd better go back inside until we figure out what's going on."

"Agent Archer." Al stepped back into view with a solemn look. "You need to see this."

Dale felt his chest tighten as he trotted along the length of the container building. He slowed before he rounded the corner, unsure he wanted to see what the SFF pilot had discovered.

"It's Mr. Youngblood." Al stepped away.

Dale flicked on his LED torch and winced. He'd seen this kind of carnage before.

Recently.

Tommy's twisted and broken body had been slammed into the side of the building, denting the heavy metal siding. Dale's torch lit up his neck and shoulders...where a particular part of Tommy's anatomy was missing.

"It's over there." Al sighed heavily. "I'm assuming that was the second impact we heard."

Dale's flashlight followed Al's outstretched arm and settled on the crushed features of Tommy's face. "Goddammit." Dale squatted and took a deep breath. "The fucking thing told us to leave and we…" he trailed off.

"What?" Al asked. "We didn't leave right that instant so it attacked?"

"If not the Alpha male, then one of the younger ones." He pushed up and stood on shaky legs. "I watched as they…'trained' a younger one how to rip a person's head off."

"Oh for fuck's sake," Al grumbled, his eyes scanning the area. "How fast are these things?"

"Fast enough." Dale cleared his throat and stepped carefully toward the corner of the building. "I think we should start making our way out of the forest tonight."

"Agreed." Al slung his MP5 and marched behind him as Dale made his way back to the bullpen.

The tent door opened again and Patricia stood in the shadows. "Was it Tommy?"

Dale paused and took a deep breath. "What's left of him." He turned, ready to read her the riot act but stopped himself. It had been his decision to wait until morning to leave, not hers.

"Is he dead?"

Dale nodded curtly. "One of the creatures tore his head off and threw both pieces against the building." He had to take another deep breath to keep from screaming. "We're loading out now and we'll be leaving shortly." He turned and faced her. "I would strongly recommend you join us."

She seemed to square her shoulders and stepped back. "I already told you, I'm staying."

Dale scoffed under his breath. "For the life of me, I can't figure out your game." He turned to face her again, his rifle dangling from his shoulder. "If you think you can get an interview with one of them, you're sadly mistaken."

It was her turn to scoff. "They probably wouldn't understand me anyway."

"Then why?" He stepped closer and gripped the open door. "Please, just tell me what it is you hope to accomplish out here on your own?"

She felt her anger start to rise again and opened her mouth to yell at him, but decided against it. "I'm not sure I could even explain it to you." She stepped back deeper into the tent. "Not in a way that you could possibly understand."

Dale sighed and pushed the door open further. "Try me."

"I…" she stammered as her brain operated three times faster than she could speak. "I can't explain it to where it makes sense."

"Just spit it out. We'll put it together like a puzzle once all of the pieces are out in the open."

She could feel her jaw quiver as she tried to piece together her thoughts and feelings but couldn't find a way to verbalize it so it would make sense to another person. "I have to…" she stopped herself and took a deep breath. "I need to face what killed my brother."

Dale felt his mouth drop open and he stared at her dark silhouette in the shadows. It took him a moment to speak and when he did, he had to force himself to remain civil. "You do realize that there is no way to know which one of them actually committed the deed." He nodded toward the tree line. "The grand majority of their numbers have left. It's only the local clan still here."

She nodded, not realizing he couldn't see it. "I understand that." She finally stepped forward and the nearly full moon highlighted her features in silver. "I just need to *see* one of them. To make it real to me."

"To make it real to you?" he repeated.

She chuckled sadly and stepped out of the tent. "I see all of this destruction. I read the list of the fallen. I studied each of the reports looking for what was left unsaid." She shook her head and shot him a tight lipped smile as she tried to keep her emotions in check. "I see all of it, but until I lay eyes on an actual angry, crazed bigfoot, none of it is really *real* to me. And if it isn't real to me, I can't make it real to my readers."

Dale sighed and hung his head. "What about what we witnessed in the woods? The funeral...thing. You replayed that video until you had their song stuck in your head."

"That isn't what killed my brother."

Dale shot her a surprised look. "The fuck it isn't. Those things are exactly what—"

"Those *things* were mourning their dead. They weren't performing a war dance or hyping each other up for a battle. They were...peaceful."

"You want to see peaceful?" He grabbed her arm and began pulling her across the bullpen. "I'll show you peaceful."

"What are you doing?!" She pulled against his grip and nearly panicked when she realized where he was taking her. "No! No! I don't want to see it!"

"You wanted to see a pissed-off bigfoot, I'm going to show you one!" He continued to drag her along the side of the logistics building with her screeching and pulling from him.

"What the hell, mate?" Al barked as he kicked open the door of the logistics building. "What are you doing?" He trotted to follow, unsure what was happening.

"There!" Dale pointed at Tommy's corpse. "You call that peaceful?!"

She pulled out of his grip and stumbled to the ground as a mix of emotions flooded her. She nearly jumped when Dale turned on his flashlight and highlighted Tommy's broken body. "Oh my god!" She turned and scrambled to her feet, running past Al.

"What the hell was that?"

Dale turned and shot him an angry glare. "She finally told me why she didn't want to leave yet. She wanted to see an ANGRY bigfoot. That was the only way to make it 'real' to her."

"*What?*" Al stared at him in disbelief then chuckled disbelievingly. "I'm not following you, mate."

"It may not be what she wanted to see, but she needed to see it." Dale slipped his flashlight back into his vest and marched past Al. "Make sure Hector is packed and ready. We're leaving in ten."

"I'm not going anywhere with him," Patricia said through broken sobs. "He's an animal."

Al clenched his jaw and nodded slightly. "We all are, technically, but we can't leave you out here by yourself.

Not anymore." He squatted beside her and patted her hand. "Before they attacked Tommy, I may have been able to leave you here to do whatever you needed to do, but now?" He shook his head. "If you stay here, it's suicide."

"You can't know that."

Al stood and held his hand out. "Tommy's body proves it. He was just a kid sitting on the roof trying to look out for the rest of us. They snuck up on him and…" he trailed off. "Well, you saw what happened."

She looked up at him through reddened eyes and narrowed her gaze. "He didn't need to drag me over there like that."

"He must have felt it was warranted." He held his hand out further. "Come on now. We need to get moving before they come back."

She clenched her jaw and took his hand, letting him help her to her feet. "What about all our stuff?"

"I'm just taking what's necessary." He held his MP5 up. "And lots of ammunition."

"Our tents and sleeping bags?"

"Not worth it," Al replied. "We don't plan on camping out along the way. Keep your pack light."

She gripped the strap of her satchel and pulled her pistol out from under her pillow. "Go light."

11

FOB Dog Town

"T-THEY REALLY KILLED TOMMY?" Hector asked, already knowing the answer.

Dale refused to speak and continued leading them away from the camp. He slowed his approach as they reached the end of the clearing and were about to walk into the thick of the woods.

Al increased his stride until he was alongside Hector. "That's right, mate. Tommy is gone," he replied in a soft voice. "Perhaps it would be best if we kept quiet, eh?"

Hector gave him a wide eyed stare. "What the hell difference does it make now? Tommy's dead!"

Al grabbed him by the shoulder and spun him around. "It would be bloody nice to hear the bastards if they try to ambush us, yeah?"

Hector opened his mouth to reply but chose to only nod. "Got it," he whispered.

The two fell back into step with the other two. Al

pulled out his thermal and scanned the trees on either side, putting the device away once he was satisfied that they weren't being followed. "We're clear for now."

Dale nodded curtly and continued his slow march, his eyes and ears scanning the pitch black woods. He could feel Patricia's eyes boring a hole in the back of his head, and he couldn't say that he blamed her. Under any other circumstance, he would have apologized by now. But under any other circumstance, it never would have happened. In his mind, he'd done what he had to do to keep her alive.

A loud wood knock echoed through the blackness and Dale froze, midstep. He could feel his heart rate increase in his chest and his throat tightened, waiting for the reply. He didn't have to wait long before another knock on the other side of the group sounded through the trees.

"Fuck," he muttered. He slowly turned and could barely make out Al at the rear of the line. "They know we're here."

"Aye, mate. And they know we're leaving, yeah?"

Dale swallowed hard and nodded. "Let's hope the invitation's still good." He refused to meet Patricia's withering gaze, instead turning his attention back to the trail. "Onward."

He could hear her huff behind him and knew that she was more angry at him than afraid of the Genoskwa. He couldn't allow himself to be distracted by her at the moment as he felt the eyes of dozens of the creatures on him.

Al had the same feeling and carefully withdrew his thermal optics. He held it to his eye and scanned both sides of the trail. His chest tightened and his pulse quickened at the number of big, fast moving creatures lurking in the darkness. He tried to get a headcount, but there was too much foliage between him and their pursuers.

He lowered the optic and cleared his throat. "We've got quite the entourage escorting us out."

Dale slowed his march and the group tightened on him with Patricia and Hector in the middle. Dale glanced behind him and saw her clutching her pistol tightly, keeping it close to her chest. "Just be careful where that barrel is pointed," he muttered, not entirely certain if he wanted to plant the notion of shooting him in her mind.

Hector pulled out his cell phone and began tapping away at it. The screen seemed much brighter in the near perfect darkness of the forest and Al pulled him back to him. "Turn that off. You'll ruin our night vision."

"I gotta message my *posse*. We need help out here."

"There's no signal this deep in the woods, Hector," Patricia chided.

Hector hit "send" and shoved the phone back in his pocket. "Yeah? Well, as soon as it gets a signal, my homies will come and pull our asses out of this fire."

"We aren't in a fire yet, Hector," Dale replied quietly. "Right now they're just watching us leave."

"And how long you think they're gonna keep that shit up, eh?" Hector cursed in Spanish and spun a slow circle. "They got us fuckin' surrounded, man. We are literally at their mercy."

"Let's keep it that way, eh?" Al whispered. "We don't want to do anything to set them off."

Hector spun and jabbed a finger at Al's chest. "You

really think my little fuckin' cell phone is gonna be the thing that sets them off? Huh?"

Al gripped his finger and twisted, bringing Hector to his knees. "Stay quiet and keep moving. No sudden movements, eh, mate?"

Hector came back to his feet and cursed again in Spanish, cradling his finger in his other hand. "Why you wanna go and do that for?"

"Because you're about to lose your shit and we can't have that." Al spun him back around and pointed him along the path. "Move."

"You wouldn't be pulling this tough guy bullshit if we were back in the hood. My homies would have your balls for keychains."

Al chuckled. "Mighty big keychains then." He slowly removed the thermal again and scanned either side of the trail. "Damn it. They're leapfrogging each other to stay ahead of us."

A loud whoop echoed to their right and Dale stiffened. "Aw, shit. Here it comes."

Another whoop to their left echoed through the woods just before the forest came alive with hoots and screams. Patricia held her hands to her ears and yelled over the din. "Why are they doing this? I thought they wanted us to leave!"

Dale grimaced at the shrieking and felt his adrenaline start to rush. "Maybe they want us to go faster. I have no idea."

He turned and began a quick walk along the trail, his LED flashlight leading the way. He glanced back and saw both Patricia and Hector bouncing as they jogged behind him. Al brought up the rear with long even strides, his head swiveling to check both sides of the trail.

Hector suddenly yelled and fell to the ground, both hands cradling his knee. "Sonofabitch!" He rolled back and forth, clutching his leg. "They threw something at me!"

Al scooped him up and hooked Hector's arm over his shoulder. "Don't slow down!" Hector cursed again in Spanish and spit epithets at the creatures as they continued along the path.

As Dale entered a small clearing he slowed and let the others catch up. "Al, check the perimeter."

Al slid Hector's arm over to Patricia and pulled his thermal optic again. He scanned both sides then clicked his tongue. "They're still paralleling us. It's just taking them a bit longer to go around the clearing."

Dale found himself breathing harder than he'd expected. "Part of me wants to push on and try to keep them to our rear."

"Yeah, mate, I don't think they're going to allow that." The two men paused, catching their breath as the creatures' war cries died down and they positioned themselves along either side of the path again. Dale pulled a water bottle out and sucked down half before handing it to Al. "They know we're leaving. Why are they menacing us like this?"

Al crushed the water bottle and screwed the cap back on. "Trust but verify? I have no idea." He slowed his breathing and checked the perimeter again. "Unless they don't plan on actually allowing us to leave."

Dale sighed and lowered his head. "That thought has occurred to me as well."

SURVIVAL

Al pulled his MP5 back up and gripped it. "They'll find I won't go down without a fight."

Dale nodded and switched his carbine for the shotgun, letting the rifle hang at his side. "I doubt a slug will fully penetrate their homemade armor, but I bet their skulls aren't bulletproof."

Al chuckled to himself. "I'm aiming for their willie."

Dale's face puckered. "Ow...that's just mean."

"Well, mate, they did pull Tommy's head off. It seems only fitting, don't ya think?"

Patricia appeared at their side. "Is this a break? I'd like to get Hector some ibuprofen if we have time."

"Go ahead." Dale flashed his light ahead and winced at how narrow the path appeared. "I'm in no hurry to go through that."

As she began rifling through her satchel Al stepped closer to Dale and lowered his voice. "That path is just narrow enough that they could reach out and touch any of us."

"I'm not worried about them simply touching." He sighed and tried to push the image of Tommy from his mind. "I just don't want them getting a grip on any of us."

"How come they only throw rocks at me?" Hector whined. "What are they prejudiced against Latinos?"

"I don't think they understand the concept of ethnicity, Hector. They're not racist," Dale replied. "They hate all humans equally."

"When my text goes through, my homies will teach these things a thing or two."

It was Patricia who chimed in this time. "*If* your text goes through, your 'homies' are hours away. Not to mention they wouldn't have a clue where to start looking for us. If I were you, I wouldn't count on anybody but us to get us out of here."

She stepped back and nodded to Al. "We're ready."

Al stepped in front of Dale. "How about I take point for a bit, eh mate?"

Dale started to argue but waved him on. "After you." He stood by and waited for the others to move past him then picked up the rear. He could hear the occasional twig snap in the distance or the crunch of leaves and he knew they were close. If he stopped moving and listened intently, he could hear the heavy breathing in the woods and it made his skin crawl. He could almost feel their hot breath on the back of his neck, and he had to fight the urge to run.

At point, Al slowed as he approached the narrowing of the trail. He slipped the thermal to his eye again and breathed a sigh of relief once he realized the monsters were still giving them a wide berth. He stepped more confidently into the near perfect blackness that the path had become.

Using the thermal, he could see where the branches of the trees had been broken off by the vehicles the Bureau had brought through. Even in the depth of autumn, with winter threatening to close in at any moment, there were already signs of the trees taking over the path once more. It reminded him of the tenacity of the jungles he'd fought in. You could hack a path through the thickest area and, an hour later, you wouldn't be able to find your own trail.

A whishing sound came from their left and Al quickly scanned the area with his optic. He could barely make out the heat signature, but a tree swayed violently back and forth as the creature shook it.

SURVIVAL

"Move..." Dale warned, picking up the pace. "Move it! Double time!"

Al glanced back and saw the others picking up the pace and decided it was best not to ask why. He began to trot, still scanning the area where the creature was shaking the tree.

A loud crack echoed through the woods and Dale reached forward, gripping both Patricia and Hector and pulling them back. "Heads up!" he yelled just as a tree shot through the narrow opening that made their escape route. The heavy pine bounced on its thicker limbs as they cracked under the weight of the trunk.

"Move it!" he yelled, shoving both of the civilians toward the tree. "Up and over!"

He brought up his infrared optic and saw Al on the other side of the fallen tree, his weapon at the ready. "Head on a swivel, Briese!"

Al quickly scanned both sides of the path as Hector and Patricia scrambled over the fallen pine. Dale followed, quickly closing the gap. "I don't think they're honoring the get out of the woods free card anymore."

"We need to put them behind us," Al stated as the group came together. He gripped Hector's shoulder and locked eyes with the man in the near perfect dark. "Can you run?"

"No, but I'll do it anyway," Hector was still huffing from the mad scramble over the tree. "Don't worry, man. I'll keep up."

Al nodded. "Then let's go." He turned and began to jog along the trail, his thermal optic showing him the tire tracks along the rocky ground.

Dale gripped Patricia's shoulder. "Help him if you can, but do not let him slow you down."

She nodded curtly then began pulling Hector's arm, urging him to move faster. Dale watched them for a moment then turned and marched backward, facing the area they had just been. He leveled the shotgun and swept it side to side. "I dare you to step out and show yourselves," he whispered under his breath.

12

Deep in the Catskills

Al stumbled over missed rocks in the path and cursed under his breath. "Watch your step. The path is rocky." He continued to move at a brisk pace, spinning around and marching backward, checking their rear as the group navigated in the inky blackness while the others struggled to keep up.

Ahead of them, the Genoskwa began warming up their war cries as wood knocks echoed on both sides while whoops and hollers cried out through the thick bush. "Shit's about to get real," Al called back.

Hector slowed, clutching his chest. "I can't breathe. I can't breathe," he wheezed. "Go on. I'll catch up."

Patricia tugged at him, urging him forward. "Come on, Hector. It's not that much further."

He pulled from her grip and walked a slow circle, his hands pressed to his sides. "I can't," he huffed between breaths. "I'm done. Stick a fork in me."

"Move it!" Dale barked as he caught up to the pair. "Unless you want to end up like Tommy."

"Hey man, Tommy ain't gotta run no more. Maybe I should trade places—"

"Stop it!" Patricia practically screamed at him. "Neither of you have any right to talk about him like that."

Hector waved her off and bent over, forcefully sucking air into his lungs. "I'm not made for this."

"Made for it or not, you can rest when we get to the trucks."

Patricia suddenly stiffened and gripped Dale's arm. "Tell me you know where Tommy's keys are."

"No idea," Dale replied. He nudged Hector. "Do you know how to hotwire a car?"

Hector suddenly sobered and glared at him. "What the hell, man? You ask me that because I'm a Mexican?"

Dale felt a sudden dislike for the man. "No, I ask you that because you cover the police beat. And your cousin is a car guy."

Hector shook it off and nodded. "Actually, I do. But only the older cars."

"Like Tommy's Suburban?" Patricia asked.

Hector shrugged, still breathing hard. "No idea, but I can try."

Dale nodded as he nudged him forward again. "Worst case scenario, I'll ride in the back of your truck."

"What the hell, mate?" Al asked angrily. "I have to backtrack fifty yards just to find the three of you holding a board meeting?"

"Move," Dale grumbled as he pushed Hector. "You can complain later."

The four of them fell back into place as Al led them

ahead and into the next wall of trees. "Hold up." He stopped and held a hand in the air. "It's too quiet."

Dale paused and strained to listen. "Even the wildlife has shut up." He spun a slow circle as he reached for his infrared and held it to his eye. "I've got nothing."

"Same," Al replied as he lowered his thermal optic. "My skin is crawling, mate. They're planning something."

Patricia's hand went to her temple and she winced. "Oh, no…not again."

The three men turned to face her. "What?" Dale asked.

Hector suddenly bent over and began to gag. "I'm gonna be sick."

Dale felt his shoulder slump as he waited for the effects to hit him. "We know it's coming."

Al groaned as he prepared for the wave of nausea to hit. "I have no idea where they are. Shooting blindly probably won't stop them this time."

Dale suddenly felt his knees go weak as his stomach turned flip-flops. "Oh, dear god…" He turned away from the group and threw up into the tall grass.

Hector heard him throw up and tried to hold back, but couldn't. He began to heave in sympathy, splattering the half dozen MREs he'd eaten across his shoes. Patricia continued to squeeze her temples and fought the urge to spew as her legs slowly grew weaker.

Al sighed, knowing it was about to come, and felt his mouth watering before the infrasound ever hit him. He began to feel queasy and his head began to throb at the same time. He turned away from the others, trying to ignore their loud heaving.

Hector gripped his stomach with one hand and his

temple with the other. With each heave, he farted loudly. As the last of the MREs emptied from him, so did his colon. He tried to hold it in but couldn't, and his khakis soon were filled.

"I can't…" Dale grumbled between heaves and he began to fire his carbine into the trees, praying he could hit close enough to the perpetrator to make them stop.

Al followed suit, firing his MP5 in short full-auto bursts into the trees ahead of them. The sound of the 9MM auto made his head want to explode, but he emptied his extended magazine into the woods and slapped at his vest for another one.

Almost as suddenly as it started, it stopped. Dale crumpled to one knee. "God, I hate it when that happens."

Hector stood frozen, his arms and legs spread. He felt his jaw quiver and he wasn't sure if it was from throwing up or wanting to cry. "No, no, no…" His voice cracked as he spoke. "I did not."

Patricia was still bent over, spitting the bile from her mouth. She'd inhaled some of the acid and kept trying to cough it up as it burned her trachea.

"What's wrong, mate?" Al asked, spitting into the grass to clear the bile.

Hector turned slightly and his jaw quivered again. "I shitted myself, man." He threw his arms into the air and screamed into the night sky. "Why!? I'm a grown ass man! I don't do this!"

Dale heard a twig snap behind him and he suddenly stiffened. "They're closing on us. We gotta move!"

Patricia was swishing water in her mouth when Dale made his announcement and quickly spit it out, tossing the bottle aside. "You heard the man. Let's go." She shoved at Hector and he nearly stumbled.

"I can't go anywhere. I shit my pants." He nearly cried when he moved. "I can feel it running down my legs, man."

"GO!" Dale shoved him hard and forced Hector into a trot. "You can change clothes when we're out of the woods."

Hector cursed in Spanish as he began moving again and squeezed his eyes shut as the discomforting feel of his ass cheeks sliding across each other hit home. "Aw, man, just shoot me now."

"Trust me, mate," Al yelled at him, "I've seen and heard of a lot worse in my day. If you really want to get back at the beasties, then fight tooth and nail to LIVE!" He turned and marched backward, eyeing the smaller man. "No matter what you have to endure, make sure you come out of this alive." He spun back around and increased his pace, trying to avoid the rocks and cracks in the trail while also scanning the trees for heat signatures.

The four of them pressed onward until the trail took a sudden turn in the thick of the woods. Al slowed his advance and continued to scan the trees on either side of them. "This is a perfect ambush location," he thought aloud.

Dale turned his attention ahead of the group and barely caught movement high in the trees. "Look up! I see something in the canopy!"

Al scanned the tree tops and froze when he saw the perfect outline of a wood ape jumping from one thick branch to another on a different tree. "Fuck me. I didn't know they could do that." He nearly dropped his optic when the creature grabbed a limb above its head and swung up into the darkness, disappearing from his thermal's view.

As if on cue, the forest erupted with another round of war cries. Loud whoops, screams and hoots surrounded the group, and Al nearly slowed to a stop as the noise level increased. "It sounds like a hundred of the bastards, but I can't find any of them now."

Dale heard the distinct sound of wood knocks intermixed with the screams and nearly jumped when the loud crack of a tree being broken ended the cacophony of noise. It took him a moment to stitch the two occurrences together and realize that the war cries were just to cover the sound of a tree being pushed over, but it was too late to react.

The fifty-foot pine crashed down from the left and landed between him and Hector, while another tall tree fell from the left and cut Patricia off from Al.

Patricia was nearly crushed under the branches and jumped back, knocking Hector to the ground. It was only then that she realized they were penned in, cut off from the trained shooters.

"Ambush!" Al yelled as he scrambled back from the fallen tree. He continued to scan the treetops, firing upon any clear heat signature.

Dale rushed to the fallen tree and was about to crawl over the trunk when a thick, hairy arm shot out from the darkness and reached for him. He barely spun away from the mighty grip, awestruck at how easily the massive arm snapped the limbs from the trunk where he'd been standing.

He rolled to the side and fell to the ground,

instantly scrambling to crawl under the trunk and away from the creature trying to grab him. "Move, move, move! They're trying to—" His sentence was cut short as something thick and solid slammed into his side.

Dale rolled away from the trunk with one hand grasping at his ribs. He had to forcefully suck air into his lungs, trying to see past the stars in his field of vision to spot what had tried to crush him.

As he rolled away and onto his back, he could barely make out a large piece of tree trunk, its ends twisted and shredded. In that instance, he realized the monsters were trying to crush him between the two huge tree trunks and his anger flared.

He gripped the barrel of his shotgun and came up onto one knee. He aimed high into the canopy and began firing wildly, praying that one of the creatures was stupid enough to stand in the open, checking to see if their ploy had worked.

Internally, Dale was screaming at the top of his lungs. In reality, he was struggling to keep the air going in and out of his body. As he fired the last shell from the shotgun, he fought to get to his feet, letting the shotgun dangle from his side, his hand automatically reaching for his carbine. He brought it to his shoulder and froze. He knew that Patricia and Hector were just on the other side of the fallen tree, even though he couldn't see them through the brush. He knew that somewhere on the other side was Al, as well. He brought the barrel of the carbine up higher and scrambled for his infrared monocular.

Scanning the area, there were no heat signatures to be found. He strained to listen, but his hearing was shot after emptying the 12 gage. It would take some time to get it back.

He stumbled forward and scanned the trees again, paying particular attention to the upper canopy. "Briese!" he called out.

He waited a moment and listened, praying Al would answer. When he didn't, Dale cursed under his breath and reached for the trunk of the fallen tree again, slowly daring to attempt to cross it.

He waited for another attack and when it didn't come, he carefully crawled over the obstacle, his ribs protesting with each strain of his muscles.

Dropping down between the two fallen trees, neither Patricia nor Hector were found. "Dammit," he cursed as he ran to the next tree and peered over the top. "Al!" he called out.

Dale suddenly felt his gut tighten and knot. One of the creatures had attempted to grab him and missed. What if they hadn't missed when attempting to grab the others?

Dale felt his arms go weak and he collapsed against the trunk of the tree, struggling to breathe. "Al!" he shouted again as his legs slowly buckled under him.

When the tree fell, cutting Al off from the rest of the group, he slowly began to back away, putting as much distance as he could between the trap and himself. He constantly scanned the forest and paid particular attention to the upper branches as he moved away in a zig-zag motion.

SURVIVAL

"Damn but these things are clever," he grumbled as he backed into a thick pine. He spun, half expecting a Sasquatch to be standing behind him. He slipped in behind the tree and continued to watch from inside the scrub.

He brought the thermal optic up and could just make out heat signatures on either side of the trail. He was about to take aim with his MP5 when one of the creatures burst onto the trail between the two fallen trees.

"Oh, no..." Al stepped out from behind the pine and was about to move forward when he heard a sharp squeal that quickly died out. The same creature turned and melded back into the woods. He could just make out flashes of it between the foliage and brambles and cursed under his breath.

"Fucker grabbed 'em," he mumbled as he slammed a fresh magazine into his weapon. He considered his options and cursed again. "No man left behind, eh, Albert?"

He burst through the scrub and tried his best to parallel the creature, keeping its heat signature in sight as the being meandered through the woods. More than once, he thought he saw Patricia and Hector draped over the monster's shoulders.

"Bloody hell." He increased his pace to try to close and gap and was just about where he wanted to be when he heard Dale yell his name.

Al turned and glanced back and realized that he had come too far to turn back now. Not if he wanted to keep the civilians in view.

With no plan on how to rescue them and no idea if they were even still alive, he made the only decision he could and fell back into step, following the creature through its own backyard to God knew where.

If Dale was half the badass that Al gave him credit for, he'd find a way to track them.

At least, he hoped he would.

13

Deep In the Catskills

Dale forcefully sucked in air and winced with each breath. He could feel a cold sweat pop out across his forehead and he feared he was about to black out. He rolled onto all fours and stretched his arm out toward the fallen tree. Once he found a branch of sufficient thickness, he pulled himself to a standing position and tilted his head back, sucking in the cold night air.

"Goddammit," he grumbled as he crawled over the last fallen tree and stood staring into the pitch black. He fumbled with the infrared monocular and could see the trail winding away from the trap.

The snap of a twig to his left had his head spinning in that direction and he scanned the trees with the infrared.

Nothing.

Dale stood in the dark, his mind going over a thousand things at once. Should he take the trail and try to bring back reinforcements? Should he follow the sounds of the Genoskwa and pray that some of his troop were still alive?

The twisting in the pit of his stomach made clear which he had to choose. He had to try to follow the beasts. He had to see if any of his people were still alive and kicking.

With a groan and a muttered curse, Dale turned and began making his way through the dense forest, pausing from time to time to listen and pray that he was going in the right direction.

AL CURSED SILENTLY as another branch caught him across the face, leaving angry red welts and thin, bleeding scratches. He hurried to stay behind the giant creature, noticing that the monster had a noticeable limp.

He kept the thermal optic to his eye and did his best to move silently. He knew he was failing miserably. He was actually shocked that one of the smaller creatures didn't intercept him along the path.

An unnoticed rock caught his foot just right and threatened to wrench his foot. He stumbled and came down on one knee, saving himself from a broken ankle, but creating way more noise than he'd have liked.

He leaned beside the tree closest and scanned ahead. He could just make out the creature as it dipped down into a low depression, and Al felt panic rise in his chest. He couldn't afford to lose sight of the beast or he'd never find it again.

He huffed as he came back to his feet, taking off as fast as he dared. He avoided as many limbs as he could, and eventually worked his way closer to the actual path the monster had been on. Once he reached it he realized the creature was using a game trail.

"No wonder he moved so quickly through here," he grumbled silently.

Al pushed harder and came to the edge of a shallow ravine. He barely glanced at the bottom, making a quick note of the large number of river rocks before he jumped over the edge and slid down the side.

The moment his feet hit the bottom of the dry creek bed, the stench struck him and the familiar sound of bones rattling under his feet had his head snapping back to the floor.

What he'd thought were river rocks were actually skulls. The entire ravine was filled with animal bones. With his stomach threatening to let go on him again, he realized that the grand majority of the bones were human. The freshest ones were, at any rate.

"Fuck me...now we know where all the bodies went."

A snapped twig farther along the ravine had him scanning the dry creek ahead, and Al had to force his attention back to the task at hand. He tried to stay above the bones, following the path until his thermals picked up another heat signature.

He watched as a creature stepped out of the ravine and crossed into a stand of woods to his right. Al scurried as quickly as he could along the bank of the creek, and at its narrowest point he jumped to the other side and scrambled to the top.

He scanned the woods again and cursed silently

when nothing was in view. He ran to the point where the creature had entered the woods then pushed through the brambles to continue the trek.

Once through the densest stretch of vines, Al opted to break out his LED flashlight. He snapped the red lens cover on and flipped the light on, scanning the forest floor, looking for any kind of sign.

He didn't have to travel far before he found an indented print on the thick, pine mulch floor. He would have missed it if the toes hadn't scraped deep indentions into the soft soil beneath the needles.

He followed the tracks up a small rise and paused as the trees broke into another clearing. He could hear a low grumbling and squatted where he was, hoping to stay out of sight.

Covering the light and silently turning it off, Al remained as quiet as he could. His mind kept screaming at him that they already knew where he was. He was too loud in the forest for them not to. But in his heart, he still prayed, hoping that he'd been quiet enough that they either hadn't noticed or thought his sounds were from one of their own.

To his left, he heard what sounded like low voices. They were guttural and sounded like the creatures were speaking during the inhale rather than an exhale. The very thought of it made him want to cough, and he had to hold his breath to keep from giving away his position.

A moment later the beasts could be heard walking off, their heavy breathing giving away their positions. Al took steady, methodical breaths and slowly came to his feet once the creatures had left.

He slipped his thermal optic back out and just caught a glimpse of one of the creatures going deeper into the forest. He groaned inwardly and stepped out into the small clearing, quickly crossing the sparse grassy area and entering the woods on the same game trail as the Sasquatch.

He moved silently over the well-beaten path, avoiding the numerous, scratchy branches that stretched out for him. He tried keeping the beast within view but quickly lost sight of it as it rounded a rock outcrop.

Al hurried along the game trail and stepped gingerly around the smaller stones at the base of the outcrop, nearly stepping out into a covered clearing where the beasts were now gathered.

He backed away silently and prayed that he wasn't noticed. *I'll know soon enough if they saw me,* he thought.

He backed further along the trail, finding a place where he could shimmy up the side of the rock. Perhaps from a higher vantage, he could see where the civilians were taken.

He planted his foot firmly in a crack in the base rock and pushed up, using the flat palms of his hands to grip until his fingers found a hold. As he neared the crest of the craggy pile, he slowly raised his head until he could finally make out what was on the other side.

The rock he was perched on was a small part at one end of a long line of rock outcropping. Another ran parallel, and the two formed solid walls to a central area that had been obviously used by the creatures for some time. There was no grass growing in the tightly compacted soil; the floor had been stomped smooth.

At the far end was another, smaller, outcropping that formed another natural wall. Just in front of that was a long, flat rock that he thought could almost be a table— or an altar.

At the far end, near the table rock, the stone giants had dumped Hector and Patricia. The two lay unconscious in a haphazard pile. The huge creature, *the alpha*, Al decided, was holding a spear like a walking cane and used its other hand to motion toward Hector while speaking to a much smaller creature.

Al watched in horror as the smaller creature gripped Hector's ankle and dragged him out of view. The tall, limping alpha bent to one knee and extended its hand toward Patricia. With a finger almost the size of her wrist, the creature gently turned her face to the side and seemed to be studying her.

Al watched as the giant used its spear to push itself back to a standing position and limp away. He could hear the others but couldn't see them. Hushed conversations in that same guttural language and the sounds of rocks being hit against each other told him that there were more of the creatures here than he'd thought.

He slid back down the rock, landing landed softly on the well-worn game path. He had no idea what to do next. The entire time he'd been following the creature, he'd tried to formulate a game plan for once they stopped, but never did his mind conceive a situation like this one.

He pulled up the sleeve of his coat and checked his watch. The sun would be up in a short while, and he'd be exposed.

He turned and stared back along the game trail, wondering if he could find Dale before it was too late, and maybe between the two of them they could come up with a plan to rescue the civilians.

He clenched his teeth tightly in frustration then

pushed away from the rock, following the game trail as quietly as he could.

He didn't realize that the Sasquatch had set a sentry.

DALE STUMBLED along the rocky terrain until he spotted a game trail. He pulled out his LED flashlight and scanned the area, looking for prints. He followed the trail for about thirty yards and stopped, unsure whether the creatures would use another animal's path. He spun a slow circle, looking for any kind of sign, and was about to give up when he spotted a pine sapling snapped at about three feet high.

Bending closer, he saw a few long, reddish-brown hairs clinging to the jagged break. "Bingo," he whispered.

He quickly extinguished his torch and pulled out the infrared monocular. He scanned the entire area, and once he was certain that none of the creatures were lying in wait, he began to follow the path again.

Dale moved methodically through the forest, using the game trail as his road sign and doing his best to avoid the natural pitfalls that Mother Nature loved to toss into the mix. A few misplaced steps and he could easily find himself the proud new owner of a broken arm or leg.

He tripped more than once over half-buried stones or tree roots that crossed the path. He met up with a Y in the trail and knew he'd taken the wrong path when he walked into a spider web.

The dance that followed as he scrambled to get the

sticky mess off of his face might have made for a viral video online. He was just happy not to be on the receiving end of the spider's wrath, once he was clear.

Backtracking the trail, he took the other leg and found himself coming to a dry creek bed. He could see tracks going along the edge of the ravine, and a certain track caught his eye. He pulled his flashlight again and smiled when he saw a crisp boot print in the freshly moved dirt. "He's gotta be going after Patty and Hector. That's the only reason I can imagine him coming this way."

As he stepped off the edge and slid into the ravine, his flashlight fell on a grisly scene, and Dale felt his chest tighten.

"It's a fucking graveyard," he mumbled as he scanned the area. "There must be a hundred..." he trailed off as the realization struck that he had known a lot of these people.

Dale felt his legs weaken and he fell to his butt in the soft side of the dry bed. His flashlight kept the boneyard lit up; he could almost hear the missing men's voices again, telling him to leave now, while there was still a chance.

He hadn't even noticed the smell of rotting flesh until he started coming out of the shock of seeing the sheer number of remains in one location. He held the back of his hand under his nose, wishing he'd thought to pack Vicks mentholated rub. It wouldn't mask the smell entirely, but it would take the edge off of the unbearable stench.

He pushed up from the soft soil and continued following what he was almost certain were Al's boot prints. "Good on you, buddy. Never give up, never surrender."

He came to an area where the prints seemed to meander and then disappear. He turned a slow circle, searching for the direction Al had gone, and his light happened to fall on the other side of the ravine. "You crossed here."

Dale turned off the flashlight and brought the infrared back into play. He scanned the area thoroughly and then leapt across the narrow section, landing almost directly in the other's boot prints.

Dale scrambled up the side of the ravine and soon found himself in a thicket. He swept the ground low with his flashlight again and could see where the boots had gone into the brambles.

I can only think of one reason for going through something this thick and nasty, he thought to himself. *You were following them.*

Dale bent low, and even with his ribs protesting, he tried bellycrawling through the thinnest area of the thicket. A few yards in he emerged into a small clearing. "This is better."

He noted that he could see the trees clearly on the other side and quickly checked his watch. "Fuck me. The sun will be up in no time."

He crawled out of the thicket and stood again, his ribs protesting as he took a deep breath. "Where'd ya go, Al?"

A loud wood knock echoed through the trees and Dale stiffened, certain he'd been seen. He ducked low and backed into the thicket again, allowing some of the leafier tangle to cover his front.

Afraid that he'd given his position away, he stood still

and metered his breathing, praying that the wood knock was not meant to announce his arrival. A moment later he heard another wood knock, this one much closer.

That's it then. They're closing on me.

Dale heard twigs snapping ahead of him and hunkered as low as he could. His hand slid to his side and gripped the carbine, slowly bringing it to bear on whatever approached him.

He heard a loud whoop in the woods ahead of him and the sound of something big moving quickly through the forest. He flipped off the safety, brought the barrel up, and pointed toward the sound of whatever it was making a mad dash through the trees.

Whatever it was grew closer and Dale pressed the butt of the carbine tight to his shoulder, preparing to aim for the head of whatever came out of the trees.

The noise grew louder and more haphazard and in his gut, Dale knew the creature was mad enough not to give a shit how much noise it made.

He applied pressure to the trigger and leveled the sites on where the creature was sure to emerge. "Come to Poppa, you smelly son of a bitch."

14

Deep in the Catskills

Al stiffened when he heard the wood knock then turned and increased his speed, traveling the game trail as quickly as he could.

Another wood knock echoed opposite the first, and he knew that he'd been spotted. He could actually make out some of the trees ahead of him as the sun began to rise and increased his speed, snapping twigs and stumbling along the trail as fast as he dared.

When one of the creatures "whooped" it felt like it was right beside him, and Al's fight or flight responded with "run like hell" mode. He slapped away at the lower branches that constantly threatened to hit him in the face and was at a full-on run when he burst into the small clearing at the base of the trail.

He nearly pissed himself when Dale suddenly appeared out of the thicket with his rifle pointed directly at him. "Woah! Slow down!" Dale reached out for him and Al spun, bringing his MP5 to bear on the trail behind him.

"They're hot on my heels!" He dropped to one knee and panned the weapon side to side.

"I nearly fuckin' shot you!" Dale scanned the trees beside him. "We should have brought IFF with us."

"Yeah, like that would help," Al huffed as he continued to pan the weapon side to side. "I swear to god, I could feel their breath on my neck. They were RIGHT THERE."

"I believe you," Dale responded quietly. "Let's say you and me back off a bit and give them a nice buffer." He began to back into the brush but Al grabbed him, pointing in the other direction. Dale glanced to their right and saw where the thicket ended. "Better around than through. Got it."

Al slowly backed away from the clearing until they felt the thicket was fully between them and the creatures. "Tell me you know where Patty and Hector are."

Al nodded then pulled his canteen and took a long pull. "Yeah, unfortunately. I followed big red up the hill here and," he paused to get his breathing under control. "You wouldn't believe where they hang their hats at night."

"I'd believe just about anything right now," Dale mumbled. "Where is it?"

"Top of that hill there. Game trail takes you right to their front door." He turned and raised a brow at Dale. "Literally."

"And they have guards going up and down the hill, don't they?"

Al shrugged. "If they were there when I went up, they missed me." He took another long swallow and then screwed the cap back on the canteen. "But they damned sure spotted me coming back down."

"Why'd you leave?"

Al shot him a surprised look. "To find you, mate. There's too many of them for me to form an effective assault." He took a deep breath and blew it out slowly. "Last I saw, they were both still alive. But big red had one of the littler ones haul Hector away."

"I doubt it was to change his diaper," Dale replied softly. He lowered his head and looked away. "I followed your tracks up the mountain. I see you found their boneyard."

"You could say that. Nightmarish." Al squeezed the man's shoulder. "I'm sorry about your mates."

"A very big part of me thinks they deserve a decent burial."

Al raised a brow at him. "I'm sure their families would want that." He gave him a knowing look. "Wouldn't you?"

Dale shrugged. "I don't know what I'd want. Thankfully, I don't have anybody in that pile that would…" he stopped himself, knowing he was lying. He took a deep breath and changed the subject. "What's the layout where they're being held?"

Al nodded and reached for a stick. "The whole place has a thick canopy over it, but there are two rock outcroppings that run parallel. At the end is another that closes it off like a—"

"Wait, is there a long flat rock at the end where it's closed off?"

"You know the place?"

Dale groaned and sat back on his heels. "Yeah. I know the place."

"You've been there, then?"

Dale nodded and sighed. "That's the last place I saw Gamboa and Gabaldon alive; you might say it was our gallows."

Al narrowed his gaze. "Come again?"

"That's where the leader of the Bigfoots let me go." Dale sat back and rested his head in his palms. "That's their home."

"Okay, good then. You know the lay of the land." He nudged him encouragingly. "Between the two of us, we can come up with a plan to get—"

"That's ALL I saw," Dale interrupted him. "I have no idea what's behind either of those outcrops. I know the ends were open near that back wall because I saw them moving in and out of the area, but…" he shrugged. "That's all I've got."

Al groaned as he sat back. "We need a bit more if we have any hope of getting them back alive."

Dale nodded. "Indeed."

HECTOR CRACKED an eye open and nearly shit himself a second time. One of the creatures had ripped away his pants and seemed preoccupied with collecting grass. He turned his head slightly and instantly regretted it as pain radiated up his neck and settled firmly in the front of his head. He could only assume that one of the monsters had knocked him cold and dragged him to this place to make a nice Mexican meal for the family.

He laid his head back slowly and closed his eyes, waiting for the waves of pain to ease. He screamed and nearly wept when the creature lifted his leg and began scrubbing him down with the dead grass. His eyes popped open wide and he attempted to scramble away. The creature's grip on his ankle was much stronger than he anticipated, and he found himself flopping around on the cold, packed ground like a fish out of water.

As Hector squealed, the creature lifted him effortlessly by one leg and spun him around. It began scraping his exposed areas with the grass and Hector's hands shot between his groin and his head, unsure which to protect.

The creature pressed him against the flat side of a huge rock and continued to scrub at him, grunting with displeasure as he tried to wriggle free from its grasp. Hector's scream caught suddenly in his throat when the beast shoved a handful of the dry grass between the cheeks of his ass, and it was only then that the creature dropped him.

Hector tried to roll away from the light-colored Sasquatch but was caught again by the other leg. He was shocked when he noticed hefty swinging breasts under all that hair. He found himself pressed again to the rock and he tried to take in his surroundings. He saw another of the smaller creatures scramble up the side of the rest of the outcropping and launch itself into a tall tree that hung over the area. He noted another female at the end of the outcrop that seemed busy with a pile of leaves.

When he looked back at the creature that had manhandled him, she had a look on her face that he'd seen many times growing up. It was the same smirking scowl his mother used to give him when she caught him doing something he knew he wasn't supposed to.

Hector dug his heels into the packed dirt and tried

to push back further, but the rock face was solid. The creature leaned forward and seemed to study him; it was only then that he attempted to do anything other than scream. "Y-you don't want to eat me, man...err...wo-woman. I'm t-telling you...I'm nothing but fat and gristle." He made a sour face, gestured at his torso and shook his head. "Seriously, look at this." He slapped his belly, making it jiggle.

The creature seemed to deliberately ignore him and came to her full height. It was only then that Hector realized, she might be smaller than the others, but compared to him, she was huge. Nearly seven feet tall and with arms strong enough to lift him from the ground one handed.

He swallowed hard and bit back a sob. "P-please don't eat me." He looked away and squeezed his eyes shut. He heard the creature grunt then with a loud huff, it moved away, nearly silently.

He held his eyes closed for entirely too long, and when he chanced peeking, the she-monster was gone. He lowered his arm from his face and craned his neck to see the other female still sorting leaves just yards away.

Slowly, he pulled his feet closer and tried to stand, using his hands to cover his privates. Once he was standing on two feet, he noted that his chest ached. Like he'd been squeezed, but not hard enough to break anything. He took a quick inventory and noted that his head was, by far, the worst injury.

He stumbled away from the tall rock and turned a slow circle, taking in his surroundings. The sun was just coming up and the area had an eerie grayness to it. It appeared that a fog was settling in around the trees.

He glanced over at the female still sorting leaves and

his mind couldn't comprehend what was happening. Why didn't she attack? For that matter, why didn't the strawberry-blonde one kill him and prepare a little Hector tar-tar for the whole fam damily?

Hector took a few wobbly steps and realized he couldn't be trotting around the woods with his favorite organ swinging for the world to see. There might be kids around.

He pulled his flannel shirt off and stood in a t-shirt, trying to figure out a way that he could use the material to cover himself. "Maybe if I tore the arms off, I could put my legs through there and..." He groaned loudly. "Then Pedro hangs out the collar."

He unbuttoned the shirt and wrapped it around him then used the arms to tie off around his middle. It might be a bit breezy in the back, but he'd deal with it.

He turned and looked for his boots. Surely they didn't use them as chew toys?

He extended his arm and braced himself against the rock as he worked his way to the end opposite the other Sasquatch. He rounded a corner and saw Patricia curled up next to a long flat stone and was about to run to her when another of the creatures suddenly appeared in front of him. He let out a little "*eep*" without realizing he'd done it and slowly backed away from the creature.

It glared down at him then stepped around him and disappeared behind the rock. Hector clutched at his chest and prayed that his heart didn't explode from fear. He stepped toward Patricia again then paused.

A massive red Genoskwa using a spear like a walking stick appeared at the other end of the flat rock and bent low to check Patricia. Hector watched in horrid amazement as the creature gently cradled her face and turned it side to side before standing again and limping into the wide opening between the two tall rock outcrops.

Hector stepped closer and peered around the corner. He wasn't prepared for what he saw.

The red creature stood with its back to Hector. Surrounding this great ape was a dozen smaller bigfoots. Hector hugged the rock and leaned just far enough around the edge to watch as the creature thumped the base of its walking stick to the ground. As he did, the others all turned their attention to him.

Hector stared in amazement as the leader began to speak, though the guttural language was uncomfortable to watch. It was as if the creature inhaled his word audibly, then growled as he exhaled.

It spoke slowly and methodically, pausing more than once, as if lost in thought, then picking up again.

Hector noticed that almost all of the creatures the leader addressed had lowered their eyes, and their heads were almost bowed.

Except one.

In the rear, a thick-bodied, younger male stood with his shoulders squared and his chin high. *Is he challenging this monster?* Hector thought as the body language the smaller male used looked anything but obedient or subservient.

The big red male motioned toward Patricia as he spoke then reached up and clutched at the thick muddy coat on his chest. He gripped it tightly, and Hector watched in amazement as the mud shielding crumbled in his hand. The big ape tossed the dirt and rock aside.

It was then that the young male stepped forward and growled something, and by the tone, the meaning was obvious to Hector. He was calling out the leader.

Hector couldn't read Big Red's face, since his back was turned to him, but he appeared to ignore the younger male. He was grumbling something else quietly and gently when suddenly the younger male whooped loudly and began to beat his chest, just like Hector had seen mountain gorillas do on the Discovery Channel.

Hector recoiled from the act, but couldn't stop watching.

The young male yelled something and slapped at his chest again, but this time, Big Red reacted. He thumped the base of his spear into the ground three times then tossed it aside, pounding his own chest as he let loose a roar that nearly caused Hector to wet himself.

I don't need to be seeing this shit. Ima get myself killed like a curious cat, he thought, yet he couldn't look away.

The Big Red reached out and parted the smaller Sasquatches before him then barked something in a very authoritative way to the feisty young male.

Hector had to remind himself to start breathing again as the challenger seemed to wither. He stepped back, lowering his head and averting his eyes.

The alpha male slapped his chest once with his right arm and one of the smaller ones retrieved his spear. Once it was back in his grip, he used it like a walking stick, limping heavily as he turned around.

It was only then that Hector noticed that Big Red had a missing eye. Its right eye socket was crusted over with matted hair and what looked like mud, or perhaps thickly dried blood. He tried not to stare, but once Hector looked at the rest of the creature's face, he realized it was looking right at him.

He felt his jaw tremble and his body dumped adrenaline in a fight or flight response, but Hector was frozen in fear.

The alpha looked away and walked back to Patricia. It studied her for a moment then turned and exited out of the gap in the rocks opposite Hector.

No longer able to remain standing, Hector's knees nearly buckled and he slid down the rock until he was kneeling. He stared at Patricia and, after a few moments, was relieved to note she was still breathing. He dropped down onto his hands and knees and felt an overwhelming desire to cry.

15

Deep in the Catskills

Dale chewed slowly on a protein bar, his mind still trying to embrace just how fucked they were. He glanced at Al and noticed that while the man ate, his eyes were constantly on guard.

"You sure they were alive?" Dale asked softly.

Al slowly shook his head. "They appeared in one piece. That's the best I can give ya, mate."

Dale popped the last of the protein bar into his mouth and gently folded the foil wrapper, stuffing it into his shirt pocket. "Just judging by how these things have acted before, if they *are* alive, I'd bet money it won't be for much longer."

"Then I'd say we need to formulate a plan, don'tcha think?"

Dale brushed off his pants and stood at his full height. "We both know what we need to do." He turned and glanced up the mountain. "We need to flank them, get the full layout, determine the number of enemy forces, and then verify that our people are still alive."

Al nodded patiently then looked up, scanning the trees. "You know we'll never get past their sentries."

Dale sighed heavily then turned and stared toward the creek. "If we give them a wide enough berth…" he trailed off, his mind going places he didn't want to dwell in. "Perhaps one of us stays here and keeps their lookouts busy."

"And which of us gets to play one on one with the mountain apes?"

Dale shrugged. "We could draw straws."

"Or you can sit here and rest while I go." Al raised a brow at him. "You think I haven't noticed how you're favoring your side? Is there something you should share with the class?"

Dale shook his head. "Nah, I'm fine."

Al nodded knowingly then leaned in close like he was going to say something softly. When Dale turned an ear to him, Al pushed him firmly in the ribs. He watched as Dale winced and gasped, nearly doubling over. "Yeah, you're fine, mate." He waited for Dale's temper to flare and was somewhat disappointed when it didn't.

"Okay, so maybe I bruised a rib or two."

Al crossed his arms. "Show me."

Dale scoffed. "Like I'm going to undress for you out here." He shot him a lame smile. "You haven't even bought me dinner yet."

"Come on, mate. Let's see the damage. We might need to address it now."

Dale groaned and pulled up his BDU shirt. When he undid the bottom buttons and pulled up his underlayer, exposing his side, even he was surprised at the angry, dark bruise. "Well, it looks worse than it is."

Al was bent and studying the bruise. "Did you get thrown into a tree?"

"Same difference." Dale pulled his shirts back down. "I had a tree thrown at me."

"Yeah, mate, you got yourself some broken ribs there. Cracked at least." He turned and dug in his pack. "I brought some elastic bandages." He tossed the ACE bandages to him. "Wrap 'em tight."

"I know the drill." Dale peeled his BDU shirt off then was about to lift his thermal undershirt but thought better of it. He began to wrap himself but found it nearly impossible.

Al didn't hesitate. He took the roll from him and handed him the end. "Hold that still." Dale held the end to his chest and Al began to walk around him in circles, pulling the bandage as tight as he dared. When he was done, he used the aluminum clips to secure the end. "That should do it. Lower your arms. Can you breathe?"

Dale inhaled and winced. "Barely."

"Good enough, mate." He patted his shoulder as he walked past. "I'll see you in about…" he trailed off, staring off at the mountain. "In about six hours."

"I'm not sure they have that long." Dale winced as he pulled his BDU blouse back over his shoulders. "These things usually kill you as soon as they get their hands on you."

Al rubbed at his chin. "Odd then, ain't it? They not only didn't kill them, but they walked them all the way up here?" He shrugged. "What could've changed?"

Dale slowly shook his head. "I honestly have no clue. Maybe they want their meat fresh?"

"Possible." Al hitched up his pants and tightened his belt. "I'm going to have to move quickly."

"And quietly," Dale added.

"That's a given." Al took a deep breath and then checked his watch. "I'll see you when I see you." He turned to leave then turned back. "If you hear gunfire coming from the woods, you'll have to make a decision."

"What's that?"

"Either head for the cars or charge that mountain."

Dale raised a brow at him. "Not, 'come after me and save my ass?' Seems to me that should be one of the choices."

Al smiled sadly and shook his head. "If you hear gunfire, mate, that's me getting in my last licks before they end me. There won't be nothing left to save."

Dale sobered and was about to say something when Al turned and marched away. All he could do was watch. He couldn't even think of anything profound to say as his last words to the man.

HECTOR SENSED movement at his side and turned slowly to see the strawberry-blonde female standing next to him. He winced when something brushed the back of his head and he ducked away as something landed next to him on the ground.

When he opened his eyes, he peered at a wolf's skin, but the strawberry-blonde creature was gone. He blinked rapidly at the skin and had no idea what to do with it. He slowly stood and held the skin up. It was soft and pliable, as if it had been tanned.

He turned around and saw the strawberry-blonde bigfoot about ten feet behind him. She made a motion with her hands that Hector didn't quite understand. He gave her a puzzled look and slowly shook his head. "I-I don't get it."

He could have sworn the creature rolled her eyes before moving toward him. With a movement so quick he couldn't have responded, she snatched the wolf skin from him and pressed it to his middle where his flannel shirt was tied. She shook it once as if to tell him, take it. Then she let go and stepped back.

Hector smiled as he picked up the skin and tried to wrap it around his middle. He held it against him, but couldn't figure out a way to tie it in place. He turned and offered a weak smile. "Thank you."

The female turned and walked away, leaving him in total confusion. He turned back and stared at Patricia for a moment then turned his eyes upward to the canopy. "If this is your way of keeping us alive, Señor, umm, *gracias*." He cleared his throat and smiled. "But I'd be even more grateful to get back home to a shower."

He nearly jumped when one of the creatures nudged him from behind. He spun to see the dark brown female that had been sorting leaves. She towered over him but held her hand out, offering him some of the leaves.

Hector stared at her hand and then up at her. "I don't know what you want from me."

She made an eating motion with her hand then thrust it out to him again. Hector nodded nervously as he accepted the leaves. "Yeah, I don't think my body can digest this stuff." He smiled at her as warmly as he could.

She continued to stare at him then made the eating motion again. Hector smiled again then lifted one of the smaller leaves to his mouth and stuffed it inside. He continued to smile as he chewed then realized it was the consistency of lettuce. His face went slack as he continued to chew, shoving another handful of the leaves into his mouth.

He began to chuckle then swallowed. He laughed as he looked up at her. "It's kinda bitter, but it's like salad." He shoved another handful into his mouth. "Thank you."

She turned and walked away leaving Hector to finish his supper. He watched her go back to her piles to continue sorting for just a moment, then he turned away. He nearly ran into the tall strawberry-blonde female and stared up at her. He stopped chewing and smiled nervously at her with green teeth. "It's not bad, really. Kind of like cilantro but juicy."

He couldn't read her facial expression, but she handed him something that he accepted without question. He watched as she huffed then she turned from him. He opened his hand and saw a strip of dried meat. "Oh, jerky." He stuck it into his mouth and pulled, ripping a piece of the meat away. He chewed it and grimaced at the lack of flavor. "Needs salt," he called out to her. "And maybe some garlic." He squatted down beside the rock outcrop and alternated the green stuff with the jerky. "Maybe some onions and black pepper. Oh, what I wouldn't give for some salsa." He continued to chew and then smiled. "And some tortilla chips."

He finished the food they had given him then stood

and glanced at the dark brown female sorting other greens. "I don't suppose you have some wild onions in there, do ya?"

She barely gave him a furtive glance before returning her attention to her work. "You know, I'm pretty handy in a kitchen. You'd be surprised what I could cook up." He wiped his hands on his t-shirt and stepped closer, still unsure if he was safe to approach.

He inched closer and closer until he was within arm's reach then bent and studied the food she had collected. "That a root?"

She looked at him momentarily then went back to sorting. Hector, not one to give up so easily, leaned forward and pointed to the tuber. "Root?"

She looked up, and when the two locked eyes, he saw a glimmer of something. The more he stared into her amber eyes, the more he knew that she was an intelligent creature. Fully aware and sentient.

He smiled at her and waited. A moment later she reached forward and nudged the tuber closer to him. Hector picked it up and sniffed. He scratched the tough outer skin with his thumbnail and touched his tongue to the moisture. "Has a bit of a pico taste to it."

He gripped the pointed end and peeled a layer of the tough outer skin off. He held it to his nose and nodded. "Oh, yeah. Definitely got some bite to it." He peeled a bit more of the tough skin off and bit the soft inner flesh. Almost immediately he regretted it. He chewed the tuber and then spat it aside. "Yeah," he choked as he tried to catch his breath. "That's horseradish."

He looked over and saw the female Sasquatch *grinning*. "Oh, you think it's funny?" he joked as he handed her back the root. "You should use that flavor in your jerky."

He reached across and plucked a round berry from a pile and was about to put it in his mouth. The female reached up and pulled his hand away, forcing him to drop the berry.

"What the heck?" He gave her a tight lipped smile. "Saving the best for dessert?"

She picked up the berry and held it up for him to see. Then she gently squeezed the berry and red juice flowed from it. She leaned forward and rubbed it across a scrape on his leg and Hector hissed. "Oh, that stings!"

She grabbed his leg and continued to rub the berry juice on his wound, then tossed the berry aside. When he looked at her she picked up another and made a motion toward her mouth then waved it off, acting like he was rubbing it on her arm.

"Oh...okay." He nodded slowly. "Not for eating. It's medicine?"

She continued to stare at him for a moment then went back to sorting.

Hector watched her for a moment then craned his neck to look past her. In the distance he could see smaller Sasquatches, children, he assumed, tossing a rock back and forth before slapping the ground and launching into the trees. He had no idea what game they were playing, but he recognized that they were actually *playing*.

He sat down heavily next to his new friend and continued to watch how the creatures interacted, his fear and trepidation fading with each passing moment.

SURVIVAL

Al trotted through the grassy areas, making as much distance as he could without creating noise. When he came to a stand of trees, he slowed as much as he dared, avoiding any fallen branches and doing his level best to remain on the dry pine needles littering the forest floor.

He crested what he thought was the top of the mountain only to realize he had much further to go. At the lower crest, where the trees were sparse, he got his bearings and adjusted his route. He checked his watch then took off again at a fast trot.

Surely they wouldn't have sentries out this far, he thought. He continued to study the position of the rising sun and made adjustments to his route. *I'm on the far side of their camp, and they haven't had any interaction with people out this way. Surely it's safe to move faster.*

As much as he wanted to break into a full run, he held back, ensuring he kept his noise to a minimum. He wasn't even sure it was possible to sneak up on these things. *This is their backyard, for crying out loud.*

Al slowed and studied the sun again. He pulled out his canteen and took a quick sip of water, conserving the rest for the return trip. Once he was certain of his position, he started breaking toward the far side of the Genoskwa's camp.

The course to their area was marked with rock outcroppings, and sharp stones littered the ground. When he'd find a clearing, he'd pause and study the terrain. If any large, two-legged creatures were roaming this area, they'd leave signs.

After finding no prints and no other evidence that

anything bigger than a muskrat had been through there, he pushed on, increasing his speed until he was certain he was closing on the area he'd witnessed them in.

He paused beneath a thick pine and hid in the lower limbs, letting them cover him from view and, hopefully, mask his scent. He slowly stood and parted the branches, peering out across the line of rock outcroppings. The trees were sparse ahead of him and his line of sight was good.

He pulled his thermal optic and turned off the thermal capability, using the lens to zoom in on the area.

At first, nothing stood out to him and he saw little-to-no movement. He waited, continuing to survey the area and, eventually, he caught sight of three smaller creatures playing. They'd throw something then leap to the rocks and into the trees, then back to the ground again.

He couldn't help but smile as he watched the little ones do what little ones do, but he needed to see where the bigger creatures were. He slowly worked his way out from under his pine cover, creeping low to the ground until he found another vantage point. Between an ancient dead tree and a rock outcrop, he wedged himself neatly in the gap and peered through the scope again.

He saw a few larger Sasquatch wandering the area. They all seemed to be doing something with purpose, he just wasn't sure what. He could only assume that their tribe had a pecking order, and menial tasks needed to be done.

He counted eight of the adults and was about to call it good when two more rounded the wall of rock, seemingly engaged in an argument of sorts. The bigger of the two seemed agitated and kept waving its long arms at the smaller one. Al felt his chest tighten when he saw the creature make an unmistakable gesture: the twisting and pulling apart motion Archer had described when looking at Tommy's decapitated body.

At that moment, he feared that both Patricia and Hector were already gone. Their lifeless bodies were stripped of meat, their skeletons prepared to be dumped in the dry ravine. Al felt his anger start to rise. He wanted nothing more than to put a bullet in the creature's head.

16

Deep in the Catskills

Al found himself reaching for his MP5, but he knew it wasn't a long range weapon. It was for close quarters battle. The 9MM just didn't have the *oomph* to reach out and touch somebody at this distance. He was certainly feeling jealous of Archer with his carbine. While deep in thought about higher powered weapons, he nearly missed the human that stepped out of the shadows.

Al had to adjust the zoom on his optic, but there was no mistaking Hector walking around with his flannel shirt tied to his waist and what looked like a grey animal skin draped over one shoulder. Al felt a jolt of elation for just a moment but then he saw a large, dark brown creature appear beside Hector.

He leaned closer and ducked low in the crevice as he watched the two. *Is he talking to that thing?*

Hector strolled alongside the creature until they came to the edge of the woods and the bigfoot squatted and pointed to something. He watched as Hector used his hands to dig and then he pulled at something in the ground. He held it up like a prize fish and the dark brown creature stood and turned to go back.

Hector followed behind it like a puppy.

Al slid down from the crevice and rubbed at his eyes. "Is he part of the fucking tribe now?" He leaned back up and watched as Hector followed the big brown back into the shadows.

It was then that he knew two things for sure.

One, Hector was still alive.

Two, there were more creatures there than he was able to count.

He slid to the ground and sighed, wiping the sweat from his eyes as his mind raced. "What the actual fuck is going on?"

He had to know more. Was Patricia still alive? Was she playing house with the monsters as well?

He groaned as he rose to a standing position and wedged himself back into the crevice. The two creatures that looked like they were arguing were still in a heated discussion. The larger one stood tall and beat on his chest like King Kong did in the movies. Al chuckled softly as he watched the creature suddenly appear more apelike. It dropped to all fours and bounced around for a moment then stood and made that same twisting and tearing motion.

Al's smile faded and he felt that familiar wave of anger begin to swell. "Fuck this." He extricated himself from the crevice and began his trek back to Archer. He'd report everything he'd seen and let the federal agent decide the best move forward.

He checked his watch and then peered at the position of the sun. "I'll be back before he knows it. Six hours my ass."

Dale paced nervously behind the thicket, occasionally peeking through towards the trees. Twice now he'd heard a tree knock, so he knew that they knew that he was still out there.

"Good. Keep your attention on me and not the Special Forces dude sneaking up your exhaust pipe." He opened his BDU blouse and adjusted the wrap slightly. His skin was beginning to itch and he wanted nothing more than to take the bandage off and bury it.

He was just starting to button his blouse back when a softball-sized stone sailed over the thicket and bounced just yards from him. "You mangy son of a bitch. You almost hit me!" he yelled from behind the cover.

In a momentary lack of judgment, he marched to the edge of the thicket and shot a double middle finger to the monsters. "You'll have to do better than that!"

He dipped back behind the thicket and paused, berating himself mentally for what he'd just done. "I'm losing my goddamned mind out here." He glanced at the sky then sighed and lowered himself to the ground. "It's gotta be a lack of sleep."

Another stone sailed overhead and bounced across the sparse grass. Dale stared at the rock and chuckled to himself. "Unless they can throw through this thick wall of green, I should be okay."

Another stone landed just feet from him and Dale scrambled to his feet. He glared through the thicket but couldn't see the hairy beasts. He knew they were staying just inside the trees.

He marched around the area, looking for a rock that he could throw without risking his ribs, and found a nice round one, the size of a softball. He plucked it from the ground and wiped the damp earth from it, smoothing it, tossing it in his hand, feeling the heft. He walked to the edge of the thicket and stared into the woods.

He waited to see if anything would come flying from there and when nothing did, he glanced at where the rocks had landed and made his best guesstimate of where the creatures were hiding. With a bunny hop, he tossed his rock with a sidearm motion and watched it sail into the shadows.

Yeah, it hurt to do it, but it felt good at the same time. "I hope that hit you right in the eye," he grumbled as he marched back behind the thicket.

He turned and peered through the thick vines, waiting, hoping to see where the next rock would come from and nearly shit himself when Al appeared next to him. "Playing catch?"

"Son of a…I could have shot you!"

Al scoffed. "Not with all of your attention on those things." He reached out and pulled Dale away from the wall of green. "You're not going to believe what I found."

"How many?"

"No idea. More than a dozen, I'd wager."

"No idea?" Dale gave him a quizzical look. "What did you find?"

"Hector." Al crossed his arms. "He's one of them now."

Dale's mouth fell open and it took him a moment for

the words to process. "Please expand on that before my brain explodes."

Al nodded then shrugged. "I saw a handful of the creatures. Then I watched Hector walk out of the shadows with a big brown one in tow. They went to the edge of the woods and dug up something then went right back into the dark."

Dale shot him a disbelieving stare. "You're not kidding around, are you?"

Al shook his head. "I didn't see Patricia, but it's a good bet that if he's still alive, then she's probably in it as well."

"Okay, but..." Dale held a hand up as he tried to wrap his mind around the situation. "But you definitely saw Hector?"

"And he was interacting with them." He seemed to stiffen and his face went hard. "But I also saw two others that..." he trailed off as he tried to find the right words. "It was almost as if they were arguing."

"Okay. And?"

"And one of them did this." Al brought his hands up, and violently mimed the gesture he'd seen. "Remind you of anything?"

Dale's face went pale. "Yeah. Either the lid was really stuck on their pickle jar or it was ripping somebody's head off."

Al nodded. "So I don't know if that's what they got planned for Hector, or if that was what they did to Tricia, or..."

"Or what they did to Tommy," Dale finished for him. He began to feel sick to his stomach and the mental image of the fresh skeletons in the shallow ravine came to mind. He slowly lowered himself to the ground and sat down heavily. "I need a moment."

"You probably need to eat something."

Dale shot him a look that wasn't missed. "That wouldn't be a good idea right about now." He sighed heavily and rubbed at his eyes. "So, what about the layout?"

Al hunkered next to him and met his gaze. "Yeah, that's a solid no-go. Even from the other side, there's enough clear space we'd never get close without being seen."

"So it's a direct frontal?"

Al shrugged. "Unless you have a better idea."

Dale checked his watch and raised a brow. "You got back quicker than you thought."

"Yeah, but it's a rough hike and not one I'm looking forward to doing again." He raised a brow at Dale. "You think if one of us came in from behind and got their attention that the other could charge from the game trail?"

"Or the opposite." He shrugged. "Once you're in position, I could start up the game trail, let the guards alert the others and when they all come running, you come in from behind and..." he trailed off.

"And rescue the humans."

"Well, okay. You could do that, *or*, you could attack from behind. Catch them off guard."

"Your plan sucks, mate."

"I know, but it's all I got at the moment." Dale sighed and lowered his head into his hands.

"Why?" Al asked as he slowly stood.

"Why what?"

"Hector. Why was he allowed to just move about?"

He rubbed at his chin. "What's changed since they ordered us off their land?"

"You're asking me?" Dale scoffed as he came to his feet. "I have no idea." He dusted off his pants and turned to Al. "From everything I know about these things, they eat people. Hector should have been a breakfast burrito by now. Instead, he's rubbing elbows with these things?"

Al shrugged. "And I didn't make a positive on Patricia. Maybe they ate her first?"

Dale shook his head. "I don't see Hector hanging with the homies if they'd just munched on Patty. I just can't see it."

Al glanced at the mountain again then raised a brow. "So, maybe we just walk up there and ask them."

Dale chuckled then turned and saw Al's face. "Wait, you're serious?"

"They let Hector move about on his own."

"Then why hasn't he taken off screaming? He could run down the hill and—"

"They'd catch him before he left the camp," Al interrupted. "This is Hector. There's no way he'd outrun them."

"Fuck," Dale grumbled. "Too many questions and not enough answers."

Al groaned and then stared at his watch. "Okay, it's just past noon. If I can keep the same pace, I can be back where I was in about two and a half hours."

"And that was…how far from the camp?"

Al shrugged. "Hundred yards. Maybe more."

"So, I give you three hours to make sure you've got time, then I make the frontal assault."

Al sighed as he slowly nodded. "And if I can get to

our people in time, I'll bring them down the way I came up."

"So, three and a half hours for you to return." He shot him a knowing look. "Hector can't move fast."

"Right." Al snapped his fingers. "It will be getting dark by the time we're back."

"And we have a long march back to the trucks."

Al held a finger up. "Oh yeah. Hector was without trou." He raised a brow. "He had his shirt tied to his waist and was wearing a sash made from some animal skin."

Dale stared at him, waiting for the punch line. "Like a prom sash?"

"I reckon." Al crossed his arms. "It's not so much the walk back that I'm worried about as I am…what if he doesn't have his keys? We'll have two vehicles and no keys."

Dale broke into a toothy smile. "Actually, I'm pretty sure he ditched the keys with the truck. He said something about the sun visor being too obvious."

"So there's a good chance we could still drive out of here?"

"Better than fifty-fifty, I'd wager."

"Right." Al stiffened and took a deep breath. "Back up the fuckin' mountain I go."

"Three hours!" Dale called to him.

Al flipped him the bird over his shoulder.

"Right. Now, where were we?" Dale turned and peered through the thicket. "What's the matter, boys? Didn't want to play catch with the Brit?" He picked up another stone and lobbed it over the thicket. "I hope you're ready, Chewie. I played shortstop on my high school baseball team!"

Patricia groaned as she tried to sit up and cradled the side of her head. "Oh, dear lord…my head."

Hector scrambled over to her side. "You're awake. I was worried."

She cracked an eye open and blinked rapidly at him. "What happened? Where are we?"

He helped her to sit up and knew the moment she spotted one of the creatures as she gasped and scrambled backward.

"Hold on, hold on!" He moved closer and helped her prop against the rock outcropping. "Don't panic," he whispered to her."

"T-t-they're right…there!" She pointed to the closest sasquatch and Hector craned his neck to see which one she pointed at.

The tall brown female approached from behind and handed him some of the berries. Hector accepted them and thanked her. When he turned back to Patricia, she stared at him with wide eyes. "What the actual fuck?!"

Hector smiled and took one of the berries between his fingers. He squeezed it and reached for her temple. She batted his hand away and glared at him. "Answer me, Hector. What the actual fuck?"

He sighed heavily as he plucked another berry from the ground and gently squeezed it. "This is a natural medicine." He held the oozing berry up and allowed her eyes to focus on it. "I think it helps keep shit from getting infected." He shrugged. "I don't really know, I just know that my really tall, big boobied friend there showed me that they're for rubbing on wounds." He

SURVIVAL

leaned closer and held the berry up. "You got a nasty cut there."

Her hand came up and touched the area. She winced as she pulled her hand back and stared at her fingers. "I see blood."

"Most of it's dried, but…" He leaned in closer and dabbed the wound with the berry. "There. Worst case scenario, it dyes your hair red."

She scooted up and leaned against the rock. "Why haven't they killed us?"

Hector shrugged. "No clue." He glanced back at the brown female. "I've spent a little time with her and I gotta say…" he smiled at her. "She's actually kinda nice."

The strawberry-blonde female walked past them and barely glanced at the pair. "But that one? Cranky bitch. Not much of a sense of humor."

Patricia stared at him. "You're kidding me right now, aren't you? We're dead, right? This is like some unknown level of Hell where we have to live with the ones who murdered us."

Hector chuckled again. "Hey, blondie over there wiped my ass." He cringed slightly. "Not the best bedside manner, though." He tugged at the wolf skin. "But she gave me this. I think she wanted me to wear it."

Patricia glanced at the flannel shirt tied to his waist. "So they…" she swept her hand in circles and trailed off, unable to finish her thought.

Hector nodded. "They brought us here, cleaned me up, more or less. And gave me food." His eyes lit up and he pointed to the brown one. "She's got all kinds of veggies, and the strawberry-blonde one gave me some beef jerky but it was way bland. Needed salt in the worst way and—"

"Wait, what?" She pulled at his arm. "It gave you meat?"

Hector shrugged. "Well, yeah. I mean, it was dried, you know? Like jerky. But it had NO flavor. It must be strictly sustenance because the taste? Zero stars, do not recommend."

She gave him a deadpan look. "Hector. Do you see any cows around here? You do remember that they *eat* humans, right? They killed over a hundred people in the last week. What kind of MEAT do you really think they gave you?"

Hector's face went three shades of pale and he fell back on his ass, gagging. "*Madre de dios…*"

17

Deep in the Catskills

Hector turned and wretched, trying to bring it up. "Oh, no…it's stuck inside me. It ain't coming out!"

Patricia leaned forward and patted his back. "Don't get yourself worked up. It was probably squirrel or something."

"No…" Hector wretched again and spit on the ground. "No, you were right. She probably fed me people meat on purpose."

"Hector!" Patricia pushed him and averted her eyes when he fell over and his legs went in the air. "Dammit! Cover that thing, will you?"

Hector scrambled back to all fours and tucked his shirt back down. "I can't help it. You knocked me over when I was trying to…" He urked when the thought hit him again. "I don't want to know. I coulda known who that was."

"Stop it." She winced and pressed a hand to the side of her head. "Why would they bring us here?"

Hector sat back and belched, trying desperately to remove the idea from his brain. "I got nothing." He pressed a hand to his stomach as he sat up. "I have no idea what the hell is going on. Last thing I remember, they trapped us between two big assed trees, then the next thing I know, I wake up here and they're feeding me salad and...and—"

Patricia leaned forward, her eyes darting from creature to creature. "I just had a terrible thought."

"That they're saving us for a midnight snack?"

"No." She leaned forward and whispered. "I remember reading that Native Americans used to capture members of warring tribes and turn them into slaves." Her eyes locked on his. "What if they want to keep us as slaves?"

Hector's face twisted. "Why would they do that? I mean, we're like way weaker than they are. There's not really much we could do to improve their lives around here and—"

"Hello!" she interrupted, holding her hands up. "Opposable thumbs. I'm sure there's stuff we could do that they can't."

"Well, yeah. I'm sure there's lots of stuff we can do that they can't." He glanced at the big brown female again. "I know they can't drive. She couldn't even fit in most cars, so—"

"Will you stop it!" She slapped him and the big brown female turned and glared at her. Patricia caught the look and withered back against the rock. "Just stop being an idiot, will ya?"

Hector rubbed the side of his face and scowled at

her. "Look, I don't know why they brought us here, but they did. They could have killed us at any time, but they didn't." He looked back at the big brown female and smiled again, giving her a little wave. "But don't go doing anything to piss them off, okay? I like breathing."

Patricia groaned as she sat back. "I don't like not knowing."

He turned and glared at her. "Neither do I. Especially if it deals with my staying alive or becoming a bigfoot's idea of a Manwich. So until we know more, how about we just try to keep a low profile, huh?"

She sighed as she sat back again and nodded. "Fine. But the first moment it looks like we can make a break for it, I say we hightail it out of here."

Hector gave her a deadpanned stare. "You really think you could outrun one of them? In these mountains?"

She opened her mouth to argue but quickly closed it, shaking her head.

He sat up and reached for her face again. He turned it slightly and studied her wound. "Hopefully, they didn't knock any more screws loose than you already had."

"You're not funny."

He smiled at her as he got to his feet. "Yes, I am." He hooked his chin toward the big brown female. "Just ask her. She thinks I'm hilarious."

Patricia groaned as he walked back over and sat next to the brown female. "Oh, dear god. He's got a crush on a bigfoot."

AL PAUSED and tugged a protein bar from his pack. He hated the damned things but it was energy, and his body dearly needed all the energy it could get at the moment. He quickly bit off half then folded the wrapper over the remains and stuffed it into his shirt pocket.

He shook his canteen and sighed. "Barely a third left." He decided against drinking it, pushing past his thirst.

He continued to study the sun and the terrain, doing his level best to follow the same path he'd taken earlier. It was at this time he wished he'd been a little less careful and left more of a trail.

At one point when he stopped, something small hit his shoulder and Al spun, weapon ready. He scanned the surrounding trees and it wasn't until he heard the angry barking of a squirrel that he allowed himself to relax. "Bushy tailed tree rat," he grumbled. He relaxed his weapon and pushed onward.

He kept hearing the chattering of the squirrel and soon realized the little beast was following him. He tried to throw a stone in its direction but the damned thing dodged it easily. "Shut up, will ya?" he whispered. He turned and scanned the area, just to make sure he wasn't being watched.

He even contemplated risking a single shot from his MP5 to rid himself of the wee beastie, but knew it was too high a risk to take.

As a last ditch attempt to shake the thing from his trail, Al plucked the remains of the protein bar from his pocket and tossed the wrapper side. He pressed it around a lower limb of the tree the squirrel was on and stepped away, hoping the stupid thing would investigate, decide to munch some free food and give him the chance to leave it behind.

He stepped back and waited while the squirrel stared down at the remains of the bar, then at him. As Al slowly backed away, the fuzzy tailed rat eventually darted down the trunk and sniffed at the offerings.

The moment Al saw the thing reach toward the bar, he turned and continued his march. "Must pay the highwayman," he grumbled. He continued pushing his way up the mountain and found his legs beginning to burn. Although this hike was nothing compared to what he was used to in his military days, it had been years since he'd attempted so many grueling hours traveling up and down mountains.

As he crested onto the first high ridge, he was breathing hard. He remembered exactly where he'd stood when he checked the area and moved to the same location. A quick scan with his thermal indicated nothing larger than a rabbit. Satisfied, he pushed on.

By the time he made it to the edge of clearing near the Genoskwa's lair, he was nearly out of breath. He glanced at his watch and smiled inwardly. "Record time. Even with dealing with the local wildlife." He settled into the same crevice and peered through his scope, watching the minimal activity outside the rock walls.

He smiled to himself when he saw Patricia walk out into the sunlight for a moment with Hector hovering over her. He could just make out the dark smear of dried blood on the side of her head and winced. "Let's hope you're up to high speed traveling soon, Pat."

Hector continued to stay close and more than once took her by the elbow as she seemed to waiver. Al watched as Hector turned and said something into the shadows. The same tall, brown creature appeared and handed him something that he offered to Patricia. She cautiously accepted it and whatever it was, she appeared to put it in her mouth.

Al sat back and scratched at his chin. "Maybe they thought they were cute and decided to adopt them as pets?"

Patricia stood on wobbly legs and dabbed gingerly at the bloody spot on the side of her head. "Hey, whatchu doing?" Hector asked as he approached her.

"I need to move around." She looked up at him and gave him a knowing look. "I need to move or I'll start going crazy—like, you don't want to know, crazy."

He gave her a confused look. "I...don't understand."

She licked her lips nervously. "I haven't had my medication and I'm really starting to feel it. My thoughts race from one thing to another and I feel anxious, like I need to be doing something."

Hector nodded and looked around the area. "I don't see your pack."

She shook her head slightly. "It was in the shirt pocket of my flannel."

Hector helped her to steady herself against the tall rock then held a finger up. "Give me a sec." She watched him trot over to the big brown and tried to communicate with her, mostly with his hands. He gripped the flannel material and showed the female, then pointed to Patricia. He made more motions with his hands, and Patricia realized he was trying to ask if she knew where the other shirt was.

The creature made motions back with her hands, but Patricia couldn't tell if Hector understood or not. She squinted at the pair as the clearing behind them was open and sunny, casting them into silhouette. It didn't take long for the light to affect her and she had to look away.

When Hector returned he took her by the shoulder and pulled her from the rock. "Betty's gonna check."

She shot him a questioning stare. "Betty?"

Hector smiled. "I needed to call her something other than 'hey you' so I named her Betty." He broke into an even toothier grin. "She looks like a Betty to me."

"Oh, for Pete's sake," she groaned as he walked her out and into the light.

"A little sunshine will do you some good."

"The brightness hurts my eyes. It's making my head throb."

Hector hovered over her and continued to urge her further out. "Come on, it will do you some good."

Patricia carefully walked out and let the sun warm her skin. She closed her eyes and let the rays soak in, smiling. "Tell me something," she quietly asked.

"Yeah?"

"Does Betty understand you?"

Hector chuckled. "I dunno. I mean, I feel like for the most part, yeah. But sometimes it's more like..." he snapped his fingers. "You know when you're talking to your dog and he does what you want and you're like, 'oh heck, does he actually understand me?' And then you're like, pfft, no. He's a friggin dog. He don't understand me anymore than I understand the cat. Ya know? But at the same time, you gotta wonder." His head bobbed as he spoke. "It's kinda like that."

She cracked an eye at him and chuckled. "God, you sound like me when I've gone too long without my meds."

Hector glanced back into the enclosure and smiled when Betty came lumbering toward them. "Fingers crossed she understood."

Patricia turned and saw Betty approaching and her body did an adrenaline dump, preparing her for fight or flight. Even when the creature stopped and handed Hector the pill bottle, Patricia was ready to try to run, screaming, into the hills.

Hector shook the bottle and smiled at Betty. "I knew you'd come through. Thanks, sweetheart." Betty turned around and lumbered back into the shadows and Hector handed Patricia the bottle. "She's smarter than a Labrador. I know. I had one."

Patricia twisted the cap off and fished out a pill. She tossed it into her mouth and forced it down dry. "You called her sweetheart."

Hector nodded. "Well, yeah. She's a sweetheart. She kind of reminds me of my tia Rosa. She was one big woman. Hairy, too. She could throw a *chancla* even harder than my abuela."

"Chancla?"

Hector broke into another toothy grin. "Flip flop. She could tug that thing off and have it in motion in a fraction of a second." He rubbed absently at the side of his head. "Friggin' hard, too. I think she killed me once."

Patricia giggled slightly. "Beaten to death by a flip flop. That's original."

"Nah. In my culture, it's a common thing to get nailed by a *chancla*." He reached out and began walking her toward the trees. "Come on, I want to show you something."

"Where are you taking me?"

"Not far." He pointed to the tree line. "Just over there at the edge of the woods."

She walked cautiously across the stone covered ground and as they approached the edge of the forest, she noticed green leafy plants. "This almost looks like..." she trailed off.

"If you were gonna say 'a garden,' you're not wrong." Hector bent and cleared some small stones from around a particular plant. "This one is a wild horseradish." He looked at her and smiled. "Ask me how I know."

"If you tell me that Betty told you, then I know I'm brain damaged."

Hector shrugged. "In a way, yeah." He stood and turned toward the rock enclosure. "She let me taste test some of the plants she had collected and one was definitely horseradish. Then she brought me out here and showed me where it was." He turned back and sighed. "They transplant these plants to keep them close to home. It's almost winter so she's doing what she can to harvest them all."

"How do you know that?"

He offered a slow shrug. "Well, it's getting colder and they know that. And they've been out here so long that they know when it's time to collect the things that will help them winter over."

Patricia crossed her arms. "Betty told you all of this?"

Hector shook his head. "Not in so many words, but," he took a deep breath and let it out slowly, "it's almost like…" he trailed off, unable to finish.

"Go on. I'm listening."

He turned an offered a somber smile. "It's almost like I can see what she's thinking. When we're communicating, it's like I get visual ideas."

Patricia was about to call bullshit when a thought struck her. "It's like she tells you things *telepathically*?"

Hector shrugged. "I dunno. I guess." He turned back and nodded toward the base camp. "When I told her about your medicine, I showed her my flannel shirt then I patted my pocket." He turned back to her. "But the whole time, I imagined that little orange bottle with the white cap."

Patricia fished the bottle out of her jeans pocket and rolled it across her hand. "Orange bottle with a white lid." She looked up at him and shook her head. "No, there's no way I'm going to buy that they can communicate that way."

Hector offered another long shrug. "I ain't saying they do." He turned from her and then smiled. "But I also ain't saying they don't."

Patricia rolled her eyes and then fell into step behind him, being careful of the stones on the ground. "I'd believe that she thinks of you as a pet poodle before I'd buy that they're telepathic."

Hector spun and walked backward, his arms outstretched. "It is what it is, *chica*. And I think it's about time I had me a sugar momma."

She nearly sprained her eyeballs with the eyeroll she gave him.

18

Deep in the Catskills

Patricia felt her head swooning and extended her arm, bracing against the outcropping. She closed her eyes and took deep breaths, trying to ride through the vertigo that threatened her balance.

Pushing out all the sounds and activity that went on around her, she continued to take slow and steady breaths, allowing herself time for the feeling to pass.

"You okay?"

"Yeah," she whispered gently. "Just a bit unsteady."

"Why don't you sit down and—"

"No, thank you," she interrupted quietly. "I still feel like I need to be on my feet." She slowly opened her eyes and the mountain had stopped spinning. She smiled to herself and then let go of the rock wall. "I think the worst is passed."

Hector was chewing something and Patricia raised a brow. "What's that?"

"Oh. Uh…I think it's like a wild lettuce or something. It's not terrible." He opened his hand and offered her a piece. "I guess I'm going vegan as long as we're staying with our new friends."

She plucked a leaf from his hand and smelled it. "It smells peppery."

"A little. It's pretty good, actually. I just wish I had some dressing to put on it." He closed his eyes and smiled. "Or salsa."

"Stop." She popped the leaf into her mouth and chewed. "You're sure it's not poison?"

Hector grinned. "I think I'd already be dead if it was." He hooked his chin over his shoulder. "Besides, I don't think Betty would let me eat it if was bad for me. She's the one that stopped me from trying to eat the berries."

Patricia saw the tall strawberry-blonde female lumber past and noted that her facial features were dour. "What's up with Wilma?"

"Wilma?" Hector asked, still chewing. "Which one is that?"

"The strawberry-blonde one." Patricia shrugged. "I figure if we have a Betty…well, technically Wilma's a redhead I guess, but…?"

Hector gave her a confused look. "Is that from a movie, or…" he trailed off.

Patricia scoffed. "You've never seen the Flintstones?"

Hector rolled his eyes. "No. Not exactly my flavor, if you catch my meaning."

"Anyway, what's her…deal?" She trailed off as her memory began to stitch together different pieces. "Oh, my god. I recognize her now."

Hector raised his brows. "She work in editing or legal?"

Patricia smirked at him. "She was the one I saw that night when we spied on them." She turned and locked eyes with him. "She was the one wailing so loudly."

Hector stopped chewing and turned to stare at the creature. "She was in mourning?"

Patricia nodded and stepped away, slowly approaching Wilma. She stood beside the creature and extended her hand, placing it gently on the female's arm. When Wilma turned and stared at her, her face reflected anger.

Patricia offered her best sad eyed look and gently squeezed Wilma's arm. "I'm so sorry for your loss," she whispered.

Wilma pulled her arm away and a low growl formed deep in her chest.

Patricia refused to quit and stepped closer, extending her hand. Wilma's growl grew louder.

Patricia took a half step back but continued offering her a sad smile. Without even thinking, she began to hum the Gensokwa's song which had been stuck in her head for so long.

Wilma's features instantly turned from anger to surprise. She stared at Patricia for a long moment as the tiny human vocalized their song. Wilma turned and faced the smaller female and stared at her, her confusion evident.

Patricia opened her arms wide as if to offer a hug. When Wilma's features softened, she made her move, slipping in and wrapping her arms around the thick creature's middle, still humming the song.

Hector stared in wide eyed amazement as the big

strawberry-blonde stared at Patricia's head as if it were a sudden tumor. Slowly, the creature's face softened and she lowered her arms, embracing the woman.

A moment later Wilma was singing the song as Patricia hummed. Softly, their voices carried across the encampment and Hector was shocked as more of the creatures appeared from the fringes, watching as the Genoskwa and human embraced, sharing the song of mourning.

Betty slowly approached the two and wrapped her long arms around Wilma, sandwiching Patricia between the two.

Hector moved gently toward the trio and watched as more Genoskwa appeared, joining in the quiet singing. Younglings leaped in from the overhanging tree branches to watch while older children sang along from the canopy.

Hector felt something welling in his chest and his eyes began to grow misty. He had felt a certain bond growing between Betty and himself, but at this moment, he felt that Patricia had just crossed an unseen line and cemented their relationship with the creatures, making them part of the tribe.

DALE CHECKED his watch one more time and bounced nervously in place. "So close." He glanced through the thicket and verified that the sentries were still in hiding.

He checked his watch again and groaned that it had only been seconds since the last time he'd checked.

"Aww, fuck it. If he ain't in position yet, then we'll

improvise." He marched around the edge of the thicket and instantly heard a wood knock ahead of him.

Ignoring the announcement, Dale continued across the small clearing and entered the deep shadows of the woods. He followed the game trail at a steady pace, avoiding stones and low hanging branches as he marched ever forward.

He wasn't sure if it was his imagination or if he was actually catching glimpses of the creatures moving parallel to him. Dark shadows glided on either side of him, keeping pace silently as he hiked along the game trail.

A few minutes into his advance he heard a loud "whoop" to his right. A moment later there was an answer to his left. Both felt uncomfortably close.

Dale screwed up his courage and gripped the shotgun in his hands tighter as he continued his trek, eyes forward and feet moving steadily.

He decided it was time to do a position check and stopped suddenly, his ears straining to hear the creatures on either side. The one to his left must have stopped too quickly as the sound of a twig snapping froze Dale midstep. The creature to his right, however, remained silent, leaving him unsure just how close the monsters were.

He took a deep breath and the smell that reached his nostrils told him they were much closer than he would have preferred. He felt the hair on the back of his neck stand on end and he immediately took off at a much quicker pace. He had no idea how quickly the sasquatches could move through the thick of the forest and still remain silent, but he was intent on putting a wee bit more distance between them.

Dale focused on the trail and increased his pace to the point that he was almost jogging, his cracked ribs protesting with each step.

Another tree knock just slightly behind him was followed by two more, then the entire woods grew eerily silent. Dale slowed and strained to listen. Other than his own heavy breathing and his heart pounding in his ears, there was nothing.

He swallowed hard and stared up the mountain, the game trail disappearing into the dark and hazy terrain. *Just keep pushing on. Your people are at the end of this trail.* He glanced to either side, hoping to see something that would tell him how close the sentries were.

Dale squared his shoulders and took off again, increasing his pace to a quick jog. The moment he found his pace, he heard something that sounded eerily like an owl behind him. A moment later another owl sounded ahead of him. He slowed his march and listened carefully as yet a third owl hooted even further away.

"Fuck me." He sighed heavily and dropped his head. "They telegraphed my arrival."

With a heavy groan, he shifted the shotgun in his hands and took off again. "That's okay. It was actually part of the plan, remember, Archer?" He huffed as the incline increased. "You distract them while SFF Superman swoops in and saves everybody." He ground his teeth as he pushed to increase his speed. "Everybody but me."

SURVIVAL

AL WATCHED as the creatures stopped whatever task they were involved in and turned their attention toward the shadows under the canopy. One by one they broke away and moved to the rock encampment.

He broke out his thermal optic and peered deeply into the dark area between the outcroppings. He could just make out a heat signature that slowly focused into a bipedal creature.

A smaller heat signature approached with its arms open and the two moved into a slow embrace. Al did his best to zoom in on the scene, but the scope was at its limit.

He continued to observe as a third creature, larger than the other two, moved in and combined with them. He pulled the optic away and scratched at his chin. "What the hell is going on? Group hugs?"

He checked the time and knew that Dale should be on the move, advancing on their camp. He sighed heavily as he slid back out of the crevice. *Move now or wait for them to mad dash down the mountain?*

He took one last peek at the encampment then slid down to the ground, allowing the sparse grasses to mask his advance. He began to belly crawl through the clearing, using small rock outcroppings to hide him from their view.

As closed the distance, he could hear what sounded like choral music. Al froze and slowly propped himself on his elbows, the thermal held to his eye.

Now that he was closer, he could see further into the shadows of the rock enclosure and he was shocked to see a dozen or more heat signatures, swaying to the music.

That sounds so familiar. Realization struck as he

remembered the ceremony they had witnessed. That was the song that Patricia had hummed over and over until it was stuck in her head.

Was this another ceremony? Had another of the creatures been killed?

He dropped back to the ground and slid the thermal optic into his satchel before resuming his slow advance. With his MP5 held in front of him, he wormed his way across the clearing until he was just yards from the entrance of the Genoskwa's camp. He slid in between two pines and braced his back to the thickest one, using it for cover.

He pulled his thermal again and peered deep into the darkest recesses of the enclosure. He could just make out a human standing deeper inside. But only one. He cursed under his breath as he scanned the area, praying that a second human shape would show itself. "Where are you?" he whispered.

What sounded like an owl echoed through the forest nearby and the creatures all seemed to stiffen. Al quickly brought the optic back to his eye and watched as the mountain apes began to break up and move to the exits. It was only then that he noticed a human shape had been trapped between two of the huge creatures.

That shape appeared to be female.

Al felt the corners of his mouth pull upward as a smile formed and he watched as the smaller ones scattered into tree tops and the larger ones hovered near the rock outcroppings.

A huge creature appeared from the rear of the enclosure with a good-sized stick in its hand. Al moved the thermal away just as the big red creature limped out

SURVIVAL

into the daylight. The huge stick had an obviously pointed tip, but the creature used it like a cane.

Big Red moved to the edge of the camp and whooped into the trees. A moment later another owl sound replied and Red began waving its free hand about as the others scattered, scrambling to climb the nearby tall trees or slipping behind the outcroppings that were scattered all over the mountain top like walls.

Al cursed under his breath as he realized none had strayed far from the enclosure. *How the hell am I supposed to grab Hector and Tricia and get them out of there?*

He slid deeper behind the tree he was using for cover and only then noted the heavy breathing behind him. He turned slowly to see a large, strawberry-blonde colored creature staring down at him, its eyes narrowed in an angry glare.

"I don't suppose I could interest you in a subscription to *Mountain Ape Monthly*, could I?"

19

Deep in the Catskills

Patricia felt the strawberry-blonde Genoskwa stiffen, and when the two creatures broke away, they were both on high alert. She spun and saw Hector staring at her in surprise. "What's going on?"

Hector shrugged. "No idea, but they're all acting kinda defensive."

Patricia's face went blank before her eyes shot wide. "Oh my god! Briese and Archer!"

"You think?" Hector's eyes lit up. "You think they're here to rescue us?"

"Oh, no," she groaned. "No, no, no, no…" She took off at a run and slid in the loose soil outside the enclosure.

"Where are you going?!" Hector yelled.

She spun back to face him, her face a mask of fear. "To stop a war!"

He watched her disappear as he tried to grasp her

meaning. Suddenly Hector imagined the two gunslingers marching into camp with bullets flying, expecting to save the two city idiots from the hillbilly mountain apes. "Oh, no," he groaned.

Hector took off as fast as his bare feet would carry him and cursed as he ran across the loose rocks too quickly. "Dammit! Why'd they have to lose my shoes?"

He climbed up onto one of the smaller rock outcroppings and watched as Patricia pushed past the line of Genoskwa taking up defensive positions. "Don't shoot!" she screamed into the forest. "Put down your guns! Don't shoot!"

Hector wanted to yell out as well but feared that between the two of them, it would just sound like so much noise to the hard-charging warriors. He stood as tall as he could and stared into the woods, praying.

Betty appeared next to him and stood in front of the rock outcropping, essentially putting herself between Hector and the approaching threat. Once Hector realized what she was doing, he bent forward and wrapped his arms around her neck, speaking softly in her ear, "Don't worry. They won't hurt me."

He tried to pull her back, but she was like a marble statue, unmoving.

Big Red limped to the head of the defensive line and banged his walking stick, drawing the attention of the others. He grunted something and made a motion with his free arm, sending the rest of them into hiding.

Alone, he stood at the top of the mountain, just outside the tree covered rock enclosure, and waited for whatever threat was coming up the mountain. Hector glanced at the huge red primate and a sense of awe came over him, unlike anything he'd felt before. Big Red was truly a force to be reckoned with.

Another owl noise sounded just moments before Dale broke out of the trees and approached the rock enclosure. Patricia stood on a long-dead fallen tree trunk and shouted, "Don't shoot! Put down your guns!"

Dale froze and stared at her in surprise. "Are you nuts?"

"Just do it!" She glanced over her shoulder at the huge red alpha male then turned back to Dale. "Please, Archer, just do it. They won't hurt you if you aren't a threat."

"Yeah, I think Tommy might disagree with that."

She blanched and felt her sails deflate. "Please, Archer. They haven't harmed us." She pleaded with her eyes. "Just lower your guns."

Dale gripped the shotgun tighter as his eyes darted from her to the huge red male standing behind her. The creature stared at him blankly and he realized, this was the alpha that had set him free. He could feel his heart about to beat out of his chest, but he fought his instincts and lowered the shotgun. "Fine. But I'm not surrendering it."

She turned and faced the alpha male, who continued to stare at Archer. She turned back and shrugged. "Move slowly."

Dale nodded as he tried to steady his breathing. "Yeah, slow is about all I have right now." He stepped closer and could feel dozens of eyes on him even though the alpha was all he could see.

As he crested the hill, he saw a brown Genoskwa to his left with Hector standing behind it, waving from over the creature's. "Yeah, I see you, Hector."

"She ain't wrong. Other than a smack to the head when they first grabbed us, they've been chill."

"Yeah, about that," Dale said as he approached Patricia. "Any idea why they decided to snag you two?"

"No idea whatsoever." She glanced at Hector and then back to Dale. "But we might have to fight Hector to get him away from his new girlfriend."

"You're shitting me," Dale said, turning to stare at Hector again.

"I think she wants to keep him," Patricia joked as she stepped closer. She turned and began walking him up to the alpha male. "Just move slowly and don't be aggressive."

"Don't be *aggressive*?" He nodded as they closed the distance. "Right. I'll get right on that." He glanced around the area and then pulled her to a stop. "Where's Briese?"

She stared at him for a moment then quietly asked, "He's not with you?"

Dale took a deep breath and let it out slowly. "He was supposed to have flanked the area and sneaked in to grab you two while I distracted them."

"Yeah, mate. About that." Al stated as he stepped out into the clear, a large strawberry-blonde Sasquatch holding his shoulder firmly. "They're much better at sneaking around in the woods than I am, I'm afraid."

"Great," Dale groaned. "At least the band is back together." He turned and faced the alpha male. "I'm not sure if I'm supposed to thank you or shoot you."

The creature continued to stare at the human without any reaction. Patricia turned and faced him. "He won't hurt you."

The male made no sign of moving, its eye locked on

Dale. The staring continued until it finally moved its head, nodding to the shotgun still in the human's hand. Big Red moved his free arm, motioning toward the weapon.

Dale glanced down at the shotgun then turned and nodded at the spear in the alpha's hand. "I'll give up mine when you give up yours."

The creature's eyes narrowed as it stared at him, unsure what the exchange was about. It had no clue what Dale had said until he pointed to the spear in the alpha's hand. "You carry yours, I carry mine. It's that simple."

You could almost see a light bulb come on over the alpha's head as it turned and stared at the spear in its hand. It gave a short grunt then turned and lumbered up the hill to the enclosure.

Dale glanced at Patricia. "Do we follow?"

She nodded slightly. "I think so, yeah."

The pair made a slow march up the hill, following the Big Red. "I'm shocked they haven't eaten you already."

"Same," she whispered back. "But I think we've made some uneasy connections. Looks like Hector won over his girlfriend there, and I actually had a moment with Al's new friend."

Dale looked at Al standing stiffly as the strawberry-blonde creature held his shoulder. As they approached their position, she gave him a gentle shove forward and Al fell into step beside Dale. "Yeah, mate. Hell of a plan you hatched."

"It worked, didn't it? We're all together and still alive."

Al shrugged slightly, glancing back at the strawberry-blonde female following behind them. "So far. I'm not so certain what the future may hold, though."

Once they had entered the enclosure and were surrounded by the rock walls, Dale felt an eerie sense of deja vu. "So, this is home, eh?"

The alpha turned and faced the four humans. It was only then that Dale noticed the mud and grass compress over the wounded eye.

Big Red studied them for a moment then made a motion with his arm that nobody seemed to understand. Dale glanced at Patricia who was staring at Hector. "What's he want?"

Hector shook his head. "I'm not sure." He moved closer and said loudly, "We don't understand."

The huge alpha huffed and all four of them could feel the strength of the creature in that one action. It stretched its arm out and waved over their heads, stopping at the end, then its palm opened as if it expected something to appear. Hector narrowed his eyes and slightly shook his head. "I'm not following."

The alpha repeated the gesture and Hector's eyes went wide. "He wants to know where the rest of us are." He spun and stared at Dale. "He doesn't know about Tommy."

"How can you know that?" Dale asked.

Patricia held a hand up and shook her head, "Don't ask. Seriously…don't. He just knows."

Al stiffened as he stared at the creature. "Fucker ripped his head off then asks us where he is? We couldn't carry him out of there on foot. He's right where they left him."

Hector nodded nervously then turned to the alpha. He made the motion he'd seen the younger male make in the clearing, a twisting and pulling apart movement, then pointed back towards Dog Town.

Big Red's one good eye widened and he stood at full height, his chest swelling as he inhaled. Hector cowered and turned away just as the alpha bellowed, his voice so loud that the others covered their ears.

Hector turned to Dale and shook his head nervously. "I don't think that's the answer he expected."

"Ya think?" Dale yelled back.

The other Genoskwa cowered back and some left the enclosure. Al watched nervously as the smaller ones scampered up the rock and took to the limbs in the canopy overhead. "Yeah, they're running scared."

Patricia turned and noticed that Betty and Wilma stood their ground just yards behind them. Betty appeared to be ready to throw herself between the alpha and Hector. Wilma's eyes darted between the alpha and Patricia, her nervousness obvious.

A few moments later and three young males entered the enclosure. The alpha's face twisted into a mask of anger and the four humans got to hear him speak their ancient language. He thumped the base of his spear into the ground before he broke into a loud dialogue.

All eyes were on Hector as he tried to relay what he could, reading the alpha's body language and hand movements as he barked at the younger males. "Uh, he's pissed, obviously." Hector continued to study the alpha's movements. "He wants to know if they attacked us after…" he trailed off, his eyes narrowing as he tried to put the pieces together.

"After what?" Patricia asked.

"After…something. I don't get it." He glanced at Al and Dale. "Did he tell you guys to split?"

Al stared wide eyed at him. "You understand what they're saying?"

"What? No." Hector began to stammer. "It's more like...I can't explain."

The young and aggressive male beat on his chest and stood tall, swaying side to side. It barked a reply that nobody understood until it made the twisting motion then pulled his hands apart.

"Oh shit," Hector groaned. "Little big man over there just admitted to killing Tommy."

The four of them turned and watched as the alpha's face twisted and his muscles tensed. "I think we should find cover," Dale stated quietly. "Shit's about to get real here."

The four of them watched as the alpha's volume increased, his voice literally shaking the earth beneath them. The younger, aggressive male barked a mouthy reply and launched himself toward the alpha.

Al and Hector watched Big Red's movements and both leapt to the side as the alpha threw his spear to the side. Dale grabbed Patricia and pulled her with him as he dove to the other side, rolling to the rock wall.

The pair of Sasquatch locked arms mid leap and big red slammed the younger male to the packed earth hard, landing with all his weight on the younger male's chest. He gripped the younger Genoskwa by his throat and continually slammed his head into the ground.

Dale glanced past the pair and saw the other two males nervously move back, fear evident in their eyes. They only watched the altercation for a moment before they turned and ran from the scene.

Al watched in horrid fascination as the younger male desperately tried to push the alpha off of him. His hands slapped at the older creature's face, eventually a finger finding the wounded eye. The younger male dug at the wound, scraping the mud away and trying his level best to grip the alpha by the hole in his face.

Big Red leaned away, just out of the younger creature's reach, and squeezed his throat with all his might. In a quick and decisive movement, the alpha twisted his wrist, breaking the younger male's neck in a horrific crunch.

Al winced and glanced away as the spark left the younger male's eyes. He, along with the entire gathering, watched as the creature's arms suddenly went limp and fell to his sides.

Big Red took a deep breath and let out a mournful howl that struck them all, deep in their core.

Slowly the alpha pushed up from the younger male's body and picked up his spear again, using it to support his weight heavily as he resumed his position. He squared his shoulders and barked loudly to the others.

The two other males who had been with the challenger entered and dragged their friend away as the rest of the tribe watched silently.

"I guess if you challenge the alpha, the cost is death," Hector stated quietly.

Dale brushed the dirt from his clothes and extended a hand to Patricia. "Let me get this straight. Young Kong there went against the alpha's orders and killed Tommy? And the alpha killed him for it?"

Hector shrugged. "I mean, that's the vibe I'm picking up."

Al shook his head. "That doesn't make much sense. I mean, they've killed every person who's come into this area. Why would he care if junior offed one of us?"

SURVIVAL

Hector locked eyes with him. "It wasn't because he killed one of us. He went against the alpha's orders. Then he challenged him."

"Oh my god," Patricia gasped. "His eye."

The three men turned and saw that the eye was basically gone. Some of the bone from the socket was exposed and the wound was weeping blood and puss.

"That's a gunshot wound," Al whispered.

"Wait, he was shot in the head and could still…" Dale trailed off, his mind incapable of understanding.

Patricia gave him a surprised look. "Like a frontal lobotomy. They changed aggressive humans into docile sheep, what if the gunshot changed his nature as well?"

Dale shrugged. "No idea."

"That's why they didn't eat you," Al quietly responded. "That's why he ordered us to leave instead of storming the camp and killing us."

"And the young males couldn't accept the change," Hector added. He glanced at Patricia. "It makes sense."

Dale sighed heavily. "Or maybe, as the leader of the group, he was just sick of all of the senseless killing. Blood cries for blood, right?" He looked to each of them. "It's either keep getting revenge until everybody is dead or choose to stop it." He gave a mild shrug. "Maybe he chose to stop the war."

The alpha huffed loudly as he sat on the flat rock. He sighed heavily and wiped the goo from his face that wept from the eye socket. When he looked up, he made a waving motion and Hector started to step forward. Betty gripped his arm and pulled him back as she moved in and knelt beside the alpha.

Big Red stared at the four humans for a moment then said something softly to Betty who seemed to stiffen. She turned sad eyes to Hector then turned back to the alpha. She whispered something to him but the big male held his hand up, stopping her. He made a waving motion with his hand then locked eyes with her.

Wilma moved closer and laid her hand on Patricia's shoulder. When Patricia looked up at the tall strawberry-blonde creature, she saw the same look of sadness on her face as Betty had.

"Something is about to happen," she stated quietly.

Hector felt his chest tighten. "They're letting us go." He turned sad eyes to Patricia. "Actually, the head guy is tossing us out."

"But why bring you here in the first place?" Al asked.

Patricia hung her head. "They wanted us to know that they are calling for peace."

Dale sighed as he crossed his arms. "They let a lone warrior free to warn the others," he mumbled.

"What was that?" Al asked.

"In the past. When they warred with the natives in this area, they allowed a lone warrior to live so he could go back and tell the others to stay away," he stated with a tight lipped smile. "That was what they did the first time with me."

"But we're not a lone warrior," Al stated the obvious.

"No." Hector tightened the arms of his flannel shirt. "We're family now."

20

Deep in the Catskills

After a long night of quiet singing, Al started a fire and made a stew of tubers, leaves, and other raw vegetables. They opted to skip the meats offered for obvious reasons.

The younglings were amazed by his ability to control fire, but the older creatures wanted no part of it. Although it could positively change their way of life, they had a fear…no, *respect* for fire, and refused to learn how to tame it.

Still, the humans gathered around the warm glow and allowed the fire to stave off the chill night air. Patricia wasn't shocked when she saw Hector curled up in Betty's lap, sleeping in her embrace. As she stared at the couple, she wasn't sure which one was the pet. She fished in her recently found satchel and quietly withdrew her camera. She snapped a photo then turned and showed Al the screen. "He'll appreciate the thought later."

he chuckled. "He'll think you plan to blackmail him."

Wilma gave the fire a wide berth but she approached Patricia and slipped her something wrapped in a large leaf. When Patricia opened it, she found a river rock, polished to a high sheen. Veins of shimmering rose quartz ran through it, and she clutched it dearly. When she turned to thank Wilma, she had already faded back into the shadows.

Dale sat quietly and watched as dozens of eyes reflected the firelight in the darkness. Even now, they acted timid and afraid to approach the humans. Was this simply thousands of years of habit, or was there a legitimate reason for this behavior?

He glanced at Hector sleeping comfortably in Betty's lap and chuckled. "Crazy, isn't it?" He nodded toward the pair.

Patricia rolled her eyes. "We may have to force him back to the city at gunpoint." She pointed her camera at Wilma sitting just outside the glow of the fire and snapped another, the creature appearing deep in thought.

Dale continued to stare at him. "How does he know what they're saying?" He glanced at Patricia and raised his brows. "Doesn't that seem odd?"

She nodded and turned to look at the man sleeping. "Very. I asked him but he had trouble explaining it." She turned back to Dale and gave him a snarky look. "He said it was like they had telepathy. When he talked with Betty, she could make him see pictures of what they were talking about."

SURVIVAL

Dale shrugged. "I guess anything is possible." When he noted the look of surprise on Patricia's face, he added, "I've read that wolfpacks share a type of non-verbal speech. Especially when they're hunting. I don't know if it's pure instinct or what, but it's like one of them is directing the others to break away and herd their prey a certain direction, or certain individuals in the pack know they have specific responsibilities." He shrugged again. "It's really a cool thing to watch, but at the same time, it's spooky. Maybe the Genoskwa have something similar."

"Okay," she began slowly. "But since when does Hector fit into their crowd and get to share whatever their 'non-verbal' communication is? He's just an ex-cop that writes the police beat now."

Dale gave her a surprised look. "He was a cop?"

She nodded as she leaned back and snapped pictures of some of the younglings in the canopy. "Not for long. He was NYPD, but shortly after the academy, he was directing traffic downtown while the lights were being repaired. Some asshole decides he can't wait and runs him over. Whatever happened, it messed up his hip enough that he couldn't be a cop anymore. A few years later he's writing for the Informer."

Dale had a newfound respect for the man. "I didn't know."

"He doesn't talk about it much. Being a cop was his lifelong ambition." She snapped a few more photos of the older creatures going about their nightly business. "I guess once your dreams are smashed, there's not much else to look forward to."

Al cracked an eye and rolled over. "I guess that explains why the man can't run for shit."

Dale chuckled as he nodded. "Poor guy. Messed his pants in that infrasound attack then gets manhandled by these things to get cleaned up."

Patricia broke into a toothy grin. "But he made a new friend in the process. I wonder if they'll let her keep him?"

The three of them shared a quiet laugh and then settled back, listening to the sounds of nature and the crackle of their dying fire.

A<small>L FOUND</small> he was unable to sleep and made his way silently from the camp and to the edge of the tree line. He straddled one of the smaller rock outcroppings overlooking a wide clearing, his eyes scanning the landscape, brightly lit by a nearly full moon. Knowing now what to look for, once his vision had adjusted, he could just make out the outlines of some of the sentries standing watch.

He heard something moving behind him and did his level best not to turn and look. Whoever it was, it tried to approach with stealth, and Al felt there must be a reason for it.

A few moments later one of the younglings appeared beside him, plainly staring at him with wonder. Al smiled at the youngster and patted the rock next to him. With a quiet voice, he urged it to join him. "Come on. I don't bite."

The young Genoskwa stared at him, then at the rock. When Al finally held a hand out, offering to help the Sasquatch stand, he was actually surprised when the creature took it. Even as a youngling, its hand dwarfed

Al's, and the creature was remarkably heavy. The youngster was a solid mass, obviously thick with muscle. He sat quietly beside him, and Al noted that the kid was nearly as tall as him.

"I guess when you fellows have a growth spurt, you really shoot up, eh?" The youngling turned to look at him when he spoke but showed no emotion or hint of understanding.

The pair sat quietly in the dark, staring out across the clearing for the better part of an hour. Eventually, Al turned and tried to study the creature's features. At some angles, it could *almost* pass for a human. At other angles, it definitely appeared simian. With limited knowledge of biology, Al was at a loss for how, or even if, the Genoskwa were related to humans.

Or was it the other way around? Could it be possible the Genoskwa had evolved later, from early Man?

The pair sat quietly in the dark until the first rays of sunlight began to appear on the eastern horizon. The youngling slid down from the rock and disappeared into the shadows of the woods without so much as a wave goodbye.

Al watched him trudge off and disappear and couldn't help but wonder what life might be like if they were actually neighbors. If he had come out here into the woods and built a shelter or a cabin, could the two species coexist? Would they be as accepting of them, had it not been for Hector and Patricia paving the way?

Knowing human nature and man's desire to shoot first and ask questions later, he doubted that they'd be friends, much less neighbors. The creatures would have killed him or run him off before he ever got the foundation made for whatever house he intended to live in.

The thought actually made him sad.

AT THE EDGE of the Catskills

HECTOR SAW the bright yellow pickup stand out in the early morning sun the very moment they rounded the bend. "I never thought I'd be sad to see a way home."

Patricia was still dealing with seeing Tommy's Suburban parked just outside the trap used to stop the Bureau from withdrawing from the area. The vehicles, personal items, and weapons were still scattered just like they'd found them. It didn't appear that anybody had been through the area since they had entered.

Dale had to fight the urge to collect the weapons and lock them up in one of the vehicles. He knew it would be a while before a team could come out and sanitize the area, but he also knew that it would take the better part of the entire day to secure the location.

He checked his phone and wasn't surprised that he still didn't have service. He nodded to Al, "Any chance you have cell service out here?"

Al shook his head. "No phone, mate. I knew it would be sketchy out here, but I didn't want to risk it sounding off at an inopportune time, either."

"Makes sense." Dale saw Hector rubbing the side of the yellow truck. "Hector, you got cell service? I need to check in with the boss."

Hector pulled his phone out and powered it on.

"Oh, hey. My text to the *posse*..." He grinned broadly. "I guess I don't need to send it now, do I?"

"Yeah, unless you want your buddies to shoot up your new girlfriend," Patricia replied sarcastically.

"Umm...how do I 'unsend' something?" Hector held the phone out.

Dale groaned and reached for it. "It sent already? When?"

"I'm not..." Hector trailed off. "I'm not sure if it did."

"If it did, you need to text whoever this is and let them know you don't need rescuing." Dale searched the phone and sighed. "Yeah, no service here."

Hector quickly tapped out a text and hit send then slid the phone back in his pocket. "Okay. Everybody ready to get the hell out of here?"

"Gladly," Al said in a tired voice.

Hector pulled open the door and reached behind the seat, rifling through old clothes. "Ah, just what the doctor ordered." He held out a pair of overalls and began putting them on. "Not that I mind a flannel kilt, but it's a bit breezy on the buns."

Once he had the overalls buttoned, he tossed the wolf skin in the truck behind the seat and then hopped up into the cab. "All aboard the Tijuana Express!" He slammed the door and rolled down the window, staring at Archer and Briese. "Only fits three in the cab. Somebody's gonna have to ride in back."

Dale clapped Al across the shoulder. "I'll volunteer for the back." He smiled mischievously at Al. "You can ride up front and listen to him chatter all the way back."

Al's face fell and he gave Dale a sour look. "You're a twat, mate."

"We could draw straws," Dale said as he climbed up onto the rear bumper and hooked a leg over the tailgate. He suddenly spread his arms wide. "So much room. You could ride back here with me if you want."

Al considered it strongly before shaking off the idea. "I think I like the idea of a heater instead. If he gets to be too much, I'll make him stop and ride back here."

"See ya soon." Dale sat behind the cab and crossed his outstretched legs, resting his head and shoulders on the rear window.

Hector started the big yellow truck and revved the engine a few times. "Nothing like a Chevy V-8 early in the morning." He chuckled as he made a forty point turn around and headed for the main road. "I think I'm actually going to miss this place."

"You mean Betty, right?" Patricia asked, trying to hide her smile.

Hector's grin turned into a frown. "Do you think they'd let me keep her? I could have her lie down in the back on the way home. Keep her in my apartment. Teach her to use the bathroom and…" he trailed off, trying to imagine a seven foot tall, hair covered creature trying to use the tiny toilet at his place. "Yeah, never mind."

"Maybe weekend visits?" Al offered, hiding his mirth.

"You could ask for joint custody. Take her every other weekend and alternate holidays," Patricia added.

"You two should take your act on the road," Hector deadpanned. He suddenly brightened. "I saw that you and Wilma were getting kinda close. Maybe you could bring her to the city and you two could have a girl's day? You know, the spa, mani-pedi, the works." His grin widened. "Imagine the look on everybody's face when you brought her back and she had a perm. And green and pink stripes in her hair."

"Yeah, comedy isn't your forte, mate," Al quipped. "Stick to being the brunt of the joke."

"I should make you both ride in the back," Hector muttered under his breath.

Albany, New York

Dale stepped out of the shower and began to towel off. He wasn't surprised his telephone was ringing from the moment he exited the bathroom. Picking up the receiver, he stated, "Archer."

Interim Director Stanton breathed a sigh of relief when he heard Archer's voice. "It's about damned time."

"Director, I literally just walked in the door and took a shower. Trust me, you'd prefer it that way before I came into the office and—"

"We didn't know if you were alive," Stanton cut him off. "And I've got great news."

"Oh yeah? What's that?" Dale asked as he scrubbed the towel over his wet hair.

"The Regional Director had an interesting phone call with the governor." He waited a moment for the news to sink in. "They're activating the National Guard. They said they'd level the damned mountain if need be to ensure that every last one of those things are killed."

Dale dropped the towel and stared at his reflection in the mirror, the angry bruise along his ribs starting to yellow along the edges. "Sir, don't do that. Not yet. We need to talk."

"So talk."

Dale shook his head. "No, this has to be face to face. Tell me you can call it off." He began pulling his jeans on as he scrambled around his bedroom looking for clothes.

"I, uh…" he chuckled into the phone. "I don't think I have that kind of clout, Archer. This decision was made a lot higher than I'll ever be."

"Sir, give me twenty minutes and I'll be there. Try to get the Regional Director on the line. If he's the one that spurred this, then he can call it off."

"Call it off?" Stanton stared at his phone. "Are you nuts? Didn't these things kill all of your friends on the SWAT team?"

"Sir, please. I'll be there in twenty minutes. Just promise me you'll try to get the Regional Director on the horn. You both need to hear my report."

Stanton was unsure what to say. "I'll do my best." He checked his watch and sighed. "But you'd better hurry."

"On my way."

21

Albany Field Office, Albany, NY

Special Agent Archer was leaning across the edge of Interim Director Stanton's desk, having just given an oral version of his report.

"Let me get this straight, Agent Archer," Regional Director Latham stated over the speakerphone. "The very same creatures that killed nearly one hundred and fifty of our best men are now all warm and fuzzy and we should just let bygones be bygones?"

Dale groaned low in his throat. "Sir, it's not that simple." He glanced at Director Stanton who raised a questioning brow at him. "I mean, in a nutshell, yeah. The situation on the ground has changed." He cleared his throat nervously. "I think it was all just one big misunderstanding."

"A 'misunderstanding' that led to the deaths of how many highly trained operators?" Latham asked.

Dale hung his head. "Yes, sir, I know how it sounds, but—"

"But nothing, Agent Archer." The agitation in his voice was not missed. "These creatures are dangerous. Those woods will never be safe to travel in, and do you have any idea how many tourists come to New York every year just to camp and hike in the Catskills?"

Dale sighed as he sat back in his chair. "Fine. Then that makes it a state matter, does it not? These creatures live in a state park, so the federal government doesn't need to—"

"That's why we called the governor, Mister Archer. He's calling in the National Guard. Both are state entities. Satisfied?"

"No sir!" Dale came to his feet and glowered at the telephone. "I'm telling you, sir, things on the ground have changed. The creatures have…changed. They're not aggressive like they used to be."

"And what changed them? Let me check my notes on this conversation here…oh, yeah. You said the leader had been, and I quote, 'appeared to have been shot in the eye. Patricia Murphy believes the damage to be like a frontal lobotomy, changing the creature into a more docile hominid', unquote." The creak of a leather chair could be heard and Dale knew the Regional Director was leaning forward to disconnect the call. "Our decision stands, Agent Archer. I suggest you either get on board or get the hell out of the way."

Dale wasn't surprised when the line went dead and he slowly sat back down. He looked at Stanton, who still had a brow raised. "Ballsy move, speaking to the Regional Director that way; very heartfelt."

"Yeah, but why couldn't I convince him to call off the attack?" Dale asked quietly.

Stanton sat forward and gripped the edge of his desk. "Because he's not wrong." He held a hand up to cut Dale off before he started. "Let's assume that everything you stated is correct and factual. Let's assume that the alpha male leader of this clan or tribe or whatever you want to call them is indeed of a changed mindset." He leaned forward and lowered his voice. "The thing was shot *in the head*. Most beings don't survive that. So what happens when this leader of the Genoskwa eventually dies? Does the group still accept his proclamation that they not be aggressive? Or do they switch back to their centuries old way of things?" He sat back and locked eyes with Dale. "It's a legitimate concern, Dale."

Archer sighed and rubbed a calloused hand across his unshaven face. "David, I think this is the wrong move. If we send soldiers in there, they'll just call back the reinforcements they had, we'll lose dozens, maybe hundreds more, and it won't end until eventually we'll kill all of their kind."

Stanton shrugged. "Okay. And?"

Dale gave him a surprised look. "And? We've shut down entire industries because of a spotted owl or a three-toed newt. Now we're okay with making an entire sentient species extinct?"

Stanton held a hand up. "We can't know that they're sentient."

"We can know that. I'm telling you, they are." He leaned closer and took a deep breath. "They have music and language and care for their own."

"So do pigeons. We've made more than one species of them extinct."

"That's not..." Dale stopped and bit his tongue. "You know exactly what I mean. These things have a soul. You can tell by the way they act."

"Tell me how to quantify that and I will personally intercept any National Guard unit that is deployed to the Catskills myself."

Dale hung his head and squeezed his eyes shut. "You know, before I went back out there, I would have been thrilled if you'd told me they were going to level the mountain with them still on it." He looked up and locked eyes with his boss. "But now that I've experienced what I have? I can't let you do this."

"*Let me?* This isn't *me*, Archer. It's the federal fucking government." He paused and shrugged. "Actually, it's the state government of New York. Yes, it was spurred by us, but it's out of our hands now."

Dale slowly stood from his chair and looked down at his boss. "You do realize that Murphy's sister has all of our reports. She has hundreds of photographs. She has her own experience dealing face to face with these things. There's no telling what she's liable to write in her article."

Stanton shrugged. "Out of our hands as well. She's a free citizen in a free country. As long as she stays within the standards of ethics within her own field, she's got every right to publish whatever she feels she has to."

Dale nodded curtly. "So be it." He turned and reached for the door.

"Archer," Stanton stated, stopping him. "If you really think this is the wrong move, maybe you should take a few more days off." He gave him a knowing look. "You know, to recover from such a harrowing ordeal. And if you happen to bump into Ms. Murphy and the two of you hatch something, I don't want to know anything about it."

Dale studied him for a moment, ensuring he read him correctly. "Yes, sir. I think I'd like to take a few days off. To…recover from this…"

"Harrowing ordeal. Understood. Take all the time you need."

Dale smiled. "Thank you, sir."

Residence of Patricia Murphy

"No, the governor is activating the National Guard," Dale repeated, looking over Patricia's shoulder. "The FBI can't do that."

She marked out her notes and rewrote them. "Then how did they convince the governor to activate them?"

Dale sighed and sat down across from her in the cluttered living room. "They relayed the body count. As soon as the governor heard the number of highly trained shooters were killed and how? He didn't need much convincing."

"And you're certain about this?"

"I heard it directly from the regional director in the city." Dale rubbed at his eyes. "Where the hell is Hector? Shouldn't he be here to help? He writes for the paper as well, doesn't he?"

"He's working on his piece at the office. He's penning it from a law enforcement perspective."

Archer narrowed his gaze at her. "Do what now?"

"He's covering the original story that I was going to do. How the Bureau went out there and faced these creatures."

"And failed miserably. Leading to the deaths of hundreds of good men."

She shrugged. "I hope he doesn't put that spin on it."

"So what story are you writing?"

She sat back and took a deep breath. "That they're real. And they're intelligent and live in family units and…" She trailed off, looking away. "And we're both hiding the location to keep people from going out there to find them."

"Tell me you can twist the story. Find a way to stop the state from sending in troops."

She stared at her computer screen for a moment and shook her head. "I think the direction I'm going is the best way to do that."

He raised a brow at her. "How's that?"

She smiled as she clicked her computer and brought up the photos she had snapped in the woods. "Here." She spun the camera around to show Hector splayed out in Betty's lap. "What could possibly humanize them more than this?"

Dale leaned back and sighed. "He could be dead in that picture for all we know."

Patricia rolled her eyes. "Fine. How about this one?" She spun the screen back to show Briese and a young Genoskwa sitting on a rock, the moon in front of them, casting them both as silhouettes.

"That's actually pretty good." He leaned closer and stared at the photo. "When was this?"

She turned the screen back to her and tapped at her

keyboard. "The last night. Al got up and went out there and I was going to check on him when I saw this fella trying to sneak up on him. At first, I was worried, but Al knew he was there. They sat like that for a long time." She shrugged. "Looked like a great shot to take."

"I'm glad you did." Dale sat back and wiped a rough hand over his weary face. "I tried to call the governor's office on my way over here. They wouldn't even take a message."

She checked her watch and then raised a brow at him. "I don't know how fast they're going to act, but we need to hurry." She shut her laptop and picked it up, heading for the door. "I need to kick Hector in the ass and get him going, too."

"Wait, what?"

She paused in the doorway and gave him a nervous look. "Swaying public opinion doesn't happen overnight. We need to get these stories into circulation as fast as possible. Otherwise, it will just be me and you standing out there trying to stop the Guard from doing what they're told."

Offices of the Daily Informer

Hector almost went into full panic mode once they told him what was about to happen. "I gotta go back. I gotta warn them." His eyes pleaded with her. "*Betty*."

"We can help them best by getting our stories out as fast as possible."

"But…" he stammered, staring with fear in his eyes. "What if it's not enough."

"We'll deal with that when the time comes." Dale straddled the chair next to him. "Type."

Hector lipped his lips nervously then flipped open his notebook. "I haven't even gotten my outline finished, man."

"Wing it." Dale crossed his arms, staring at the man.

Hector sat frozen at the keyboard and turned to look at him. "I can't go if you're watching."

"Oh for…" Dale came out of the chair so fast that he nearly upended it. "Don't dawdle." He paused at the opening to Hector's cubicle and gave him a knowing look. "Betty needs you to step up right now."

Hector nodded nervously then began tapping at his keyboard. Dale found Patricia sitting at her computer, working.

"What can I do to help?"

She slid him a UDB drive. "Go through all of the pictures and delete the fuzzy ones. The paper will only allow the clearest shots."

Dale paused, thumb drive in hand. "Wait, you mean the creature photos or *all* of the photos?"

Without stopping she said, "All of them. We can use a lot of the camp photos as well."

Dale rolled his eyes and sat in an empty cubicle. He stared at the computer for a moment and nearly jumped when she set her laptop in front of him. "That's Eric's station. You'll never get into his system, so use this."

Dale opened the laptop and inserted the thumb drive. He checked his watch and groaned internally. "This is going to take all day."

"Possibly," she muttered. "But the sooner you start, the sooner you're done."

As he began going through the digital photos, he remembered the carnage. The blood stains. The damage done to the vehicles when they first entered the woods. With each passing picture, other images flashed in his mind and he felt his heart hardening.

He paused his task and sat back, his mind going in circles. "What if they're right?"

"Excuse me?" Patricia asked absently.

Dale sat up and sighed. "What if they're right?" He pushed the laptop away and swiveled the chair to face her. "What Stanton said. About when the alpha for this clan finally dies and another has to take his place?" He sighed heavily. "What's to stop them from falling back on centuries of tradition?"

She pulled the pencil from her mouth and set it down gently. "And what if they don't?" She shrugged at him. "Seriously, what if this is the first step to something huge? A day when man and Genoskwa can be friends or, barring that, at least polite neighbors?"

Dale turned his head and stared at the destruction on the screen again. "And what if we're wrong?"

She huffed as she spun back to her screen. "I'd rather err on the side of peace."

Dale stared at the back of her head for a moment then turned back to his duties. He continued to click through the assortment of photos and paused when he came across one of Tommy, hamming it up in a crooked selfie.

His mind immediately jumped to Tommy's body and what had occurred while the kid stood watch. He tried closing his eyes to make the image go away, but instead it only intensified the gory details.

"I can't do this." He pushed the computer aside and stepped away from the cubicle. Patricia turned to yell at him when her eyes fell on Tommy's cheesy grin on her laptop.

She suddenly felt her emotions tugging her in two separate directions. She stood from her desk and watched Archer pull the door open before he stepped out into the stairwell.

She turned back to her laptop and slowly sat back down. With a heavy sigh, she continued tapping away at the story she hoped would change her world.

22

Albany, New York

Dale drove without thinking. His mind wandered as he traversed the city streets and he thought of all of the good men who had given their lives in the line of duty. Not just those who were felled by the Genoskwa, but all the people he'd known since he became a member of the Bureau.

Without realizing it, he'd arrived at David Ford's house and pulled into the driveway. He shut off the engine of the non-descript sedan and sat quietly, staring at the front of Ford's place.

Completely lost in thought, he nearly jumped at a light rap on the window. He turned to see an older woman holding a small dog in her arms.

Dale lowered the window and the woman suddenly appeared even older than he originally assumed. "Are you a friend of Agent Ford?"

Dale offered a wan smile. "You might say that. We went back a long way."

Her hand went to her mouth and her eyes saddened. "I was afraid of that."

"Of what?" Dale asked, honestly confused.

"You used a past tense when speaking of him." She stepped back slightly and peered at the front of the house. "I haven't seen him in well over a week, so I've been assuming the worst."

"You are...?" Dale asked.

"His neighbor." She pointed to the house next door. "Harry and I have lived on this block almost our whole lives. I can't tell you how relieved we were when an FBI man moved in next to us." She smiled sadly and shrugged. "It just made us feel safer."

Dale reached for the door handle and stepped out of the car. "He was a good guy."

"One of the best." Her tight-lipped smile indicated she was about to cry. "We always invited him over for dinner, even though he rarely took us up on it." She leaned closer and lowered her voice. "Personally, I don't think he cared for my husband's cooking, but Harry thinks he's a master chef. Who am I to tell him differently? He might stop doing it." She laughed at her joke.

Dale stood straighter and sighed. "I'm not sure why I'm here."

She waved him over. "We have his spare key, if you need to go inside."

Dale stared at the front door and slowly shook his head. "I don't think the answers I'm searching for are in there."

"What answers do you need?" she asked.

Dale shrugged. "I'm not even sure what the questions are. I just know that I could really use his advice right about now."

"Try me," she said, turning and leaning on the front fender of the car. "I was a school teacher for thirty-five years. There's not much I haven't seen or heard in that time."

Dale chuckled and shook his head. "Oh, I doubt you've had much experience in this." He crossed his arms and continued to stare at the house. "He used to invite us over for barbeques in the spring."

She nodded. "Oh, I remember those. Harry and I would stop by quick; we didn't stay long. We knew it was meant for family. Still, the smells that wafted over the fence…couldn't help grabbing a quick bowl of his chili." She smiled at the memory.

"We weren't exactly family."

Her eyes widened and she patted his arm. "Yes, you were. He told us how the people he worked with were the closest thing to family he had." She pushed off the fender and stared at the front of the house. "He'll be missed."

"He already is." Dale reached for the car door. "I'm sorry to have disturbed you."

"No, honey, you didn't disturb me at all." She rubbed his arm and moved in closer for a brief hug. "I hope he wasn't in any pain when he went."

Dale opened his mouth to reply and found he couldn't. "That much, I really don't know. I'm going to assume he went down swinging, though."

"I know better than to ask how it happened. But can I ask where?"

Dale shrugged, deciding to lie. "I just know it was in state someplace."

She patted his arm again. "Maybe we'll hear about it on the news. Thank you. For stopping by and letting us know."

"You're welcome." He opened the car door and slipped back in behind the wheel. He watched her walk away slowly and his eyes were drawn back to the front door. "She's not wrong, brother. You will be missed."

Offices of the Daily Informer

Hector pushed back from his computer and rubbed his eyes. "How does this sound? 'FBI Discovers Sasquatch While Performing Training Exercises; Over a Hundred Dead in the Aftermath'. Is that confusing?"

"Hundred what? Agents or Bigfoots?" Patricia asked.

Hector sighed heavily and rubbed at his eyes again. "I can't put the entire story in the headline. I just need to hook 'em, not reel them in."

Patricia pulled the pencil from her mouth and stood, peering over her cubicle. "Just say 'FBI Discovers Bigfoot' and leave the rest for the story."

Hector winced. "That's a tiny hook."

She sat back down and stated loudly, "What does Roger always say? Short, sweet and..." she trailed off.

"To the point." Hector groaned. "It still feels lacking, though." He pushed away from his computer and came to his feet. "I can't be rushed. I hate being rushed. I don't do my best work when I'm being—"

"Just do your best!" she shouted, cutting him off. The others working in the office turned to give her dirty looks. She seemed to wither a bit then stood again. "Time is of the essence, Hector. We have to push these stories through quickly, to get people's support."

"I know this." He continued to rub at his eyes. "Maybe we should just go back out there and tell them what's coming. Maybe they could leave the area until the soldiers are gone. Or they could find a place to hide and ride out the storm."

"Where?" She spit the pencil back onto her desk and rounded the corner to face him. "We know there are natural caverns and old mines out there, but so does anybody else with access to those files." She glanced around and then lowered her voice. "The best thing we can do right now is push the truth out so people can take a stand. If enough of the public demonstrates or, or…I dunno, tries to stand up to them, the better the odds the Genoskwa will be left alone."

He turned sad eyes to her. "You really believe that?"

She nodded as she spoke. "I have to," she sighed. "It's all we have."

He groaned as he sat back down. "Give me your eyedrops. I need…" he trailed off, seeing trouble approaching.

Sports reporter extraordinaire, Mike Kenny, rounded the corner. "Heads up, children. Roger is headed your way. Seems he got an odd phone call from some bigwig at the FBI." He leaned against the edge of the cubicle. "Seems like you two stirred up a hornet's nest."

"Great," Hector moaned. "Just what we need."

As predicted, Roger Whitaker entered the bullpen and marched straight to Patricia. "Guess who I just got off the phone with. Wait, you don't have to guess. I'll tell you."

"The FBI," she moaned as she sat on the corner of Hector's desk.

"No, the…wait. Yeah. How'd you know?"

"Mike blabbed," Hector replied quietly.

"Well, they're threatening to hit us with national security violations if we proceed."

Patricia crossed her arms. "Did you tell them that one of their own was with us the entire time? Besides, there was nothing out there that affected national security."

Roger growled low in his throat. "Your email earlier simply said that you were taking the story in a different direction. What does that mean?"

She hooked a thumb toward Hector. "He's going to report on the FBI pooch screwing. I'm reporting on the creatures themselves."

Roger's features twisted. "Why?"

She glanced at Hector who simply shrugged. "Tell him."

She leaned closer and lowered her voice. "The agent that went out there with us, he came in earlier and said that the head office convinced the governor to activate and call in the National Guard." She raised a brow at him. "They want to *exterminate* all of them."

Roger narrowed his gaze at her. "Again, why?"

"Revenge," Hector stated. "Cop killers gotta pay the price. It's been that way since the first cops put on a badge."

SURVIVAL

Roger groaned and crumpled the paper in his hand. "And you're hoping your story will garner enough public support to stop them."

She nodded. "That's the play. Are you still on board?"

Roger tilted his head back and sighed. "Fine. Do what you feel is best, but I don't see how you're going to go from 'mountain apes kill over a hundred FBI agents', to 'let's save the bigfoots in the Catskills'. If you can pull that one off, you're a better writer than I'll ever be."

Patricia smiled. "I have some photos that might help."

Roger stiffened. "You have photos? Of actual bigfoots? Not fuzzy, out-of-focus stuff like always gets put on the 11 o'clock news?"

She stepped around him and handed him the printouts. "And I have digital copies for the presses, but yeah."

He opened the file and began to flip through them. "Dear lord." He looked at Hector disapprovingly. "Are you *snuggling* with this thing?"

Hector broke into a toothy grin. "She's not the best looking, maybe, but she has a beautiful personality."

He slapped the file down and held his hands up. "You're burning daylight."

"We know." She kicked Hector's chair. "Move it, amigo."

OUTSKIRTS OF NEW YORK CITY

. . .

Albert Briese pulled his Range Rover into the main building of his "office," a converted plane hangar on a private airstrip. He shared the runway with two other small companies, both of whom were hardly ever present.

He pressed a button on the sun visor and the doors to the hangar began to open. He could see the small crew he kept employed at this location busy inside.

A voice came across the overhead speaker of the car, "You're early, sir. The helicopter is almost ready. It's being prepped as we speak."

"I see that, Godfrey. By chance has Tricia Murphy or Agent Archer called yet?"

"I'm afraid not, sir."

Al pulled the Rover inside and parked it at the far wall between his armored Bentley and Jaguar. As he stepped out of the vehicle he handed the keys to Godfrey and picked up the mug of Earl Grey. "I expect to hear from either of them at any moment."

"So you will be returning to the mountains with them, sir?"

Al sipped the tea and nodded. "When the time is right, yes."

"Shall we send our standard condolence package to Mr. Youngblood's family, sir?"

"The attorneys have already taken care of that, Godfrey." He took a long drink from the mug and sighed. "Now that's what I've been missing."

"Well, sir...that and a shower." Godfrey raised a brow at him.

"Correct as usual, Godfrey." He peeled his outer jacket off and dropped it to the floor. "I'll be inside if you need me." He spun around and pointed at his valet, who was picking up the jacket with sugar tongs. "Notify me the moment they call."

"Of course, sir." Godfrey turned and cleared his throat. "Shall I burn this, sir?"

Al paused at the door of his apartment and turned to face him, a smile forming. "Not this time, ol' chap. That jacket holds particular memories."

"Perhaps I should seal it in plastic, sir. To, uh, preserve those memories."

Al's smile widened. "Just hang it in the closet by the small door."

Godfrey's face fell as he turned away. "Very good, sir."

Al wasted no time scrubbing days' worth of sweat, dirt, and grime away. He quickly shaved and toweled off before setting out his clothes for the day. He intended to be ready for another mountain adventure. An adventure that he was certain was in his future.

The drive to his New York home was just a bit over three hours, but traffic had been unusually light. Al knew that he was operating on borrowed time. He hadn't slept more than a few minutes over the past three days, and the caffeine he'd been taking would only get him so far.

He set the clothes aside and stared at the bed. He knew that the moment he fell into it, he would be lost to slumber for the better part of the day. He pressed the button beside the bed and asked again, "Any word?"

"Not in the last twenty minutes, sir."

"Very well. If they call, you'll probably have to use the cattle prod to wake me."

"Huzzah," Godfrey deadpanned. "I so look forward to using it, sir."

"Good night, Godfrey."

"Good *morning*, sir."

Al turned and fell into the bed, bouncing into position before pulling the pillow to him and jerking the comforter up and over him.

As he suspected, he was out just moments later.

23

Albany, New York

Dale drove the familiar streets of Albany, his mind wandering as his body drove. He didn't intend to end up at the VFW, at least not consciously, but here he sat.

He stared out of the windshield of the agency car and remembered all of the times he'd come here with his dad. The VFW post was his father's home away from home, and after Dale's mom passed, his dad had spent most of his waking hours here, reliving the past with his comrades.

Dale sighed heavily and was about to back out of the parking lot when a burly black man tapped lightly on his window. He rolled it down and saw the man squinting at him. "Dale Archer? Is that really you?"

Dale cracked a smile and nodded, reaching for Charles' hand. "Chuck. It's good to see you again."

"What's it been? Twelve years?"

Dale nodded. "Since Pop passed, yeah."

"Get your butt outta that car and get inside. The boys would love to see you again."

"Actually, Chuck, I was just about to—"

"Never take no for an answer," Chuck laughed as he reached for the door. "You'll make their day."

Dale dropped his head and nodded, sliding out of the seat. "Maybe for a minute."

After Dale made the rounds, shaking hands and receiving hearty back claps, he found himself sitting alone with Charles. "What brings you by, son? You look like a man with a lot on his mind."

Dale nodded. "Yeah. I just…I've got a decision to make and it's not an easy one. I started driving around and somehow ended up here. I guess in the back of my mind I was wishing I could talk to Pop again."

"Talk to me." Charles leaned in and lowered his voice. "I know I ain't your pops, but we was friends for…ever. Maybe I can impart some wisdom on you that'll help you do what you gotta do."

Dale smiled inwardly. "I appreciate it, Chuck."

Chuck reached into his jacket and withdrew a silver flask. He unscrewed the top and handed it to him. "Don't worry. It's the good stuff."

Dale pushed it back. "It's too early in the morning for—"

"Son, that is single malt Scotch," Chuck interrupted. "It is never too early for a good single malt." He pushed it closer and Dale picked it up.

"Cheers." He took a short pull and felt his eyes begin to water. After he swallowed the spirits he nodded, trying to catch his breath. "Smooth," he whispered hoarsely.

Chuck laughed as he took a long pull and then screwed the cap back on. "Go on, now. Talk to me."

Dale breathed through his mouth, trying to get his eyes to quit burning. "I'm not really sure where to start."

"The beginning is always best."

Dale took a deep breath and leaned close. "Let me ask you something. After the war, did you ever run into any of the men you were fighting against?"

Chuck gave him a confused look and shook his head. "I'm not sure I'd know them if I did run into them. Why?"

Dale felt his shoulders slump a little. "Let's say you did, and they were just, you know, normal guys. Would you be able to…work with them? Help them in any way?"

Chuck sat back and gave Dale a wary eye. "War ain't personal, son. To soldiers on a battlefield, it's all business. Our job is to win. Theirs is to lose."

"What if it ends up more of a tie?"

Chuck's eyes widened. "We ain't talking 'bout no 'Nam here, right son?"

"No, no, no…not 'Nam. Nothing like that."

Chuck sighed and propped his elbows on the table. "Just tell me what's rubbing you raw, Dale."

Dale took another deep breath. "Let's just say that there was this group, and they were just trying to protect their land. Their people. Their way of life."

"Okay…"

"And say the government came in and *inadvertently* stirred up a hornet's nest with these people."

"We talking Ruby Ridge stirred up? Or Waco?"

Dale stared at him a moment then shook his head. "I'm sorry, is there really a difference?"

Chuck sat back and chuckled. "Of course there was. Ruby Ridge, they snuck up on the man and tried to ambush him after they'd set him up. Waco, they scared them people into barricading themselves into a building before they set it on fire."

Dale opened his mouth and then paused. "I guess, a little of both, maybe."

Chuck rolled his hand at him. "Carry on. We'll figure it out along the way."

Dale blew his breath out hard, trying to think of how to explain the situation without giving up too much information. "So, let's say some government people got killed during the initial confrontation."

"Uh-oh. That ain't good for nobody."

"Right. So, the government sends in even more people."

"To teach them folks a lesson, I reckon."

"Right." Dale cleared his throat. "Except, the government lost again. By, a lot."

"We must be talking hillbillies, because them folks can shoot."

Dale nodded. "Yeah, something like hillbillies. They're a pretty basic group."

"Okay, go on."

"So, let's say a small group of people, civilians, went out there to verify stuff."

"*Verify?*" Chuck asked, his eyes narrowing. "Verify what?"

"Well, there was a couple of reporters that wanted to gather intel facts for a story. They were escorted by one of the government people and an ex-soldier."

"Once a soldier, always a soldier, son, but carry on."

Dale sighed again. "So they get up there with the

hillbillies and this government man realizes that they're actually decent folks. They just want to be left alone."

"Makes sense. Most folks just want to be left alone."

"Right?" Dale glanced to either side then lowered his voice even more. "So when the government man gets back, he finds out that his bosses are about to call in the National Guard and they intend to flatten this...*hill* where the hillbillies live."

Chuck sat back. "And now you're uncertain." He gave him a knowing look. "I'd be a fool to not think you was that government man." He took a deep breath and crossed his arms. "Other than fighting with the government folks, have these hillbillies broken any laws?"

Dale shook his head. "No. They're just out there living their lives."

"So what's a lone government man to do?" He tapped at his chin as he thought.

"Well, here's the rub though. There's things I might *could* do, but I'm torn."

"Over?"

"Well, on one hand, these people killed my friends." He shrugged. "Like, a lot of my friends."

"Ah, okay. Now I see. And you're wondering if maybe doing the right thing means you're betraying your friends."

Dale gave him a confused look. "The 'right' thing?"

Chuck shrugged. "Sounds to me like it is. You say these folks just wanna be left alone, right? And the government sent folks up there to poke the hornet's nest without provocation, right? 'Cuz these hillbillies didn't do nothing illegal to bring the government to their doorstep, right?"

Dale nodded, trying to follow the logic. "Right..."

"And now you want to do something to help these hill folks, but since your friends ended up dead, you ain't sure if helping them is the right thing. Right?"

Dale shook his head. "Yeah, I think."

"Son, you got yourself all twisted up inside for the wrong reasons." Chuck leaned forward and whispered. "Follow your heart. You know what's right and wrong. Your daddy made sure of that." He leaned back and crossed his arms again. "Tell me this. When you came down off that hill and you learnt them hillbillies was about to get hit hard, what was your first instinct?"

"To stop it."

Chuck nodded. "But since they hurt your friends, part of you wants vengeance. Now you got a crisis of conscience."

Dale nodded, hanging his head. "Pretty much, yeah."

"It ain't never betraying nobody to do what's right." He reached out and took Dale's hand. "Listen to me, son. You follow your heart. The Lord will know that you did what you had to do. Ain't no shame in that." He locked eyes with him. "No shame at all."

"But if I do nothing?"

Chuck shrugged. "You're the one has to live with that decision." He gave him a knowing look. "You gonna be able to sleep at night if you do nothing?"

Dale thought of Betty and Wilma, all of the younglings playing in the tree canopy and even Big Red, the old alpha male that let him go, not once, but twice. He shook his head. "No. I couldn't."

"There's your answer, son." Chuck stood from the chair and held his arms open. "Get in here."

Dale accepted the bear hug and even grunted when

Chuck set him back on the ground. "Thanks. I think I needed that."

"You bring your skinny ass back here anytime you need to remember your old man. We'll share some stories with you that'll make you feel he's still with us."

Offices of the Daily Informer

Patricia chewed nervously at her thumbnail as Roger went over her story. She nearly jumped when he opened the door to his office, the papers still in his hands. "Is any of this true?"

She nodded quickly. "Every word of it."

He handed her back her copy. "Send it." He wiped at his eyes. "You got me wanting to go tromping through the woods to stand with them against the army."

She felt the smile tugging at the corners of her mouth. "Really?"

Roger nodded and waved her on. "Send it. It's ready for print." He turned to Hector. "Now yours…"

Hector stepped forward, grinning. "It's ready too, right?"

"It's more red ink than black." Roger sighed. "I sent you an edited version. Make the changes and resubmit." He checked his watch. "If you hurry, you can still make the morning edition."

Hector groaned as he turned back to his computer. Patricia fell in alongside him. "Come on. I'll help."

"I told you I don't like to be rushed."

"We'll fix it." She nudged him. "We've got time."

"He does this every time," Hector groaned. "I bet if I had a chest like yours he would accept it just fine."

Patricia laughed. "My work speaks for itself. Anyway, man boobs would not become you."

"No, I meant…" he trailed off. "Oh, ha ha ha. You know what I meant."

"Yo, Pat." Patricia looked up to see Kelly Morgan holding her phone. "I just got news you're going to want to hear."

"Go ahead," Hector walked past her. "I think I can handle a few edits by myself."

"I'll be right back." She held a finger up to him before turning for Kelly. "What's up?"

She held her hand over the speaker of her phone. "I've got a source with the National Guard. "They're being spun up for…" She paused and checked her notes. "'In state mountain maneuvers.'" She raised a brow at her. "Sound familiar?"

Patricia felt her heart sink. "When?"

"First thing tomorrow." She lowered her voice and leaned closer. "Word is that they've placed State Police at the roadblocks going in now."

Patricia threw her head back and groaned. "Okay, thanks, Kel." She trotted to Hector's desk. "We got a problem."

"Don't we always?"

"Listen. The Guard is being activated for mountain 'training.' We both know what that means."

Hector's face went pale. "But Betty is—"

"I know." She crossed her arms over her chest. "I know we wanted both stories to go out at the same time, but I think that if we're going to get any public support, we need to push mine out in the late edition."

"Go!" Hector shooed her off. "Do it. My story can be a follow up."

She spun and darted across the bullpen. She threw open Roger's door. "I need to push my story tonight. It needs to go out in the late edition."

Roger set down his pen and gave her a confused look. "You know our readership is a lot lower in the late edition."

"It can't be helped." She pulled the door shut behind her. "They've activated the Guard."

Roger's face went slack. "Okay. We push it onto the late edition and run it again in the morning." He snatched the phone up from his desk to call the press room. He held his hand over the receiver, "Make sure you have the digital photos ready."

She jerked open the door and ran to her desk, prepping her story packet to be sent to the presses. She felt chills run up her spine as she clicked "send".

24

FBI Field Office, Albany, New York

Dale Archer pushed open the glass door so hard that it slammed into the far wall. He ignored the noise and the weird looks he received as he marched across the floor to Director Stanton's office. He could see through the glass wall as Stanton looked up and waved him in.

Dale opened the door and slipped inside, shutting it behind him. "We have to find a way to stop the governor from attacking the mountain."

David Stanton set down his pen and leaned back in his chair. "I'm afraid we're too late. He activated the National Guard this morning." He glanced up at the clock. "They've probably finished their initial briefings and are gearing up for insertion to the woods."

Dale felt his chest tighten and his ribs ached. He sat down gingerly and wiped a heavy hand over his face. "I have to do something." He looked up at Stanton, his eyes pleading. "I can't stand by and let them annihilate the group."

"It's out of our hands, Archer. We are completely out of the picture here."

Dale shook his head and pointed to the phone. "The Regional Director could call the governor back and—"

"Harold Latham is the one who got the ball rolling on this. You heard him yourself. He's not going to backtrack now." Stanton pushed his chair back from his desk and crossed his legs, getting more comfortable. "And I'm at the point where I believe it's the right call as well."

Dale scoffed. "Revenge is what this is." He sat back and huffed. "We invaded their territory. We picked a fight and they won." He clenched his hands together to keep from shaking. "Even I wanted a pound of flesh when I heard about..." he cleared his throat and lowered his voice. "When I heard what happened to our people."

"But," Stanton stated flatly, "you got to hang with the cavemen and caught a little Stockholm, didn't you?"

Dale's eyes narrowed. "That isn't fair. You weren't there."

"No, but these creatures are murdering beasts and—"

"It can't be murder unless you acknowledge that they're more than animals. Otherwise, that's all it is, an animal attack. Same as mountain lions, bears or wolves."

Stanton shot him a tight lipped smile. "Fine. You can call them whatever you want, but the point is, they killed over a hundred men. They will pay the price."

"How do we know it was them and not some of the other clans that have already departed the area?" Dale shot back at him. "It could be that the ones that did the actual killing are in a completely different state right now."

Stanton nodded. "You're right. They could be."

"Are we supposed to kill them all?" He came to his feet and pointed at the map of the United States on the wall. "What about the ones in Oregon or Washington state? What if some of them killed hikers or hunters or—"

"That's enough, Agent Archer," Stanton stated firmly. He stood from behind his desk and locked eyes with him. "I'm not the one who needs convincing. I gave you time off so you could do whatever it is you feel you need to do. However, you need to realize that neither I, nor this office, is in any position to assist you in your endeavor." He pointed out the door. "It was the Regional Director that made the call. He's like five people over me, and I'm just a fill-in until they find the right person to take over for Davidson." He planted his hands on the edge of his desk and leaned forward. "I shouldn't be the one to tell you this, but your name was mentioned for this position." He raised a brow at him. "I cosigned that suggestion."

Dale fell back into his seat. "But only if I play ball."

Stanton sat back down and shook his head. "I don't think anybody expects you to roll over for what you believe in. And yes, there are a lot of other people's names in the hat for the job." He leaned forward and tapped his temple. "Be smart in whatever you decide to do. Leave yourself some plausible deniability."

Dale scoffed again. "Yeah, with what I need to do, there is no plausible deniability." He came up out of the seat and reached for the door. "You realize that for me to stop them, I'll be lucky to keep my job, much less be considered for promotion."

It was Stanton's turn to scoff. "This is a federal agency. Do you have any idea just how many people 'fail upward' in federal agencies? It's easier to promote them than it is to fire them." He raised a brow at him. "Just don't screw up so bad that they are *forced* to fire you or throw your ass in the pen."

Dale rolled his eyes as he pulled the door open. "I'll see you once this is over."

"Cover your ass out there." Stanton watched him walk away and sighed. "And for the love of god, take this stupid job so I can get out of here."

OFFICES of the Daily Informer

HECTOR SUBMITTED his article again and paced outside Roger's office. Patricia approached slowly with two cups of coffee and handed him one. "Anything?"

"Not yet." Hector took the coffee and continued to stare at the door, waiting for Roger to either give his approval or order another rewrite. "Why do I feel like a kid in school waiting for the semester grades to be posted?"

"It's not that terrible," Patricia said as she sipped the bitter brew.

"Easy for you to say. Does he ever require you to rewrite your submissions?"

She nodded, unsure when the last time actually was.

"Sure. All the time," she lied.

Roger's door opened and he handed Hector the article. "You're too late for this afternoon, but it will go out in the morning." He planted his hands on his hips and smiled at the two reporters. "We've already gotten feedback on yours, Pat. The pressroom updated the website the moment we gave it the green light." His smiled widened. "You might get picked up by the AP on this."

Patricia's eyes lit up and she turned to Hector. "Do you know what this means?"

Hector's smile faded. "Yeah, your name will get out there, some big organization is going to poach you and we'll never see you again."

"No, stupid!" She punched him in the arm. "If it goes national, we'll have all kinds of public support for them." She grabbed Roger's arm. "You have to let me know if they pick it up. I don't care what time it is."

"You know it." He turned back for his office. "Go on. Go celebrate. I'll just stay here and keep working like the good little worker bee I am."

"What's to celebrate?"

They turned to see Dale standing behind them. Patricia gave him a questioning look. "Where did you run off to?"

Dale shrugged. "I had to see a guy about a dog."

Her features creased and she shot him a questioning stare. "Do what?"

"Something my dad used to say. I'll tell you about it later." He stepped closer and looked at Roger. "What are they celebrating?"

"Oh, the feedback on her article. It went live on the website right away and there's been quite the activity. There's a possibility that the AP will pick it up."

"Well, I should think so." Dale replied. "Proof that Sasquatch is real?"

"And living in New York of all places." Roger shook his head. "You kids have fun. I'll let you know if it goes national."

Patricia nearly jumped up and down. "If the AP picks it up, we'll have public support from all over. Maybe even international support."

"I just got word that the governor activated the Guard units. They're probably already in motion," Dale quietly stated. "I have no idea what to do about it."

Patricia turned to Hector. "What about your *homies*?"

Hector gave her a blank stare. "What of them?"

"Would they help us block the road going in?" She shot Dale a questioning look. "I mean, if we blocked the road…"

Dale shook his head. "It wouldn't stop them, but it might slow them down, like chaining yourself to a redwood tree."

Hector reached for his phone. "Just gotta slow them down long enough we can warn the Genoskwa. Maybe get Betty to safety."

Patricia pointed at him. "You round up your *posse*, I'll call Albert."

OUTSKIRTS OF NEW YORK CITY

"YES, Miss Patricia, he is in, but he's sleeping. He told me to wake him if you called." Godfrey deadpanned.

"This might take a moment. Shall I have him return your call?"

"Yes, please."

"Very well, madam. As soon as he's up. Thank you for calling."

Godfrey hung up the phone and sighed. He knew that Al wasn't teasing about the cattle prod. He just hated to resort to the vile instrument.

He walked into the master bedroom and tugged the comforter from him, exposing his skin to the chill air. Al grunted and slapped a hand around, searching for the cover.

"Miss Patricia telephoned, sir," Godfrey stated loudly. "She wishes for you to return the call."

Al groaned something and rolled over, pulling the pillow over his head.

Godfrey sighed and strolled to the closet to grab the cattle prod. He stood in front of Al and hit the button twice, letting the electric sizzle sound next to the man's ear. "Please, sir. Don't force me to use this damnable device."

Al grunted something unintelligible and Godfrey pressed the dual tongs to the back of the man's thigh. "Last chance, sir."

When Al refused to respond, Godfrey pressed the button then stood back as Al literally leaped from the bed, swinging and cursing. "What the bloody hell do you…" he trailed off, staring at Godfrey. "Did they call?"

"Miss Patricia did, in fact, call you, sir. She wishes for you to—"

Al dove for the side of the bed and reached for the phone. "Last number on the list?"

"Of course, sir." Godfrey turned and quietly placed the prod back in the closet. "Will that be all, sir?"

"Yes. No! Coffee. Please. Black and strong."

"I shall prepare the Black Rifle coffee, sir. Extra strong."

Al listened as the phone rang and did his best to not sound excited when she answered. "Hey, Tricia. Godfrey said you called."

"The wheels are in motion, Al. We need all hands on deck if we're going to stop a massacre."

"I've got the chopper fueled up and ready. Just tell me when and where."

He could hear her cover the phone and speak to someone. "There's a helipad on top of the FBI's Albany field office. How soon can you be here?"

"Give me an hour. I'll see you there."

Al hung up the phone and dug through the clothes he had left sitting out. He donned the thermal undershirt, t-shirt and flannel, tucking them all into his khakis. He pulled on his boots then reached for his leather flight jacket. "Time to get rotary."

TIA LUCIA'S CANTINA, Albany, New York

HECTOR'S TIRES screeched to a stop outside the cantina. He slammed the door and ran inside, looking for his cousins. "Where's Miguel?"

Tia Lucia hooked her thumb over her shoulder. "They're in the back, *mijo*. What's going on?"

"No time. We need to hurry." Hector pushed past her then slid to a stop. He leaned in and kissed her cheek. "*Te amo!*"

She watched him disappear into the kitchen and heard the back door slam a moment later. She muttered to herself in Spanish as she finished clearing a table. "Nearly forty years old and he's still a boy."

Hector stepped into the alley and broke into a toothy grin. "Now, that's what I'm talking about." Cars and trucks were lined up on both sides of the alley.

Miguel approached him. "What's the deal, bro? I called everyone." He glanced at his watch. "Some are still driving in."

"Perfect!" Hector pulled him closer and kissed the top of his shaved head. "We gotta go, bro."

"Woah, Popo, back it up. Where we going?"

"It's a long story, *cabrón*. I'll tell you on the way." He opened the passenger door of the classic Malibu and fell into the seat. "Come on, man. We need to hurry."

25

FBI Field Office, Albany, NY

Dale slid the door shut on the UH-1D Huey and fell back into the barely padded seat. "Tell me you're licensed for this thing," he said sarcastically.

Al pointed to the head seat dangling in front of him. "Use those if you want to talk."

Dale pulled the headset on and adjusted the mic. "Tell me you're licensed for a damned gunship!"

Al broke into hearty laughter. "The Huey, yes. But the guns aren't real." He lifted the craft from the roof of the FBI building and began to gain altitude. "The guns are mockups. The only thing they fire are lasers for specialized targets. I use this for insertion training with military and police units here in the states."

Dale nodded to himself and sat back next to Patricia. "Well, to be honest, this is one time I actually wish it was armed."

"We wouldn't last ten seconds against the US military. Not even a National Guard unit."

Dale shrugged. "Oh, I dunno about that. I happen to know a lot of Guard guys. You'd think they were members of Meal Team Six."

Al's head bobbed as he considered the statement. "Okay, you got me there. But as far as their equipment? Yeah, we're better off not bluffing."

"How long a flight is it?" Patricia asked.

"Not long at all," Al replied. "Even if the Guard has a good head start, they're limited to the highest speed of their slowest vehicle. We'll beat them there with time to spare."

She sat back and gripped the edges of her seat tightly. "I certainly hope so."

Dale noted the white knuckles. "Afraid of flying?"

She nodded nervously. "Oh yeah. My whole life." She turned her attention back to Al. "How often do these things crash?"

Al smiled behind his aviator sunglasses. "Usually only once." He glanced over his shoulder at her. "But the spare parts can keep other choppers in the air for a long time."

"Very funny."

"Agent Archer, what's the plan?" Al asked.

Dale sighed heavily. "Right now I'm going by the seat of my pants. I have no idea what to do once we get there."

"Too bad Hector isn't with you. He could tell the mountain monkeys to skip town until the Guard is gone," Al quipped.

"He's driving there with some friends," Patricia stated. "I have no idea what we expect a half dozen people to do to stop the National Guard, but like Archer said, we have to try something."

"Roger that." Al leaned to the side and studied the changes in landscape as the city gave way to suburban areas. He could see the patchwork quilt design of the country quickly approaching. "You can say goodbye to cell service soon."

"Are we there already?" Patricia asked, craning her neck to peer out of the Huey.

"Not even close, but we're approaching the open countryside. If you have any calls to make, you should do it now."

Miguel stared at Hector open mouthed. "You're not lying."

Hector shook his head. "Would I shit you? I'm telling you, man. They're real."

"And we're going there to stop the Army from killing them all?" Miguel slowed the Chevy and prepared to turn around. "Ain't no way I'm standing toe to toe with the Army."

"Hey!" Hector reached over and pressed his leg down. "Keep going!"

Miguel pulled the Malibu to the side of the road and a line of classic cars behind him followed suit. "I ain't about to get shot over a bunch of bigfeets that I ain't never even seen, man. You're *loco*!"

"No wait…we gotta go! Betty needs me, man."

"Who the hell is Betty?" Miguel asked, glaring at him.

"She's one of the bigfoots, man. She's my *amiga*." He locked eyes with Miguel. "We need a show of people out there. With enough public support, the military will have no choice but to stand down."

"A bunch of *posse* from the hood ain't gonna stop them, Hector. You need to wake up and smell the *enchiladas*." Hector reached for his phone and speed dialed a number. "Who you callin'?"

Hector pressed to phone to his ear. "Mario."

Miguel's eyes widened. "Why would you call him?"

Hector sat stiffly in the seat beside him. "Maybe he'll back my play since you don't have the *huevos*."

Miguel's eyes narrowed. "You wanna see *huevos, chinga cabron?*" He grabbed the gear selector and slammed the car into drive, spraying loose gravel as he accelerated. "Call in Mario and his merry band of crazies? What the fuck is wrong with you?"

Hector lowered the phone and slipped it into his shirt pocket. "I should call him anyway. We need as many people there as we can get."

"Then use the internet, fool. Your paper puts all their shit online anyway, yeah? Tell the people to go there."

Hector felt the corners of his mouth begin to curl into a smile. "You're as genius as you are beautiful!" He pulled his phone out again and went to the website. "I'ma tell the whole world where to go."

Miguel shrugged. "Well, maybe not the whole world. A good slice of New York, maybe."

SURVIVAL

Somewhere in The Skies of NY

Patricia felt her phone vibrate and plucked it from her pocket. She scrolled through a line of instant messages and froze. "Oh, no. What were you thinking, Hector?"

"Problem?" Archer asked, leaning towards her to peer at the screen.

"Hector just told everyone where we're going. He posted a comment after my article and pinned it to the top of the message board." She squeezed her eyes shut as she darkened the screen. "What was he thinking? We went to so much trouble *not* to mention where they lived."

Dale smiled at her and patted her hand. "Right now, we need public support more than anything, right? Keep them alive, worry about keeping people away from them later." His smile broadened. "Hector is putting the word out so we'll have that public support actually present."

She lowered her head and sighed heavily. "We'll never keep people from trying to contact them now."

Dale shrugged. "Let's figure out a way to keep the National Guard out first. Then, if we have to, we'll figure out a way to move the clan to a different area."

She nodded weakly and slipped her phone back into her pocket. "It's going to get really messy out there."

"Not necessarily," he replied as he squeezed her hand. "The road in to where the camps are is rough. Like, you need an off-road vehicle to get to it. If we set down right where the trail exits onto the paved road, then we block ingress and keep everyone a safe distance from the tribe."

She turned and stared at him. "How far is it from the road to the camp?"

Dale shrugged. "Probably ten or twelve miles." He leaned forward and patted Al's shoulder. "Hey, what's the distance from the paved road to the camp?"

Al thought for a moment. "About twenty clicks."

"There ya go," Dale grinned. "Twenty clicks is about twelve miles. That's a lot of distance to search if you're looking for something, and the Genoskwa are really good at hiding."

She nodded slowly then pulled her phone back out. She scrolled to where Hector's pinned message was and smiled. "And he gave them the highway marker from the main road." She darkened her phone again and leaned her head back with a smile. "I think we're good."

"See? No harm, no foul. And who knows? Maybe people will actually show up."

"That would be nice."

En Route to the Catskills

Miguel and Hector grabbed the ends of the "Road Closed" barriers and spread them apart. "I'm pretty sure Patty said there's a state patrol sitting at one of these now." He wiped the sweat from his brow as they gripped the second orange and white barrier. "What do we do about that one?"

Miguel grinned as he pulled his cell phone. "Pedro, get your truck up here to the head of the line."

SURVIVAL

About a half mile back, a big wrecker pulled out of the line and drove in the oncoming traffic lane. "Sup?" he asked, as he put the truck in park.

Miguel clapped Hector on the back and shoved him toward the truck. "Show him where to go." As Hector scrambled into the cab, Miguel approached the driver's window. "There's more of these ahead. Don't ram them. We got lowriders coming behind you. Just ease up and push them out of the way so we can follow."

"You got it, bro." Pedro gave him a thumbs up then turned to Hector. "I take it there's cops ahead?"

Hector nodded. "There was when we came out. I'd bet money they're still there."

Pedro broke into a toothy grin. "Let's go piss off some popos." He paused and cleared his throat. "No offense, bro."

"None taken." Hector slapped the dash. "*Àndale!*"

AT THE EDGE of the Catskills

AL PULLED off his headset and tossed them into the seat as he stepped down from the Huey. Dirt and dust still hung in the air as the rotors continued their slow deceleration.

Dale and Patricia kept their heads low as they trotted from the side door of the chopper. "We're the first here," she said excitedly.

Al inspected the Huey's position and nodded

approvingly. "They'll have to have a tank to get around this."

Dale stepped back and studied how the helicopter was situated. With the rocks and trees on either side there wasn't room to go around it. "Unless they flatten this thing or figure out how to go over it, it should work as a blockade." He glanced along the trail and sighed. "Should one of us go in and try to warn the Genoskwa of what's coming?"

Patricia sighed. "Where's Hector when you need him?"

Al smiled broadly. "He's on his way. I saw a line of quite colorful vehicles on the main road coming in. I'd give him about thirty minutes…if he can get around the state police roadblock."

Dale spun on him. "The roadblocks are manned now?"

"I saw a patrol car with the lights flashing at one on our way in, so I'd assume there's an officer with the vehicle."

Dale wiped a heavy hand over his face. "We may not be able to count on Hector or his buddies helping."

Al stifled a smile. "I've seen what can happen when people are determined. I can't imagine the officer shooting someone over a roadblock, but…this *is* America."

Dale turned and gave him a concerned look. "Should we provide air support while they try to get past the cop?"

Al shook his head. "If they're not here shortly then we can consider it. But something tells me they won't need our help."

Dale's eyes narrowed. "What makes you say that?"

Al shrugged. "Let's call it intuition."

SOUTHERN ROADBLOCK near the Catskills

SERGEANT DEREK BRENNAN fought to keep his eyes open and checked the coffee cup on the dash. With a wide yawn he settled back into the driver's seat and allowed his eyes to flutter shut. Alone, in the middle of nowhere, the car slowly warming in the early sun, and bored nearly to death, sleep called gently and the young officer enjoyed the siren song.

His head lolled to the side just as something large drove past his cruiser, a loud crunching noise snapping him awake.

He blinked the sleep from his eyes and instantly sat up, his head spinning as a line of brightly colored vehicles slipped past his roadblock.

"What the hell?" He reached for the door handle, stopping himself as more cars zipped by. He leaned towards the middle of the car and peered over his left shoulder. The line of cars seemed to stretch forever, and he was afraid to open his door, lest he cause an accident.

He reached to flip on his overhead lights and realized they were already on. He instinctively reached for the sirens and turned them on, waiting for the drivers to obey his warning and pull over.

The biggest part of him wasn't surprised when they refused to stop.

Derek reached for the radio and reluctantly keyed

the mic, calling dispatch. "Mary Twelve David to control, we have an issue at the southern roadblock."

"Go ahead Mary Twelve David," dispatch responded.

"Yeah, uh…I got a line of cars that have blown through the barriers and, uh…yeah, they're not stopping."

After a moment of silence, the dispatcher came back over the radio. "Did you get the tag numbers of the vehicles?"

"Uh, negative dispatch. There's too many of them and they're running pretty close together."

It took the dispatcher a moment to piece together what was said. "Mary Twelve David, are the cars still driving through?"

"Yeah, that's affirmative, dispatch." He bent low and peered through is side mirror. "We're talking a lot of cars here."

"Stand by Mary Twelve David."

Derek lowered his mic and felt his heartrate increase as the line of cars continued to zip past. "How the hell am I supposed to write this one up?"

26

Edge of the Catskills

Hector broke into a grin and made a slow approach, his arms out wide. "Huh? Whatchu think? I told you I'd bring my *vatos* and look." He spun around and gestured towards the convoy pulling onto the dirt road and attempting to find parking spaces on either side of the trail.

Al fought the smile forming and simply nodded. "I hope it's enough."

"Hector, it looks like we're having a car show," Patricia stated as she stepped beside him. "How many people are there?"

Hector shrugged. "Not enough. I posted on the Informer's website about—"

"Yeah!" she interrupted, poking him in the chest. "About that. I thought we were keeping their location a secret?"

Hector backed away slowly. "Too late for that, *chica*.

We needed public support. You said this yourself." He spun a slow circle, his arms stretched wide. "Well? This is public support."

"I'm talking about announcing the location of the Genoskwa online."

He smiled at her. "What, this? This location is a far cry from where Betty and her family live." He leaned close and lowered his voice. "Most folks aren't gonna trek twenty miles into the woods just to snap a picture of a bigfoot."

She glared at him. "It's entirely too close."

"You're both right," Dale said quietly as more cars pulled into the area. "We may have to move the chopper to make room for all of your friends."

"Friends?" Hector laughed. "This is *familia*."

"Regardless…" he trailed off. He turned to see Al already sitting in the cockpit and knew that he had the same thought. "You might want to warn your friends… er, family, that it's about to get windy and dusty around here." The whine of the helicopter's engine slowly increased in pitch as the rotors began to turn.

Hector trotted back to the line of cars as Dale and Patricia ducked low and stepped out of the clearing and into the woods for protection. Dale leaned close to her ear and nearly had to yell, "Any idea how many of your readers will respond?"

She shook her head and squeezed her eyes shut as Al brought the helicopter up from the ground. Once he'd passed overhead, she stepped out of the woods and watched as he took the craft about two hundred meters over the woods and slowly began to set it down in another small clearing. "I have no idea how many might show up. I mean, who would bother to come all the way out here? Still, according to my boss, the phones and server were both lit up the moment the article went online." She turned to him and shrugged. "Being a keyboard commando is one thing, but actually driving to a remote location to fight the government?"

"Understood." Dale took a deep breath and let it out slowly. "We might not be able to stop them." He turned and gave her a knowing look. "I think we need to be ready to accept that."

Patricia gave him a tight-lipped smile and shook her head vigorously. "I refuse to give in. I refuse to believe that the military will roll right over us to—"

"Good," he interrupted. "Stay positive and help boost everyone else's spirits. Keep them motivated."

"Where are you going?"

He turned and shot her a mischievous grin. "To see if Al and I can slow them down even more."

She watched him disappear into the woods and had an uneasy feeling. She was about to call to him when Hector grabbed her arm and startled her. "Hector! I nearly jumped out of my skin!"

"Come here. I want you to meet some people." He tugged at her until she finally turned away from Dale's retreating form. She rounded a small stand of trees and nearly froze. "Is that a food truck?"

Hector broke into a toothy grin. "The army can't do nothing stupid if they're busy eating, can they?"

"Oh, you might be surprised," she groaned.

"We want to park it where the helicopter was. You know, block the road and shit. Then my cousin can fire up the grill and the fryer and start making *carnitas*." He leaned closer and bumped her shoulder. "It's a genius plan, really. We fill them up, pour a few beers down their throats, make them sleepy, we win!"

She tried not to laugh at the simplicity of his plan but the idea of food and a party atmosphere appealed to her. Slowly she began to nod. "Do it." She reached for her phone.

"Who you gonna call?"

She held the phone up, trying to get a signal. "If I can get through, I'm calling the radio stations."

"The what?"

She shot him an evil grin. "We make this a party. Invite the whole world, tell them we got tacos and beer and give them the opportunity to 'stick it to the man'. At least, that's the plan."

Hector pointed at her as he walked backward toward the truck. "I like the way you think!" He spun and slapped the side of the taco truck. "Miguel, Rio, let's move the truck and get the grill fired up. We're a go, man!"

FBI Field Office, Albany, NY

Interim Director David Stanton picked up the phone. "This is Stanton."

The growling voice of Regional Director Harold Latham immediately caught his attention. "What the hell kind of monkey shit fight are you running down there, anyway?"

"D-director?" Stanton fought the urge to come to his feet. "I don't understand what—"

"Have you not read the damned papers?" Latham barked.

"I, uh…" He cleared his throat nervously. "No, sir. I have not."

"It seems that reporter woman…Murphy. She ran an article that implied we went into the woods to shoot a bunch of unarmed teddy bears that were previously believed to be a myth!"

Stanton groaned inwardly. "We had a man go with her. He was supposed to redirect her from—"

"Oh, I'm quite aware!" Latham cut him off. "One of our own." His voice grew angrier as he spoke. "The very man you suggested be promoted to your position!"

Stanton hung his head. "Sir, the circumstances on the ground have shifted."

"You don't say!" Latham was screaming into the phone. "From what I understand, your boy Archer is out there with her, right now!"

Stanton groaned inwardly. "Sir, I'm certain he's trying to redirect Ms. Murphy and her associates away from—"

"You better heel your dog, Stanton!" Latham screamed into the phone. "I mean it. I will not have a member of our team end up on the eleven o'clock news!" Latham suddenly became calm and quiet and that alone put fear into Stanton's mind. "If I see or hear Agent Archer in an interview or even milling about in the background of a news report, I'll personally bury you both."

Stanton opened his mouth to reply when the line went dead. He banged his head on the desk as he dropped the phone back into its cradle. "Somebody get Archer on the line! See which sat phone he checked out and CALL it!"

Southern Roadblock

State Police Sergeant Derek Brennan opened the door of his car and pushed it shut behind him. He peered past the line of cars still approaching and sighed heavily. The traffic continued to grow and the people behind the wheels had changed demographics. What began as a colorful parade of customized lowriders and lowrider sedans had morphed into college students stuffed in Subarus, families in minivans, and men in hunting gear driving lifted pickups. He saw more than one news van drive past the roadblock.

Sergeant Brennan reached through the open window and grabbed the radio handset, keying the mic. "Mary Twelve David to control, we have an even bigger issue at the southern roadblock." He paused for a moment and squinted in the early morning sunlight as it reflected off of hundreds of windshields. "The line just keeps getting longer."

"Mary Twelve David, stand down from your position. If possible, follow the vehicles and prepare to operate as crowd control."

Derek stared at the radio in surprise. "Crowd control? Be advised, control, I'm a one person unit out here. There are literally hundreds of people driving *through* my roadblock here."

"Mary Twelve David, understood. Be advised that the north side roadblock will be joining you at the scene."

Derek hung his head and scoffed. "Two uniformed officers in a crowd of how many?" He turned and tried to guesstimate the number of people closing on the location. "For the love of…" He sighed heavily then keyed the mic again. "Copy that, control. Abandoning southern roadblock and proceeding to…wherever these people are going."

He tossed the mic back through the window and opened the car door as more vehicles whizzed by. "I am not paid enough for this," he grumbled as he started the car and put it into gear. "Out of the frying pan."

Fort Hamilton, Brooklyn, NY

Major Patrick O'Dell slammed the door of the hardened Humvee and tugged his helmet off. "Let's move," he barked. He thumped the helmet down on the center doghouse and clenched his jaw. This "operation" was, in his honest opinion, the biggest bunch of bureaucratic hogwash he'd ever heard of. Go to the Catskills and kill a bunch of "feral bigfoots." He glared at his driver. "Have you ever heard of such bullshit before?"

The young sergeant shook his head. "Sorry, sir. This is a new one on me."

O'Dell grumbled under his breath. "Kill a bunch of feral…you do realize that very statement implies that there are domesticated…" he trailed off, unable to actually say the word.

"Personally, sir?" The sergeant pulled the lead Humvee from the motor pool parking lot. "I'm thinking they're testing us. I mean, everybody knows there's no such thing, right? So, this is the Guard's version of a snipe hunt."

The major turned and raised a brow at the man. "A snipe hunt?"

"Yeah. I mean, yes, sir. You know. A snipe hunt. When you take somebody out in the woods and—"

"I know what a snipe hunt is, Corporal."

"Um, sir? I'm a sergeant."

The major shot him an evil grin. "Not if you keep talking like that." He leaned back in the seat and propped an elbow up on the door. "Do you know a Lieutenant Colonel Mayfield?"

"No, sir. I've not had the pleasure," the sergeant replied cautiously.

"He's supposed to be flying in to take command of our unit." The major ground his teeth. "I can't believe the governor not only authorized this activation, but he pushed for it. Of all the hairbrained bullshit ideas. Talk about a waste of resources."

The corporal in the rear seat leaned forward, "Major? There's a radio call for you."

"Who is it now?" O'Dell grumbled as he reached for the handset. "Major O'Dell."

"Major, the state police have reported a caravan of civilian vehicles have blown through their roadblocks and are converging on the insertion point."

O'Dell sat forward and pressed a finger to his other ear. "Say again your last."

"State police have reported a caravan of civilian vehicles that have gone through their attempts to close the road, sir. They're converging on your insertion point."

O'Dell stared at the radio in confusion. "How the hell would a bunch of civies know where our insertion point is?"

"I have no idea, Major, but Colonel Mayfield has verified that the roads leading to the mountain are nearly bumper-to-bumper civilian traffic."

O'Dell gripped the handset tighter then nodded. "Understood. Are there any viable alternate routes?"

"Negative, sir. However, the colonel did advise that the oncoming lanes appeared clear."

"Understood. O'Dell out." He handed the radio back to the corporal. "Driver, we may have an issue getting to the insertion point."

"Sir?"

O'Dell sat back and crossed his arms. "When we hit traffic, pull into the oncoming lane."

The sergeant shot him a confused look. "Major?"

"Just do it." O'Dell rolled his eyes. "This day just keeps getting better and better."

27

Edge of the Catskills

Dale felt a knot form in his stomach when a military Boeing CH-47 Chinook banked over them and made another low pass, pausing to land just the other side of Al's helicopter. "Why did I imagine they'd come in with tanks and Humvees?"

Al huffed and crossed his arms, his aviator sunglasses shielding him from most of the prop wash. "Showoffs," he grunted. "Of course they'd arrive by air. It's faster and puts on a hell of a show."

"We're fucked, aren't we?"

Al shrugged. "I'm not seeing armaments on that craft. I'd be willing to bet it's just a transport." He lowered his face and stepped to the side, allowing his Huey to act as a block from the twin rotor debris.

Dale squeezed his eyes shut and listened as the rotors began to power down. "Christ, I can't see a thing. How many?"

"How many what?" Al asked, still having to shout to be heard.

"How many soldiers are getting off that thing?"

Al craned his neck and peered through the windows of his chopper. "I only see three."

Dale opened his eyes and blinked rapidly, trying to clear the dust from his vision. "Three? Surely they'd send more than that."

"Let's go say hello," Al shoulder bumped him then stepped out into view. "Oh, a light colonel."

Dale fell into step behind him. "He don't look that light to me." He smirked at his pun. "How are we going to handle this?"

"Follow my lead," Al whispered as he approached Lt. Colonel Mayfield. "Colonel, I'm Major Albert Briese, Her Majesty's Royal Marines," he extended his hand.

Colonel Mayfield raised a brow. "Isn't it *His* Majesty's Marines now?"

Al offered a tight lipped smile. "Not when I served, sir." He held his hand out again and Colonel Mayfield peered past him to the man standing in his shadow.

"Are you, by chance, Agent Archer?"

Dale stepped forward, "I am, sir." He held his hand out as well and felt the same cold shoulder that Al had received as Mayfield turned to the two uniformed officers in tow.

"Let's get the perimeter secured and arrange to remove those cars. The convoy isn't far behind and we'll need clear access." Mayfield turned back to the two men and removed his sunglasses. "Agent Archer, I've been instructed to inform you that your services are no longer required here. You are free to leave."

Patricia had made a silent approach and listened to the conversation. Her eyes darted between the three men as Hector slipped in behind her.

Dale shot the soldier a surprised look. "Do tell?"

Mayfield stiffened and gave him a stern stare. "Actually, it was Director Latham that asked me to relay that message. I'll consider it received." He stepped closer and his features turned to stone. "Now I suggest you remove yourself from the premises before I have you physically removed."

Patricia scoffed and crossed her arms. "You and what army?"

Mayfield's brows narrowed as he stared down at the small woman. "Do you not see this uniform? I *am* the Army."

She rolled her eyes. "Pfft. It's gonna take a lot more than you and those two paper pushers to remove him from this mountain." She glanced at Al and smiled. "And I'd pay good money to see you try to remove our pilot. He's Special Forces."

Mayfield's face reddened and Dale stretched out his arm and pulled Patricia back a step. "Looks like it's about to blow," he mumbled.

Al sighed and stepped between them. "Colonel, sir, I think there might be a misunderstanding here."

"Oh, you're goddamned right there's been a misunderstanding. In this situation, my word is law. If you don't all cease and desist, I'll have each and every one of you arrested and thrown under the jail!"

Al winced and shook his head slightly. "Sir, we're trying to act as a buffer between the good people of New York and your soldiers. You see, there's the possibility of a PR nightmare about to unfold here and—"

"And I don't give a tinker's goddamn what you think you're doing!" Mayfield took a half step back and counted to himself. "You will direct those people to remove themselves and their vehicles or every damned one of them will be impounded."

Al winced again and shook his head. "Yeah, that's not going to happen." He turned to Dale and shrugged. "This isn't going as I'd hoped."

"Captain!" Mayfield barked. "Arrest these people and order those civilians out of the area!"

A burly young man in a pilot's uniform trotted toward the group and Al groaned. "I really don't want to hurt your man, Colonel."

"Get these people the fuck out of here!" Mayfield turned back to the chopper and reached for the door when the sound of a scuffle caught his ear as his pilot was slammed against the side of the Chinook, and slid to the ground unconscious. He spun and glared at them. Hector shook his head nervously and pointed to Al.

"As I was saying, Colonel, there's the opportunity to avoid a PR nightmare."

"He isn't going to listen, Al," Dale said as he stepped alongside him. "I say we arrest him ourselves and let the Genoskwa decide what to do with him."

Al raised a brow and nodded. "Interesting thought, but…no. I think that might not be the best step forward, mate."

"And who the fuck is this *Genoskwa*? Local Indians?"

Patricia rolled her eyes again then stepped forward and poked him in the chest. "You were sent out here to kill a clan of indigenous beings and you don't even know their name?"

Mayfield brushed her hand away and felt his anger

bubbling again. "Somebody get these lunatics the hell out of here," he growled. "Before I do something I can't take back."

Dale plucked his handcuffs and let them dangle from a finger. "Uh-yeah. Sounded like a threat upon a federal officer to me. What do you think?"

Al sighed and threw his hands up. "Certainly what I heard, mate."

"What the hell do you think you're—"

Dale slapped a cuff onto his wrist and spun the colonel's arm around behind his back. "In case you haven't heard of Miranda, it requires me to inform you that you have the right to remain silent."

"Let go of me!" Mayfield barked as Dale clicked the cuffs to his other wrist.

The second flight officer came running when he heard the colonel yelling and Al stepped in front of him. "Na-uh. Unless you want to be arrested along with your boss, you'll do the smart thing and stay back."

The young lieutenant stood back and stared at the scene. "Sir?"

"Get these crazy people off of me!"

Dale reached for his weapon and held it loosely in his hand. "I'm fresh out of handcuffs, but I can always put one in your kneecap if it keeps you out of the way."

The lieutenant took a half step back and shook his head. "Uh, no sir."

"You realize you just pissed away your career, don't you, Mr. Archer?" Mayfield hissed as Dale spun him around and pressed him to the side of the Chinook. "I was activated by the governor himself to come here—"

"I don't care who sent you," Dale replied. He used his forearm to hold the colonel in place then turned to

Hector. "Get your ass up that mountain and make them understand that we can't hold these assholes off forever. Advise them to leave."

Hector's eyes widened. "They're not going to listen to me. This is their home."

"Make them understand!" Dale took a deep breath and brought his voice back down to a steady level. "They called in the other clans to fight armed men before. I don't think they have the resources to do that again. You need to make them understand that this time, they'll use big weapons and level the mountain from afar. The Genoskwa won't have anybody to fight because they'll be miles away."

Hector swallowed hard and looked to Patricia. "I don't think I can convince them."

"Fine. I'll come with you." She shot Dale a defeated look. "Wilma and I sort of made a connection. Maybe I can convince her."

Dale turned to Al. "Can you get them closer?"

Al opened his mouth to argue then closed it and smiled. "Actually, I found a clearing a couple hundred yards from their camp. It's rocky as hell but I think I can find a place to put her down."

Dale raised a brow at him. "That's if they don't spear your ass first. Remember what happened to the gunship pilot."

Al shrugged. "Nothing ventured, mate."

"I'll have your head for this, Archer," Mayfield hissed. "If you somehow avoid prison, you won't be able to find a job as a fucking mall cop."

"I'll take my chances." Dale pulled him roughly from the side of the chopper and perp-walked him toward the group of lowriders. "I'll hold him and his people back as long as I can."

Deep in the Catskills

Al felt his chest tighten as he made a slow approach to the clearing. His eyes darted from tree line to tree line looking for any sign of a bigfoot wielding a spear.

He found the clearest area that he thought might make a good place to land and brought the Huey in low and slow. As the skids touched ground, Hector was already tugging the door open then disappeared from view. Al cursed silently to himself as he began the shut-down procedures and nodded to Patricia. "Go on. I'll catch up."

She hopped down from the craft and attempted to navigate the rock strewn clearing while simultaneously trying to keep an eye on Hector.

She had almost caught up to him when he entered the shadows of the camp. Hector slid to a stop and spun a slow circle, yelling, "Betty!"

A young male stepped out from the longer outcrop with a spear in his hand. Hector locked eyes with the creature and pleaded, "Please! Tell me where Betty is!"

Patricia grabbed his arm and pulled him back. "He isn't looking friendly, Hector."

"I don't care," Hector replied through gritted teeth. "I have to find her."

A loud "whoop" echoed through the trees and Hector's head spun around. He ran to the end of the rock wall and caught sight of Betty as she stepped out of the woods and made her way past the makeshift garden toward him. Hector's face lit up and he ran to her, arms outstretched.

Patricia watched in awkward fascination as Hector ran into the arms of the female Genoskwa, wrapping his arms around her belly. "I found you!"

Patricia made a slow approach as Hector tried to speak to Betty. What amazed her most was that Betty responded in their strange, growling language.

She stood at the edge of the clearing and watched as the creatures slowly appeared from the shadows of the woods. She stared at the clan as they approached Hector, and Patricia searched for Wilma.

When she saw the strawberry-blonde female emerge from the brush, she smiled and made her way in that direction. "I know you probably don't understand me, but you need to take your people someplace safe." She reached out and Wilma took her hand. In that moment, it was as if her message was received. Wilma stiffened and stared at her.

Patricia tried to explain, mental images of the soldiers and weapons they would use flashed through her mind and she could see her fears reflected in Wilma's eyes. "They won't stop."

Wilma peered over Patricia's head and stepped toward the clan's patriarch. The towering, red haired, one-eyed male that had released them stood at the edge of the woods with the same thick spear in his hand.

When the two females stood before him, Patricia noted that Wilma kept her head bent and her eyes averted as she spoke softly to him. Patricia wished she had brought her recorder as the two conversed in their guttural language. After a few moments, Wilma turned to her and took her hand again. She mumbled something and the image of the mine entrance flashed through Patricia's mind.

It took her a moment to realize what was happening and Patricia felt an elation she couldn't express as she finally understood what Hector was trying to explain to her. Somehow, the creatures could project mental images as they spoke and although the message wasn't entirely clear, Patricia was able to piece together the intent.

She shook her head, "No. The mines won't keep you safe." She imagined jet planes and missiles. Helicopters and tanks. Large munitions that could level the mountain and any living thing on it or in it. "They have horrible weapons." She swallowed hard and turned to the clan patriarch. "Could you stay with another tribe of your people until the humans leave your mountain?"

The huge male stared at her then turned to Wilma who seemed to translate. Patricia tried to study their features, hoping to get an inkling of their thoughts. When Wilma's head slumped, she knew the answer.

"You don't understand. Many humans were killed during…" she paused, trying to think of a word that put the altercation into context. "War. Their leaders insist on blood."

Wilma's eyes watered as she did her best to explain, and Patricia watched as Big Red accepted her answer. He closed his eyes and leaned his head back, letting the sun wash over him. When he turned his attention back to the pair, he mumbled something and Wilma let go of Patricia's hand, cutting off the mental images.

"What? What did he say?" she asked. She reached

SURVIVAL

for Wilma's hand again. "What is he going to do? Where will you go?"

Wilma turned to her and she saw a single tear run down the side of her simian face.

"Please, tell me."

Wilma gave her a sad smile and patted the side of her face. With a mighty arm she pointed back down the mountain and made a motion with her hand. The message was clear. "Go back."

28

Edge of the Catskills

"What am I supposed to do with him?" Miguel asked, staring at the angry soldier with a gag in his mouth sitting at the rear door of the taco truck.

"I don't care," Dale replied. "Just don't let him go."

"We could stuff him full of *carnitas* and beer," Rio offered, an evil grin crossing her features. "Or put him to work slinging shredded pork."

Dale turned and gave her a dissatisfied stare. "Now's not the time."

"Why should he get to sit in the shade and do nothing?" She sneered at the older man. "I bet he hasn't done an honest day's work since he enlisted."

Mayfield struggled against the gag, spitting it free from his mouth. "I'm an officer," he corrected.

She mocked him with wide eyes. "Ooh…an officer." She scoffed then slung the towel back over her shoulder and sauntered inside the truck. "Just stay out of my way or I'll dump hot grease on you, *cabron*."

Dale checked his watch then sighed. "Somebody tell me something. I hate not knowing what the hell is going on."

"Uh, sir?" Dale turned to find the younger pilot holding a handheld radio. "The convoy is approaching. I just thought you should know that things are about to get really messy for you if you don't release the colonel."

Dale groaned and blew his breath out hard. "I'll deal with that when it gets here."

"There's not a rock you can hide under, Archer," Mayfield sneered at him.

"Oh please. You're a light colonel with the national fucking guard, not some Joint Chief or SecDef." Archer waved him off. "If you're so damned important, maybe I'll just hold you hostage."

"You already are, dumbass," Mayfield growled.

Dale sighed and finally turned to face him. "I can make this get really ugly, really fast. Keep running your mouth and...son of a bitch." He stepped towards the man and pulled the gag back up and stuffed it into his mouth. "And keep it there."

The young lieutenant sighed heavily and held the radio up where Mayfield could see it. "I brought Major O'Dell up to speed, sir."

Mayfield rolled his eyes and leaned back against the truck, waiting for his troops to arrive and release him.

Dale paced a circle in front of the taco truck then finally turned to Miguel. "Can you have your friends block the road?"

Miguel stared at him blankly for a moment then

nodded. "Yeah. I'm sure they can. But the soldiers will just make a new road."

"So, let them. Even if it slows them down a little. I need every minute I can get."

Miguel whistled and called Pedro over. "Gather the homies and send word down the line. Have them block the roads as far back as they can." Pedro shot him a thumbs up then ran for his truck. He grabbed the mic from his CB radio and called out to whomever was listening. When Miguel turned his attention back to Archer, he lowered his voice. "You know that won't buy you much time."

"Hector needs every second we can give him."

Miguel grinned as he leaned closer. "Tell me something. He really get all buddy-buddy with the bigfoots up there?"

Dale chuckled. "Yeah, he really did." He glanced to the side to make sure nobody was close. "According to Patricia he got real chummy with a lady 'squatch."

Miguel's brows rose and his features twisted. "Like… monkey love?"

Dale laughed and shrugged. "I dunno man. It was more like he was her pet human. She actually rocked him to sleep."

"With a big ass rock, I hope," Miquel added. "Hector has always been a bit *loco*, ya know? But cuddling with a…" he trailed off, unable to say it aloud. "Man, I'm gonna bust his *huevos* over this. I promise."

"First, let's get these things to a safe place." Dale took a deep breath and sighed when he saw the cars still on the road begin pulling into the oncoming lane and blocking the road. A slow smile crept across his features and he nodded with approval. "Okay. Step one complete."

"Yeah, uh…Agent Archer?"

Dale turned and faced the young flight officer. "What?"

"Yeah, uh…they've pulled onto the shoulders of the highway. The major says they'll be here in fifteen mikes."

Miguel shrugged. "It was worth a try, *amigo*."

Dale sighed and leaned against the taco truck. "How about a cold one?" He glanced at his watch. "Nothing like beer for breakfast."

Miquel handed him a Corona. "On the house, Archer. Free beer for the condemned man."

Dale smacked the cap off on the side of the door handle and took a long pull. "Yeah, thanks. I'll try to enjoy this. Something tells me they don't serve these in prison."

Deep in the Catskills

"She wouldn't tell me anything," Patricia said as they made a slow walk back to Al and the Huey. "But I finally get it, Hector. What you were talking about earlier. It's like I could 'see' what she was saying."

"I know, right? It's fucking incredible, isn't it? How do you explain that to people?"

Patricia shrugged. "I've got no idea. But after she

projected to me, I realized I had to visualize what I was trying to say to her for her to understand me." She sighed heavily and glanced back over her shoulder. "I don't think I got my message through to Big Red, though."

"Big Red? The boss?" Hector waved her off. "Trust me, he's the boss for a reason. He knows what's what."

"He can't though." She paused just meters from the chopper as Al started the engine again. "I mean, yeah… he's faced soldiers and the Bureau with their guns and explosives, but he had a ton of backup. This time it's the military, and they're coming in heavy."

Hector hung his head and squeezed his eyes shut. "I told Betty goodbye." He looked up at her and had to wipe his eyes. "It was like she knew I'd never see her again."

Patricia nodded and clapped his shoulder. "Wilma got teary on me, too. She wouldn't tell me what was going on, so I have no clue what to tell Archer."

Hector stiffened and squared his shoulders. "We tell them that they agreed to leave." He turned to her as the idea took root. "Yeah, we tell them that they left everything behind and just took off through the mountain tunnels…or a game trail, or…something. They left to go live with their cousins in Guatemala or some shit."

Patricia broke into a toothy grin and pulled him toward the chopper. "How about they went to stay with another tribe in Vermont?"

"Okay, whatever." Hector slid into the chopper and pulled his headset on. "But you know Guatemala is farther away, and I don't think the National Guard has jurisdiction there."

"Yeah, but they'd have to cross the country...they'd definitely look for them. I'll take my chances with Vermont," she laughed. She turned to Al, "We're done here. We can go back."

Al twisted in his seat. "What was that about Guatemala?"

Patricia smiled and shook her head. "The Genoskwa wouldn't tell us what they were going to do so we're going to report that they've already left the mountain."

Al raised a brow at her. "You really think they'll buy that?"

She shrugged. "We'll have to sell it to them."

"I still like Guatemala," Hector stated firmly. "I'm telling you, the Guard can't do shit there."

"Take us home, Al," Patricia patted his shoulder then sat back. "Put on our game faces boys. We got a hard story to sell the military."

NEAR THE CATSKILLS

"CHRIST, Sergeant! I think you actually missed a bump back there."

"No worries, Major. I'll hit it twice on the way out."

Major O'Dell gripped the dashboard as the Humvee bounced along the side of the highway. He ignored the confused or angry faces that glared at him as the vehicles passed the long line of autos parked on the highway.

He noted dozens upon dozens of people on foot and walking towards the insertion point. Some carried folding chairs and coolers, while others came with just their families. "Like they're going to a fucking carnival," he grumbled.

"Sir?" the driver asked as he tried to navigate the rough and overgrown shoulder.

"These civies. Making a day of this like it's some kind of twisted joke."

"Well, sir…" the sergeant chuckled. "They think there's bigfoots out here." He shot him a toothy grin. "I mean, come on."

"This is a military operation, Sergeant. We're going to have to turn every stinking one of these people back and seal the damned roads once they're gone."

The sergeant nodded as he drove. "Yeah, that could take a while." He turned and saw the disapproving stare from the major. "I mean, uh, that could take a while, sir."

O'Dell rolled his eyes and turned away from the sergeant. "Tell me something, Sarge. What do you do in the world when you're not pretending to be a soldier on weekends?"

The sergeant felt his hackles rise and almost opted not to reply. Instead, he decided to be honest. "Well, *sir*, after six years in the Army and three tours in the sandbox, I figured it was time to come home and actually try to be a husband and father." He turned and gave him a stoic look. "But I still put my life on the line daily. I'm a firefighter. I decided to go with the Guard instead of the reserves because I wanted to serve my community."

O'Dell sighed. "So admirable," he grunted. "I'm sure the retirement benefits don't hurt either."

"You're not wrong, Major. Might as well put those six years to good use, don'tcha think?"

O'Dell sat up and nodded ahead. "Is that it?"

The sergeant slowed the Humvee and twisted in his seat, looking at the corporal in the rear. "Is this it coming up?"

The corporal scanned the map then looked up. "This should be the road the Bureau took to insert, Sergeant."

"This is it, sir."

"It's about damned time," O'Dell pulled his helmet on and fastened it. "Time to meet this light colonel and find out what this op is really about." He chuckled under his breath. "After we bust him out of federal custody."

FBI Field Office, Albany, NY

Interim Director Stanton paced his office. "No answer at all?"

"Sir, the calls go directly to voicemail," the disembodied voice declared over the speaker. "We've been trying to reach Agent Archer since the minute you told us to call. I don't know what else to do short of going out there and tracking him down."

Stanton hung his head and sighed. "That's just what we need. To put somebody else's head on the pike alongside Archer's."

"Sir?"

"Never mind. Just…keep trying." Stanton reached across his desk and hung up the call. He fell into his chair and rubbed hard at his temples. "There's got to be a way to reach him. Latham wasn't joking about hanging us both if Archer brings bad press to the Bureau."

A knock at his door had Stanton lifting his head. "What now?" he groaned.

"Sir," an agent spoke nervously. "I activated the tracking on the sat phone assigned to Agent Archer."

Stanton sat up straighter and grasped at the lifeline. "Where is he?"

"He's in the Catskills, sir." The agent rubbed nervously at his neck. "But, uh…he's moving. Fast."

"Excuse me?"

The agent handed him a laptop. "The program pings the phone every five seconds. It gives us as close as we can get to real time movement and, while it will wear the battery of the phone down a lot faster, it still—"

"Just give it to me." Stanton pulled the laptop from his hands and set it on his desk. "What is this?"

"Uh, that's the speed that he's moving at, sir. Approximately ninety kilometers per hour."

Stanton squinted and leaned in. "There's not a car out there that can traverse that landscape that fast." He rolled his eyes as he sat back. "That's why he isn't answering. He's in a plane or a helicopter. He can't hear the damned thing ringing."

The agent nodded nervously. "My assessment as well, sir."

Stanton handed him back the computer. "He can't stay in the air all damned day. Keep trying to call him.

The moment that phone is stationary, I expect him to answer."

"Yes, sir." The agent plucked the computer from his hands and disappeared quickly.

Stanton leaned back and rubbed at his eyes. "For the love of...answer the damned phone, Archer."

29

Edge of the Catskills

Al landed the Huey deftly beside the big Chinook and did his best to block the narrow trail that cut deeper into the forest. He tugged the headphones off and tossed them into the seat next to him and reached for the door as the rotors slowly wound down to a stop.

He paused and tilted his head, listening to a sound that shouldn't be there. In his peripheral vision he could see Hector and Tricia making their way back to the growing crowd of people and he wanted to fall into step with them, but that annoying buzz was going to eat at him.

He clambered over the gear bags and sat in the rear compartment. "What the hell is that?" He leaned forward, listening to the incessant buzzing and narrowed it to a small duffle bag.

He pulled the duffle to his lap and unzipped it, fishing around for the source of the noise. He felt the plastic brick buzz against his hand and withdrew the object. "A sat phone?" He glanced at the number and racked a grin. "Forty three missed calls? Somebody's impatient."

Al reached for the side door and clipped the phone to his belt as he made his way toward the crowd of people. By the time he found Archer, Tricia and Hector, they were deep in conversation.

Al approached carefully, listening to Tricia as she explained the situation and slipped the phone to Dale. Archer felt the thing buzz in his hand and glanced at the screen before holding a finger up, cutting her off. "This is the office; it might be important. Give me a second."

Patricia groaned as he stepped away and turned to Al. "He said the military will be here any moment. We need a viable story to sell."

Al glanced at Mayfield handcuffed to the side of the taco truck and gently tugged her aside. "In case the old man's hearing is better than mine."

When Archer stepped back into the group, his face was fallen. "I'm not to do anything that could give the Bureau a black eye."

Hector scoffed then laughed out loud. "Like you could do anything worse than they've already done to themselves."

"Not now, Hector." Archer wiped a heavy hand over his face and sighed. "Somebody tell me that there won't be any news crews out here."

Patricia's face fell and she stared at him blankly. "I may have already messaged my contacts at several radio and TV news stations."

He nodded as he clipped the phone to his belt loop. "I was afraid you were going to say that."

"It's not all bad, mate," Al smiled at him then nodded toward the road entrance. "The military is here just in time to escort you away to a black site. The chances of getting on the news then are pretty much nil."

"Thanks for that, bud."

"Don't mention it." Al reached out and gripped his upper arm, pulling him aside. "I think you need to disappear."

Archer pulled his arm free and stood his ground. "Screw that. The colonel was interfering with an official investigation. That's an arrestable offense."

"Yeah, I think you're going to be outgunned, Archer," Patricia replied quietly. "Maybe Al is right. Make yourself scarce while we deal with the incoming soldiers."

Archer glanced over his shoulder then looked at Mayfield, struggling to get to his feet. "Yeah, maybe you're right."

"Oh, no…" Hector groaned. "When it rains it pours, man." He nodded towards the road where a news van cut in between incoming Humvees.

"Great," Dale groaned.

"Yeah, that settles it, mate. Time for you to go for a walk in the woods." Al hooked his chin toward the tree line. "Just hide in the shadows and keep an eye on things."

"Come on, man. I'll go with you," Hector walked past him and waved him forward. "Come on. If it's good enough to hide Betty and her people, I'm sure the two of us can disappear, too."

Dale rolled his eyes and sighed. "Fine." He fell into step behind Hector and just caught a glimpse of one of the soldiers approaching Mayfield with something in his hands. Cuff keys, no doubt.

Dale slipped behind a long rock outcrop just yards inside the tree line and settled in next to Hector. He could just make out the crowd of people in the clearing as loud *música Mexicana* began to play.

Hector groaned. "Great. I can smell the taco truck."

Dale gave him a confused look. "Nothing is keeping you here."

Hector shot him a surprised look and broke into a toothy grin. "Want a taco?" He stood and stepped aside, preparing to go back. "A beer?"

"I already had the beer." Dale glanced at Mayfield brushing the dirt and grass from his uniform. "And my guts are all butterflies right now. But you go ahead. I'll stay here and keep watch."

Hector nodded and stepped out. Almost immediately Mayfield pointed at him and two soldiers took off to catch him.

To his credit, Hector played it cool. He let the soldiers grip him by the arms and lead him back to Mayfield. "What's wrong? Why you manhandling me, man?"

"Where is Archer?" Mayfield hissed.

Hector shrugged. "No idea." He glanced around the area and shook his head. "He was here just a minute ago."

Mayfield glanced toward the tree line. "What were you doing over there?"

Hector squared his shoulders and locked eyes with the man. "You see a porta potty around here? I was dropping a deuce." He laughed and hooked his chin back toward Archer. "Go check it out. It's one for the history books, I tell ya." He looked at one of the soldiers still holding him. "That shit happen to you too, man? When you eat those MREs? Man, they clog my pipes like you wouldn't believe. And the gas!"

"That's enough." Mayfield continued to stare at the ever growing crowd. "Lieutenant, call in as many tow trucks as you can. And grab those two state patrol officers. I want them escorting people out of the area immediately!"

Hector pulled away from the soldiers and shook his head. "You can't do that. This ain't a military base. It's a state park. People are free to assemble wherever they want to and—"

"And shut this guy up!" Mayfield barked. He stepped away from the two soldiers and locked eyes with Al. "And you. You need to move that Huey. You're blocking the trail."

Al sucked at his teeth. "And wouldn't you know it. I just ran out of gas." He shrugged. "I put in a call to Triple A, but they said it might be a while. Apparently the roads are all blocked."

Mayfield's jaw muscle flexed as he ground his teeth. "You can move that bird, or I'll have it moved. And I promise you, you won't like how I do it."

Al nodded slightly. "I think I read you, loud and clear, Colonel. But I still need the fuel."

Major O'Dell appeared by his side. "Colonel, I'm having my men round up the civilians and ordering them back to their vehicles."

"Very good, Major. Drag them out by their goddamn hair if you have to." Mayfield forced an evil smile. "And have some of your men use a transport to drag that Huey into the trees. Clear our path, Major. We have monsters to kill."

"Copy that, sir."

"Now, hold on just a minute," Al began.

"No, you had your chance," Mayfield interrupted. "Now we'll do things my way."

Patricia held her recorder up and clicked the button on it, stopping the recording. "This is going to play so well on the eleven o'clock news."

Mayfield reached for the device and she pulled it away. "I don't think so, Colonel. Freedom of the press and all that."

"You're wasting your time anyway, man," Hector stated firmly. "We warned them you were coming." He grinned at the soldiers and crossed his arms. "They've already left. Heading to Guatemala as we speak."

"Vermont, you idiot," Patricia groaned. "They're headed to Vermont."

"Whatever," Hector continued smiling. "They can move through those trees like ninjas. And if they think you might come close, they'll disappear into the mines or the natural caverns that run all through these mountains. You'll never find them."

Mayfield took a deep breath and let it out slowly. "You'll forgive me if I don't take your word for it. It's been my experience that people aren't always completely honest when it comes to—"

"It doesn't matter," Patricia interrupted him. She nodded to the large group of people still milling about. "All of these people came out here to support *protecting* these creatures. How well do you think it will play on the news when we show you and your soldiers trying to hunt them down to exterminate them?"

Mayfield ground his teeth together and leaned close to her, his voice a growl. "You won't be able to, Miss Murphy. There won't be any civilians left on this mountain to report anything that we do." He leaned back and sighed. "We have our orders and they aren't optional."

"And where did these orders originate, if you don't mind me asking?"

"The governor himself."

She held up the recorder again and clicked it off. "Thank you for that quote, Colonel."

Mayfield rolled his eyes then turned to O'Dell again. "Get these people the hell off this mountain, NOW, Major!"

"On it, sir." O'Dell reached for Patricia's arm and Al gripped his wrist, pushing him away.

"No need to get physical, Major." He raised a brow at the man. "I'll escort her myself."

Mayfield waved his young co-pilot over and pulled him closer. "Find Archer. I don't care if you have to take to the air and scan using infrared, find that son of a bitch and bring him to me. In chains."

Dale watched from the shadows and could only pick up pieces and parts of the conversation. When Mayfield was mad and throwing around threats, his voice carried fine. But when the man got really angry and lowered his voice, Archer could only guess what he was saying.

Once Al pulled Patricia away, she broke free and ran into the sea of people. The military didn't seem to notice as she melted into the crowd only to emerge near the first news van that had entered the clearing.

Dale was bewildered at her actions until he saw her embrace a young woman dressed for broadcast. The two chatted quickly and Patricia handed her something. Dale was just far enough away that he couldn't identify what it was.

"What are you doing?" he asked out loud. He noticed a soldier approaching his area and ducked quickly, praying the man didn't see him. He duck-walked to the end of the rock outcrop and rose just high enough to see the soldier approach the other end. He paused at the other end of the outcrop and pulled his sidearm. When he bounced around the edge and peered behind the stony wall, he found it empty. He glanced around then quickly holstered his weapon.

Dale watched as the man slowly sauntered back out of the trees and made his way toward the crowd again. It was only then that he noticed the man standing atop the lead Humvee with a bullhorn in his hand. "Attention! Attention!" He lowered the bullhorn and slapped at the side. "Attention, people. I need you all to get back into your vehicles and vacate this area immediately. We have called in wreckers to tow at the owner's expense any vehicle that fails to comply."

Dale smiled as people waved him off and a few swore epithets at the man. "Hearts and minds, dumbass," Dale grumbled.

"This is a military operation and you are not permitted to be here," the man stated through the bullhorn. "The state police have radioed for backup and anybody found not complying will be subject to arrest."

This statement earned the speaker a round of half

empty beer cans launched in his direction and a wave of negative shouts from the crowd. Dale had to stifle a laugh as the man scrambled down from atop the Humvee. "Okay, fine! Don't say you weren't warned!" He tossed the bullhorn into the open window of the Humvee and stormed off.

Dale glanced up at the blue sky peeking through the tree canopy and uttered a silent prayer. "We're going to need all the help we can get."

30

Edge of the Catskills

"I HAVE AN IDEA," Patricia whispered as she pulled away from Al. "Call it a Hail Mary pass." He watched her disappear into the crowd only to emerge near the newly arrived news van.

Patricia approached cautiously and stared at the back of the woman's head dressed smartly in a dark blue blazer. "Becka?"

Rebecca Williams spun around and her eyes shot wide. "Trish!" She reached out and embraced her like a long lost relative. "What are you doing here?"

Patricia gave her a crooked smile. "Hector and I broke the story on the Genoskwa…remember?"

"Of course!" She tapped the side of her head and crossed her eyes. "Duh." She sobered and gave her a fake smile. "But seriously. Why are you out here?"

She held up the recorder. "We're trying to save the Sasquatch from the military."

"From…the military are here to hurt them?"

Patricia's face fell. "Why else did you think we made a public cry for help?"

"Oh, I wouldn't know about that. My producer shoved a microphone in my hand and pointed us to the sticks. Said to follow up on some story that Hector Ramirez broke."

Patricia hung her head. "Tell ya what. I'll make you a deal."

Becka leaned closer. "I'm listening."

She held up the recorder again. "I have the leader of the military admitting that they were sent out here by the governor to commit genocide." She raised a brow at her. "And I'll give you an exclusive interview, along with unpublished photographic proof of the Genoskwa…if you'll help me put a stop to this."

Becka's face went stoic and she stared at the recorder then at Patricia. "I want to hear what's on there first."

Patricia raised a brow at her. "And if you like what you hear?"

"We have a satellite uplink. I can cut in at any time." A slow smile started to form. "If what you say is on that recorder, and IF you can provide the picture proof… then you have your deal."

Patricia couldn't stop the smile from spreading. "We don't have time to waste." She pushed past Becka and climbed into the news van. She handed the recorder to the tech inside. "Set this up for her. We have a lot of work to do."

FBI Field Office, Albany, NY

The Interim Director picked up his phone and cautiously answered, "Stanton."

"I need your help."

Stanton stared at the receiver a moment. "Didn't I just hang up on you? You have your orders, Archer."

"And I understand those orders, sir. I'm just…" he trailed off, trying to think of any way they could legally stop the Guard from rekindling a centuries old war that had finally found peace. "We have assets on the ground. Physical assets, sir. Equipment, vehicles, weapons, personal belongings…" he sighed heavily. "Can't we call this a crime scene and close it off? At least until we have a chance to recover what's ours? It will buy the Genoskwa time to relocate."

"Are you kidding me right now?" Stanton slowly came up from his chair. "I understand you're all buddy-buddy with these things, but do I really have to remind you of the personnel losses we suffered at their hands?"

"No, sir, you don't." Dale huffed and paced between the trees. "Sir, things have changed here on the ground. The 'squatches are…" he trailed off again, unable to find the words.

"They're what, Archer? Kinder and gentler now? Just because they let you go twice doesn't mean that we can consider them allies. They're *animals*, Archer. They're beasts that can rip a man's head off and let's not forget that they eat people."

"I don't think so, sir. Not anymore." He leaned against a thick pine tree and rubbed at his eyes. "Director, I'm telling you, they've changed."

"Interim director," he corrected. "And I have to ask you, Archer. If a bear didn't kill you and eat you would you suddenly consider it friendly?"

"That's not fair, sir. These creatures are intelligent. They mourn their dead. They, they…" He sighed again and slid down the tree, sitting in the pine needles at the base. "They may not be human, but they're damned close. Unrefined, uneducated, uncouth, yes. Yes, to all of it. But they have souls."

"You can't know that, Archer. Any more than you could know if a human has one."

"Then they have a conscience. They know right from wrong, and the leader is forcing them to change. When we were in the camp, he made an appearance and made it clear that we were to leave. We didn't leave that night, and Tommy Youngblood was killed."

"You just made my point."

"No, sir. You don't understand. It was one of the younger males that acted on his own. He killed Tommy, and when we made that known to the leader, he killed that male." Dale ground his teeth in frustration. "His order was for us to leave. Not die. And when that young male took it upon himself to act, the leader removed a threat from his clan. I believe he did it because he now sees killing as wrong."

"Archer," Stanton groaned, "you can't know that. I can't even hazard a guess how you communicated with this leader of theirs. Much less how much of what you told him he actually understood."

"Sir…I'm not asking you to go to war with the Guard. Just help me make the case that the entire mountain is a crime scene. Just…buy us some time."

Archer listened to the silence on the phone and if he

hadn't heard Stanton breathe, he'd have thought the man had hung up on him. "I don't think I can sell this idea of yours."

"Then make it your idea, sir. Don't even mention me unless you have to." Dale pulled himself back to a standing position and crept towards the rock, peering out at the military trying to corral citizens. "They're already trying to clear people from the scene, and once the public is gone, there's nothing we'll be able to do to stop this."

Stanton groaned loudly. "Son of a bitch. Why are you putting me in this situation, Archer?"

"Believe me, sir. I wouldn't ask if I didn't believe they were worth saving."

Stanton huffed over the phone. "Fine. I'll make some calls."

"And?"

Stanton paused while he thought. "I don't know if I can sell Latham on this, but…for now, consider it an order to secure the mountain as a crime scene."

"Yes!"

"Don't…don't even celebrate this bullshit idea of yours yet. Because I promise, if this shit rolls downhill and jeopardizes my career? If I get stuck as the director of this fucking office, I will make your life a living hell."

"I'll be there to mop up your tears, sir. I promise."

"Yeah, right." Stanton groaned again. "Agent Archer, you are in charge of securing that mountain until we can get a cleanup team up there to secure our property. Meanwhile, I'm going to call Director Latham and pray that the man doesn't rip me a new asshole. If the governor wants to send the Guard in after we've released the area, he is more than welcome to."

"Understood, sir." Archer heard the line go dead and he ended the call. He stood tall and made his way around the stony outcropping. "Now I just have to convince these trigger happy idiots that I'm in charge."

AL HAD MADE his way to where the news van was and craned his neck to see inside. Patricia was leaning forward, pointing at a screen. "There. Roll sound from there."

The colonel's voice was loud and clear as he stated, "There won't be any civilians left on this mountain to report anything that we do. We have our orders and they aren't optional."

Patricia could be heard asking, "And where did these orders originate, if you don't mind me asking?"

Mayfield sounded smug when he stated, "The governor himself."

Patricia leaned back with a satisfied smile. "Good enough?"

Becka sighed. "That's good enough to explain where he got his marching orders, but he didn't admit to being there to kill the bigfoots."

Al stuck his head in. "Go back further. Right after he threatened to have my chopper pushed into the trees to clear their way."

Becka gave Al the once over. "And who is this strapping fellow?"

Al shot her a winning smile. "Just your friendly neighborhood chopper pilot, ma'am." He reached up and tilted the brim of his hat. He nodded to Patricia. "A couple minutes before that last quote."

Patricia worked the mouse and traced back the digital recording. Mayfield's voice was loud and clear, "...push that Huey into the trees. Clear our path, major. We have monsters to kill."

Al smiled at Becka. "Voila. One threat to kill the Genoskwa."

"Genoskwa..." Becka shook her head. "That doesn't really roll off the tongue, does it?"

Al shrugged. "Sounds better than 'bigfoots.' If you ask me, it gives them credibility as a tribal culture, a sentient race."

Becka broke into a toothy smile. "I love the way you talk. Where are you from?"

Al chuckled. "All over, actually."

"Ahem." Patricia shot her a serious look. "Time is of the essence here, Becka."

"Right." She stiffened in her chair and reached for her microphone. "Tony, grab the camera and let's roll some footage."

Tony reached for the shoulder-held camera and slapped a fresh battery into it. "What are we doing? B roll?"

"Oh, no. We're going to talk to the good general and see if he'll admit on camera to what he said on tape."

"Colonel," Al corrected. "He's actually a lieutenant colonel."

"Gotcha." Becka stepped down from the van and glanced through the crowd. "Now which one is he?"

Al pointed to the side of the taco truck. "The guy with the sunglasses ordering the other soldiers? That's him."

Becka took a deep breath and straightened her skirt. "Let's go catch us an asshole."

Hector made a slow and sneaky approach on Dale and grabbed his arm, pulling him into a thick group of people. "What are you doing, man?" You're supposed to be hiding."

Dale smiled as he shook his head. "Not anymore. I just got off the phone with my boss. The whole mountain is now a federal crime scene. The military cannot enter it until we've concluded our investigation and cleared out all of our belongings."

"Wait…what?" Hector broke into a wide smile. "Like, they can't go up there until you guys pick up all your shit?"

Dale shrugged. "Something like that." Dale took a deep breath and peered over the crowd. "Now I get to tell Colonel Whatsisface to get the hell off my mountain."

"Oh man! I definitely want to watch this." Hector trotted to catch up to him and took up a position at his side. "This is gonna be good."

Dale slowed as two soldiers spotted him and started towards him. He recognized the young co-pilot from their earlier confrontation and smiled. Exercising his authority over the young butter bar lieutenant should be a piece of cake.

"Agent Archer, you need to come with me," the soldier stated.

SURVIVAL

Archer squared his shoulders. "Only if you're escorting me to your commanding officer."

The soldier shot him an evil grin. "Oh, that's exactly where we're taking you."

"Good." Archer locked eyes with him. "I need to tell him that I just got off the phone with my boss and this mountain is under the jurisdiction of the FBI."

"Fat chance, buddy." The soldier reached out to take his arm and Archer gripped his wrist, pulling him into an arm bar.

"Oh, I'm not bluffing." He shot a serious look to the co-pilot and shook his head. "Unless you both want to be arrested and charged with obstruction, I suggest you escort me to your boss."

Hector couldn't stop the giggles that erupted. He arm pumped the air then bent low to look the soldier that Archer was holding in the face. "Sucks to be you right now."

Archer shot him a disapproving look. "Let's keep this professional, shall we?" He let up on the pressure and allowed the soldier to come up from a bent position. "Promise me you're going to play nice and I'll release you."

"You're still under arrest, Archer," the soldier said through gritted teeth.

"Sorry pal. I don't think you have those powers." He released the soldier and locked eyes with him. "Now. Take me to your boss."

The soldier rubbed his arm then slapped at the young co-pilot. "You just stood there."

"Yeah, I'm not stupid," the co-pilot replied.

Hector tried to stifle his giggles as he followed the three of them across the clearing. He saw Mayfield's eyes light up when Dale came into view and Hector was counting the seconds until the shit hit the fan.

As Mayfield stepped towards Archer, a young woman shoved a microphone into his face. "Lieutenant Colonel, would you mind commenting on your previous statement about being here to kill all of the Genoskwa in these mountains?"

Mayfield shot her an angry stare. "I don't have time for this."

"So you're not denying that you and your soldiers were sent here, by the governor, with the sole purpose of killing an entire tribe of gentle giants?"

"What?" Mayfield flustered. "Where did you get such a wild idea?"

Becka smiled and held the microphone closer. "From your own words, Lieutenant Colonel." She nodded at Patricia who clicked on the recorder, playing back Mayfield's words.

Mayfield felt his face flush and he glared at Patricia. "That isn't my voice. I never said those words."

"Now, Colonel…" Patricia waved a finger in his face. "Tsk-tsk. We both know you said this and I have witnesses."

"I never—"

"Colonel Mayfield, sir?" The co-pilot stated as they approached. "We have Agent Archer."

"Finally. Arrest that man and put him in chains." Mayfield smiled at him smugly.

"Yeah, I don't think so, Colonel." Archer stepped forward and held the satellite phone in his hand. "I just got off the horn with my boss. This entire mountain is now under FBI jurisdiction."

"Like HELL!" Mayfield barked. "The governor himself sent me here to—"

"It's an active crime scene!" Archer yelled over the man. "You and yours are to vacate now or risk being arrested." He turned and waved at the two state patrol officers who had paused working crowd control to observe the altercation. "Gentlemen, will you please escort the colonel and his people from this area. This is an active Bureau crime scene."

The two state patrol officers looked at each other and shrugged, unsure who they took orders from.

"Archer, you are under arrest for—"

"No, Colonel!" Archer yelled, his face turning red. "We can stand here all day long arguing who has jurisdiction, but I can guaran-goddam-tee you that you will lose." He lowered his voice and took a breath. "I suggest you call your superiors and get your new marching orders."

Mayfield glared at him as he slapped at Major O'Dell. "Get on the radio and find out if there's any merit to his story." He turned his eyes back to Archer. "And you better pray to whatever ungrateful god you believe in that you're right." He sneered as he leaned closer. "Or I will thoroughly enjoy putting you in chains myself."

31

Edge of the Catskills

"This is going to play so well!" Becka cheered for herself as they continued recording. "Ready Tony? Okay." She took a deep breath and put on her camera face.

Tony held up three fingers. "In three, two…" He pointed to her.

"We are here at the foot of the Catskill Mountains with literally hundreds of citizens who have all come out in support of the alleged tribe of New York Bigfoot. Reports of previous altercations between these legendary creatures and both FBI Special Agents and contracted military personnel have filtered down to us thanks to special news reports filed by Patricia Murphy and Hector Ramirez of the Daily Informer.

"These reports were backed by a myriad of photographs and first-person accounts of interactions with the creatures, which, with a call for public support, have brought citizens from all walks of life to this once serene park, all in the hope of saving these creatures from potential military genocide.

"According to Lieutenant Colonel Mayfield of the National Guard, his unit was activated by the Governor of New York to respond to previous acts of violence, supposedly carried out by the 'Genoskwa,' an indigenous tribe of Sasquatch that call the Catskills home."

Patricia smiled to herself as she slowly backed away, allowing Becka to do what she did best: sell a story.

She turned and saw both Major O'Dell and Agent Archer on phones, pacing as they spoke. She knew that the whole thing could come down on either side. She could only pray that the influx of public support would be enough to sway opinion, perhaps forcing the governor's hand into recalling the Guard.

She spotted Al and made her way toward him. "Any word?"

Al shook his head. "From what Dale explained, the Director of the Albany office made the decision, but the original call for military action was pushed by someone above him. A...regional director?" He sighed. "I dunno. I just know that it will come down to the letter of legality."

"What do you mean?"

Al took a deep breath and let it out slowly. "Whether the Albany guy has the power to declare this a crime scene or not. I think Dale's on a three-way call between the regional guy and the Albany guy."

"So this could all go south anyway," she stated in a defeated tone.

Al shrugged. "Or not." He glanced around the crowd. "Have you seen Hector? He was stuck to

Archer's side like glue then suddenly he's off somewhere."

She waved him off. "Probably went to get food. He can eat like there's no—" Her words were cut off as the crowd emitted a collective gasp.

Both she and Al studied where they were looking and followed their gaze. Patricia felt her breath catch in her throat and she rushed to Dale's side, pulling the phone from his ear.

"Hey, I'm on the line with—"

"Shut up and look!" She pointed towards the Chinook and Dale felt his blood run cold.

"Oh, no." He lifted the phone to his ear again. "I gotta call you back. Shit's about to go down."

Al appeared beside them. "We need to get them out of here." He urged Dale with his eyes. "We need to go. NOW!"

"It's too late, Al." Patricia noted the crowd all staring, low murmuring travelling through like a soft wave. Her eyes fell on Becka, still broadcasting, except now she looked terrified.

"Come on," Dale tugged Al's arm. "We need to get between them and the military."

O'Dell stared open mouthed as Hector and Betty made a slow, tentative approach from behind the helicopters. "Son of a bitch. They *are* real."

REBECCA WILLIAMS GASPED THEN SPUN to her cameraman, her eyes wide. "They're really real," she whispered. "Come on. We have to get closer!"

"I'm on your heels!"

She pushed her way through the crowd without so much as an 'excuse me' and forced her way in behind the military. She spun again and faced the camera. "Place me in frame, but make sure you keep the animal in the shot," she whispered.

The cameraman adjusted the focus then gave her a slight nod. "You're good."

Rebecca turned to a forty five degree angle where she could see the action as it unfolded then brought the microphone to her mouth, commentating on the scene as it occurred.

Hector held Betty's hand and had to crane his neck up to look at her, speaking softly as he led her down the trail to the people. "Come on," he urged her. "It's going to be okay. They just need to see you the way I see you."

The big female had to force herself to take each step, her eyes darting between hundreds of shocked faces. More than once she hesitated, tugging at Hector, begging him with her eyes to leave.

"We have to show them," he argued. "That you're not a threat. That we can be friends."

Her entire body shook with fear as Hector urged her forward. He made sure he stood directly in front of her, acting as a literal human shield. "She's not gonna hurt nobody!" he shouted. "She's friendly."

Betty froze just yards from the edge of the clearing and seemed to relax when she saw Patricia, Dale and Al trotting toward them. She actually smiled and gripped Hector's shoulder gently.

"Get her the hell out of here!" Dale yelled as they rushed to their side. "This isn't over yet! The jurisdiction play might fall through!"

"For God's sake Hector!" Patricia called, stomping her feet as she came to a stop. "What were you thinking?"

Hector swelled his chest and set his jaw. "They need to know. They gotta see that Betty ain't a threat." He looked up at her with pride in his eyes. "She trusted me enough to come with me."

Al stared with wide eyes. "How did you get all the way up the mountain so fast?"

Hector shook his head. "I didn't. She came down the path to check on me and…" He looked up at her again and smiled. "I could *feel* her out there. Watching me." Betty rocked back and forth nervously as people slowly moved closer to get a better view. She grabbed each of Hector's shoulders and he could feel her grip shaking. "I went to her and convinced her that the only way this could be over was to show them that she's not a monster."

Dale groaned and leaned closer, whispering "That was a stupid move, Hector."

Al gripped Dale's arm. "The soldiers." He nodded behind them.

Dale spun and saw the military men fanning out, their weapons at the ready. He stepped toward them and held his arms out, shouting, "No! Don't shoot!" He pointed to the closest soldier, "Don't you fucking dare! I swear to god, I'll drop you where you fucking stand!" He pointed to another, "Lower your goddam weapon!"

Colonel Mayfield and Major O'Dell waded through the men and stood between the soldiers and Archer. "You lose, Agent Archer." Mayfield crossed his arms over his chest and sneered at him. "My command just verified our orders from the governor. The same governor, I might add, who is on the phone right this moment with *your* chain of command, getting your boss's ass chewed for making such a dumbass move."

Dale locked eyes with him and ground his teeth. "Until my boss calls me and tells me to relinquish this area to you, this is still a federal fucking crime scene."

Patricia nudged Dale and pointed to Becka and her cameraman. "They're broadcasting."

Dale smiled as he turned back to Mayfield. "Smile, Colonel. You're on live television." He stepped toward him then turned and pointed at Betty, still swaying nervously. "You gonna risk hurting this creature in front of thousands of American viewers? In front of all of these witnesses?" He scoffed. "Even you can't be dumb enough to believe that she's a threat. Hell, they walked here holding hands. Does that look like a threat to you, Colonel?"

"Doesn't matter what I think or what you believe, Archer. I have my orders!"

With that statement, the crowd erupted into a low booing session. One lady, a decided flower child, marched up to him and publicly chastened him. "Shame on you. Wanting to harm one of God's beautiful creatures. Shame!" She turned to the crowd and puffed her chest. "The only monsters I see here are wearing green and carrying guns!"

The crowd liked that and began to close in on the handful of soldiers, murmuring epithets as they closed the distance.

Dale stepped forward again and held his hands in the air, yelling for their attention. "Woah, hold on people! Hold on!" He stepped toward the hippie and gave her a sad smile. "Enemy of my enemy, I get it. But we can't have any violence here today." He gave her a knowing look. "None. We can't give them a reason."

The woman studied him for a moment then turned and stared at Betty. A slow smile relaxed her angry face and she nodded, backing away.

Dale stepped back closer to Betty, keeping his arms raised. "Lower your weapons. Now. There will be no bloodshed today."

"That's not your call, Archer!" O'Dell yelled. "The colonel is well within his rights here."

"What the hell?" Al stepped forward and glared at the military men. "Tell me something. Did any of you sign up with the intent of hunting down and killing unarmed civilians? Because I can promise you that once word of these creatures gets out, they'll be protected by every means. Do you want your claim to fame to be that you gunned down a rare, exotic, intelligent creature, a legend, simply because some bureaucrat sitting in an office hundreds of miles away told you to?"

"Where are the rest of them, Archer? They damned sure aren't on their way to Guatemala."

"Vermont, asshole," Patricia corrected him.

Archer shrugged. "These two have a…" he glanced at Hector and grinned. "A special bond. Betty here just came off the mountain to make sure Hector was safe."

"For fuck's sake. You named them?" O'Dell scoffed.

"Hey, Betty happens to like her name!" Hector yelled. He turned and gripped her hand again. "She's my friend."

"Right." Mayfield turned to O'Dell. "Major. Do your duty."

O'Dell smiled and lifted his rifle. "Yes, sir."

"Hold that weapon!" Dale stepped forward again,

raising his hands. "There's no threat here!"

"I'll gun your ass down, too, agent," O'Dell sneered at him.

"You'll have to," Dale shouted back to him.

"Yeah. Me, too," Patricia stood beside him.

"And me." Al moved to Dale's other side.

There was a low murmur across the crowd when the flower child lady stepped between O'Dell and Archer. "And me."

"And me," another stated, moving beside her.

"And me."

"And me."

"And me."

"Us, too."

O'Dell paled and glanced back to Colonel Mayfield. "Sir?"

Mayfield ground his teeth and his face began to redden. "I told you men to clear this goddamn mountain of all civilians!"

The two state troopers moved next to Dale and crossed their arms, silently pledging their support.

Hector watched a small child slowly approach, his eyes locked to Betty. He could feel her trepidation as the young boy gently moved to stand in front of her and held his arms out.

Betty looked to Hector who gave her a silent nod.

With a slow deliberate movement, Betty bent and lifted the child, cradling him against her bosom. Patricia felt her eyes well and turned to ensure that Becka had caught the moment.

She wasn't disappointed.

"Enough of this bullshit!" Mayfield yelled. "Get these people OUT OF HERE!"

A loud crashing sound echoed through the woods and the forest fell silent. The crowd died down and the soldiers stiffened as wood knocks echoed around them.

Dale looked at Al with fear in his eyes. "They've surrounded us."

Once the wood knocks died down, a loud "whoop" called from one side and was answered by another on the other side. The soldiers began to lose their nerve as war cries broke out, indicating the humans were all surrounded.

Grunts, hoots, whoops and screams echoed across the clearing, increasing in volume and tempo until the civilians found themselves covering their ears and bending down, some falling to their knees.

As if by some unseen prompt, the noise abruptly ended, leaving the area in an eerie silence. The only sound was the rustling of the few remaining leaves on the deciduous trees.

"What the hell was that?" Mayfield asked.

Dale stepped forward and shook his head at the man. "That was Betty's people letting you know that they won't let you harm her."

Betty crouched low and set the little boy down, nudging him away with the back of her hand. When she stood again, she stood tall, her head held high and Hector noted that her hands were no longer shaking.

The sound of branches breaking and heavy footfalls sounded to their left and Dale barely caught a glimpse of Big Red emerging from the forest.

The crowd emitted another collective gasp as the towering giant moved purposefully between Betty and the soldiers, his walking stick held firmly in his grip.

"Good lord," Mayfield gasped. "He's huge."

Big Red turned and looked at Betty. He emitted a barely noticeable grunt and she immediately lowered her head, averting her eyes.

"What does this thing want?" Mayfield asked.

Hector released Betty's hand and stepped forward. As he approached Big Red, he caught the giant's eye. Hector held a hand out and the giant Genoskwa didn't attempt to move. Hector reached out and touched the creature's arm, making his connection.

"He's come here to avert...war," Hector stated plainly. He looked up at Big Red and gently shook his head. "No, you...you can't mean that."

"Mean what?" Dale asked.

Hector turned to him and shook his head. "I'm not...I mean, I can't..." He found breathing difficult and had to force air into his lungs. "He can't mean that."

"What does it want?" Mayfield asked.

Hector took a deep, shaky breath and turned to face him. "If you must have blood..." he swallowed hard. "He's here to give you that."

Mayfield's features twisted. "What are you saying?"

Hector felt his jaw quiver and he stared up into the face of the giant once more, just to ensure he had the message right. "Are you certain?"

Big Red grunted and Hector felt a sadness overwhelm him. "If you have to have your pound of flesh for everything that's happened here, he's offering himself," his voice cracked as he spoke.

"What the fuck?" O'Dell scoffed. "Like this guy can read the ape's mind? Tell me you aren't falling for this bullshit."

Big Red grunted and shrugged off Hector's hand.

He lumbered forward until he stood directly in front of O'Dell.

Slowly, the giant extended his hand and gripped the barrel of O'Dell's rifle and pulled it up to his chest. With a solid tug, he pressed the barrel where his heart would be. O'Dell could feel his entire body trembling and his mouth had gone dry, the metallic taste of fear nearly overpowering.

Hector trotted up beside Big Red with tears in his eyes. "Tell me you don't understand that sign language, you prick," he hissed. He turned and locked eyes with Mayfield. "They're not stupid beasts, Colonel. They have families. They love. They mourn their dead and care for each other in ways that…" he choked on his words. "In ways that I think humans have forgotten how to." He felt his jaw quiver as he spoke. "If it means you'll leave his family alone, he's willing to sacrifice himself to save them."

Mayfield was shaking his head in disbelief. "No…no, that can't be right."

"Don't you get it, Colonel?" Dale asked as he slowly approached. "He understands that humans feel the need for revenge. Blood for blood. He's willing to give you that if you'll just let his family…survive."

"What's it going to be, Colonel?" Becka asked, pointing the microphone in his direction. "The people of New York want to know."

Mayfield opened his mouth to say something then quickly closed it. He cleared his throat nervously and looked at the crowd of people, all staring at him, wondering what his next words would be. He glanced back at the giant red beast and felt his own jaw quiver as he tried to speak. "S-stand down, Major."

O'Dell shot him a confused look. "Sir?"

"You heard me." He seemed to pull himself taller and thrust out his jaw. "Stand down." He turned and looked over the crowd. "All military personnel, stand down."

"But, Colonel, we have orders."

Mayfield looked up at the one-eyed giant and shook his head. "I see no monsters here today, Major. Gather the gear, load up and let's return to base."

The crowd erupted in cheers and Big Red jolted at the noise. He took a half step back and glanced at Hector, who quickly took his hand and told him, "It's over. You can go home now."

Big Red seemed to deflate and sighed as he stepped away. He looked off into the line of trees and offered a single "WHOOP!" before turning and marching back into the shadows.

Hector rushed to Betty's side and wrapped his arms around her. "It's over. It's all over now." He could feel her body relax and he felt her giant hand stroke his back before she pulled away.

He gave her a sad look and shook his head. "No, wait. You don't have to go." He turned and motioned to the crowd of people still coming to their feet and celebrating their victory. "They want to know you like I do."

Her eyes told him everything her words couldn't.

It wasn't meant to be.

She turned and trudged back into the trees, leaving Hector standing with his friends, tears streaming down his face. "Betty…"

She paused and offered one last look goodbye before she disappeared into the shadows.

32

FBI Field Office, Albany, NY

Dale knocked on the doorframe of Stanton's office. "Going someplace?"

Stanton folded the top closed on a box and set it aside. "After the stunt you pulled? Where do you think I'm going?"

Dale felt his stomach knot on him. "Oh, shit. I am so sorry…"

Stanton turned and shot him an angry look. "Not yet you aren't. But I promise you, you will be."

Dale stepped into the office and closed the door. "I knew there could be blowback but I never—"

Stanton couldn't hold back any longer and broke into laughter. "I had you. I so had you!"

"What?" Dale stared at him in shock. "Wait a minute. You mean they didn't fire you?"

Stanton scoffed. "Hardly. I'm headed back to Santa Fe. I have to report first thing Monday."

Dale huffed with relief and practically crumbled into the chair across from the desk. "Oh, shit. Yeah, you had me. I really thought that…" He sat up and narrowed his gaze at him. "If you're going back to New Mexico, does that mean they found a fulltime replacement for the office?"

Stanton sobered and raised a brow at him. "Yeah, and I hear he's a real son of a bitch. You may have your work cut out for you with this one."

Dale winced. "That bad?"

Stanton glanced through the glass wall and lowered his voice. "You won't be able to pull that cowboy shit I let you get away with. This guy? He'll make sure you never leave the office again."

"Great." Dale hung his head and ran a calloused hand over his face. "Who is it?"

Stanton reached into his pocket and pulled out a set of keys, tossing them to him. "You."

Dale caught they keys and stared at him in disbelief. "No way. You're fucking with me again, aren't you."

Stanton picked up the box and tucked it under his left arm. "I wish." He held his hand out. "Congratulations, *Director* Archer."

Dale took his hand and held his breath. "How? Didn't Latham lose his shit over all that?"

"Latham knows leadership qualities when he sees them. And an agent that's willing to put his ass on the line to do the right thing? You were a no brainer."

Stanton reached for the door and paused. "Oh, one last thing."

"Yeah?"

"Get to know your people, Dale. The ones that stay true? Those Boy Scouts who are willing to fall on their swords for what is right?" He nodded at him. "Those are the ones you want working for you. Don't let the shadows that have been cast on the Bureau as of late taint your heart."

Dale nodded. "Yes sir."

"Good." Stanton kicked the door open and gripped the box. "If you ever need advice, my number is on your desk." He turned and offered one last curt nod. "See ya in the funny papers."

OFFICES of the Daily Informer

"I CAN'T BELIEVE you just *gave* her all of that. That was your scoop!" Mike Kenny sat on the corner of her desk playing with a rubber band. "I mean, you had the story of the century. Proof positive that bigfoot exists, and you just signed it all over to Becka fucking Williams of all people."

Patricia shrugged. "I got what I needed from that story. Remember, I did break it first."

"Yeah, but you signed over the rights to all of your pictures, and…" he made a choking gurgling sound. "To Becka fucking Williams!"

"Okay, stop. I'm pretty positive her middle name isn't 'fucking.' And she served a purpose. If she hadn't been there broadcasting the whole thing, there's no telling what Mayfield would have done."

"Oh yeah!" He snapped his fingers. "Check this shit." He pulled up the website edition. "The online edition already has a metric shit ton of people claiming it was all fake. Look…one guy says you can see the zipper on the monkey costumes. Oh, and the center for the Knicks has already claimed that 'he was the man in the gorilla suit.' Can you believe this crap?"

She shrugged. "It is what it is."

"How can you be so indifferent about this? People are out there building their careers off your hard work and others are claiming it's all bull. I'd be super pissed."

She sat back in her chair and sighed. "I just wanted to know the truth about how my brother died."

"And that's the other thing. Those things killed your own brother and you're out there fighting for them? I'd want blood if it were me."

She nodded slightly. "At first, yeah. I did. I needed to know."

"Know what?"

"What it was that actually killed him." She sighed again and rocked her chair side to side. "But once I was out there…I dunno."

"I couldn't. That's all I'm saying. If I were in your shoes, I'd want a bigfoot skin rug in my living room."

Patricia's face twisted. "No, you wouldn't. You have no idea how bad they smell."

"Pfft!" He waved her comment off. "It couldn't be all that bad."

She reached into her duffle and pulled out a t-shirt and held it under his nose. "Here ya go."

Mike winced and pulled away. "Good lord, that reeks. What is that?"

"The shirt I was wearing when I hugged Wilma." She shot him a knowing look. "She was the strawberry-blonde colored one."

"Yeah, okay. No rug. But still...they killed your brother."

She cocked her head to the side and studied him a moment. "No. No, not really. I mean, it might have been one of them. But...the thing that killed my brother was defending its home. From armed invaders. It was a...a war. A war that has been going on for centuries." She shot him a gentle smile. "But now that war is over. We can all live in peace."

Mike scoffed as he pushed off her desk. "Yeah, right. Until the next hiker goes missing. Then some dumbass hunter is going to go tromping into the mountains wanting a scalp for it."

She took a deep breath and let it out slowly. "Let's just hope it never comes to that."

Tia Lucia's Cantina, Albany, New York

Miguel sucked on the beer in his hand and kept shooting sideways looks at Hector. "You really cried over that Wookie-looking thing?"

"Stop it," Hector warned as he pushed his plate away. "She's not a Wookie."

"She your girlfriend, Hector?" Rio teased as she sat down beside him. She leaned over and nudged him. "You two play kissy-kissy up in them mountains, *cabron*?"

Hector rolled his eyes and sighed heavily. Tia Lucia pushed open the door from the kitchen and brought out another plate of food, setting it beside Rio. "You two leave him alone. He lost a friend up there, didn't you *mijo?*"

Hector nodded sadly. "I did." He sat back and reached for his beer.

"You know where they live, man. You can go back any time and visit, yeah?" Miguel bumped him playfully.

Hector shook his head. "No, I don't think they're still there." He drained the beer and set the empty down gently. "Big Red…he knows. People know now where they are. He's got no choice but move his tribe someplace else." He spun the bottle slowly in his hands. "I'll never see her again."

Rio studied him for a moment then offered a sad smile. "You really loved her, didn't you?"

Hector thought about it and nodded. "Yeah. She was *familia.*"

Miguel sighed and sat down beside him. "You'll always have her, bro. Right here." He tapped Hector's chest. "And if you think about it, you're one lucky dude."

Hector gave him a confused look. "How?"

Miguel scoffed. "Bro! Not only did you *see* a bigfoot, you became friends with one. Like…a buddy, ya know?"

Hector cracked a grin. "Yeah, I guess it's all in how you look at it."

"Man, I can't believe my own cousin stood toe to toe with the military." Miguel clapped his shoulder. "You got *huevos*, man."

"I had to," he sighed. "I had to protect Betty. I had to show everyone that she wasn't a bad person. She's just…shy."

"I wonder why they're like that?" Rio asked. "I mean, wouldn't it be cool if we could just go to the zoo and see..." she trailed off, noting the look on Hector's face. "Never mind. I just answered my own question."

"They've always been like that, from what I could tell." He locked eyes with her and shrugged. "It's all about survival."

FROM THE DESK OF HEATH STALLCUP

A personal note-

Thank you so much for investing your time in reading my story. If you enjoyed it, please take a moment and leave a review. I realize that it may be an inconvenience, but reviews mean the world to authors.

Also, I love hearing from my readers. You can reach me at my blog: http://heathstallcup.com/ or via email at heathstallcup@gmail.com

Feel free to check out my Facebook page for information on upcoming releases: https://www.facebook.com/heathstallcup find me on Twitter at @HeathStallcup, Goodreads or via my Author Page at Amazon.

ABOUT THE AUTHOR

Heath Stallcup was born in Salinas, California and relocated to Tupelo, Oklahoma in his tween years. He joined the US Navy and was stationed in Charleston, SC and Bangor, WA shortly after junior college. After his second tour he attended East Central University where he obtained BS degrees in Biology and Chemistry. He then served ten years with the State of Oklahoma as a Compliance and Enforcement Officer while moonlighting nights and weekends with his local Sheriff's Office. He still lives in the small township of Tupelo, Oklahoma with his wife. He steals time to write between household duties, going to ballgames, being a grandfather and the pet of numerous animals that have taken over his home. Visit him at heathstallcup.com or Facebook.com for news of his upcoming releases.

GENOSKWA THE SERIES

GENOSKWA THE SERIES

ALSO BY HEATH STALLCUP

Caldera The Series

Monster Squad The Series

Hunter The Series

Nocturna The Series

Whispers Trilogy

Bobbie Bridger series

Genoskwa Series

Ain't No St. Nick

Sinful

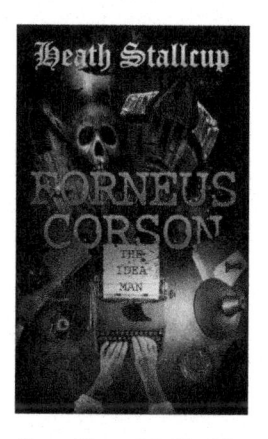

Forneus Corson The Idea Man

Mind Trip

ALSO FROM DEVILDOG PRESS

www.devildogpress.com

Zombie Fallout Series By Mark Tufo

Caldera Book 1 By Heath Stallcup

All That Remain By Travis Tufo

From The Ash by Dave Heron

Heart Of Jet By Sheila Shedd

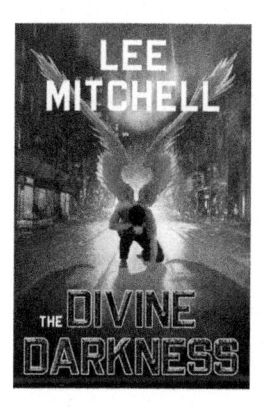

The Devine Darkness by Lee Mitchell

Shifters: A Samantha Reece Mystery Book 1 by Jaime Johnesee

CUSTOMERS ALSO BOUGHT

CUSTOMERS ALSO PURCHASED:

SHAWN CHESSER
SURVIVING THE
ZOMBIE APOCALYPSE

WILLIAM MASSA
OCCULT ASSASSIN
SERIES

JOHN O'BRIEN
A NEW WORLD
SERIES

ERIC A. SHELMAN
DEAD HUNGER
SERIES

HEATH STALLCUP
MONSTER SQUAD
SERIES

MARK TUFO
ZOMBIE FALLOUT
SERIES